A LOFTY FIGURE TOOK SHAPE AGAINST THE OPAQUE GLOOM OF THE DESERT ...

"Adam?" she whispered, rising to meet him.

"Yes, Ruth," he answered.

They clasped hands.

"Ruth, dear, I do not like this," Adam said very low.

"What? Seeing me again?"

"No. Meeting you in secret."

"But you must. I'm afraid—if you meet your—my—Guerd Larey. You couldn't avoid it. And the thought frightens me."

"I understand. I don't want to meet Guerd and I don't want him or anyone to—know I see you. Still—"

"You must meet me here. Adam, I'd never have gotten through this day but for you," said Ruth, her face pale and her great eyes mirroring the brilliance and mystery of the stars as she gazed up at Adam ...

Books by Zane Grey

Published by POCKET BOOKS

ZANE GREY

STAIRS OF SAND

PUBLISHED BY POCKET BOOKS NEW YORK

POCKET BOOKS, a Simon & Schuster division of
GULF & WESTERN CORPORATION
1230 Avenue of the Americas, New York, N.Y. 10020

ISBN: 0-671-83589-0

First Pocket Books printing July, 1981

10 9 8 7 6 5 4 3 2 1

1

The canyon, with its gleaming walls, dark as ebony on the shady side, gold where the desert sun burned, afforded some relief from the heat, if not from the sight of the infernal, endless sand—sand blowing, shifting, heaving like billows of a silver sea, rolling away dune after dune, rising in steps, beautiful, mystic, beckoning toward the cool blue heights—stairs of sand, treacherous and alluring.

Ruth Virey settled back in the wagon seat and dragged her gaze from that canyon gateway, through which the desert seemed to mock her.

Old Butch, the mule on the right, had balked. After thirty miles of travel he had become as immovable as the cliff of rock. Ruth had heard he was noted for balking, at strange times and places. He dropped now beside his mate, weary, sand-laden, obstinately set in his tracks.

The young man, Ruth's companion, had evidently abandoned any hope of starting the mule. He had coaxed, pulled and beaten, all to no avail. Then he had flung himself down in the shade, where he now sat wiping his wet brown face, and pushing back his long damp hair with nervous hand. A radiance had faded from that youthful face.

"Hal Stone, do you mean we are stuck here?" repeated Ruth, this time sharply.

"Well, I guess—for today, anyhow," he replied, grimly. "Old Butch won't budge till he gets ready."

"My grandfather told me he had heard there was only one man on the desert who could move Butch when he balked. I wish that man would happen along."

"I don't," said Stone, significantly, raising sand-reddened blue eyes that held a smouldering fire.

"How far have we come?" she went on, quickening.

"I'm not sure. Maybe thirty miles."

"If so we're still ten miles from the Indian settlement where you said we could stay all night?"

"Yes, about that, I guess," he returned, avoiding her steady gaze.

"And from there, two days more to San Diego?"

"I didn't say so."

"Yes, you did," she flashed.

"Well, since you ran off with me—of your own free will—what difference does it make, whether it's two miles or ten?" he retorted, defiantly.

"That depends on you," she rejoined, gravely. "What are you going to do?"

"What do you want to do?"

"I won't go back. Can't we walk on to the Indian settlement?"

"No. It's too late in the day. The cursed sand is still blowing. After dark I'd not be sure of the road."

Ruth saw the sand out there between the gap of the cliffs—a filmy haze, moving, streaming, thinning —and she heard it too, a soft silky seeping roar, low, strange, menacing.

"What can we do?" she asked, after a long pause.

"Stay here till Old Butch wants to move. We've water, food, blankets. We can make out quite well."

"I did not expect to camp out with you—alone, on the desert," declared Ruth.

"What did you expect?" he asked, almost harshly.

"God only knows. I never thought of anything except to get away from that awful hole—and from *him*."

Stone rose to approach her and lean over the front wheel.

"Well, you've gotten away, and you won't go back. Isn't it about time now to think of me?"

His tone was that of a lover, appealing, yet tinged with a resentful uncertainty.

"Of you?" she asked, studying the boyish reckless face with a sudden remorse.

"Yes, me," he returned, taking her gloved hand in his.

"What do you mean?"

"You know what I mean, Ruth Larey."

"I told you not to call me Larey," she said, angrily, and pulled to free her hand.

Stone held it, until seeing she would not soften, he flung it from him.

"You let me make love to you—kiss you," he burst out. "You said you would love me. You've run away with me."

"I know, Hal," she returned, contritely, reaching out as if to give him her hand again. "I'm to blame. But can't you see it with my eyes? You happened along. I was lonely, sick of the desert, distracted. I—I think I did love you. And I was certainly glad to run off with you. But I never would have—if I'd suspected you'd be so selfish and swift in—in your demands."

"Humph! You're a funny woman," he said, with faint sarcasm. "Lead a fellow to risk his hide by eloping with you—then flout him when he wants what he had a right to expect."

Ruth's self-reproach, that had prompted her toward warmth, suffered an eclipse. This escapade of hers, which had promised deliverance, began to take on another aspect. She had thought to escape the desert, as she had yearned to for years, but the desert had betrayed her. Dare she go farther with this young man, whom she had known only a few weeks, and therefore not at all? Could she force herself to return to Lost Lake? Almost anything would be preferable. Remembrance of the freighting post in its ghastly setting, and the man she hated and feared roused such revulsion that she shook.

Meanwhile Stone lifted the canteens and baskets, and a roll of blankets out of the wagon, and carried them to a flat rock at the base of the shaded cliff. Then he returned to help her out of the high-wheeled vehicle.

"Come. You might as well be as comfortable as possible while we have to stay here."

Ruth stood up, and leaned to reach his hands, intending to jump down, but he pulled her, and she stumbled on the wheel and fell into his arms. Then he swung her away toward the cliff, unmindful of the undignified disarray of her apparel.

"Put me down," she commanded.

Not only did he not comply with her demand but he clasped her close and bent low, trying to kiss her lips. Ruth, suddenly furious, beat at him, and wrestled so effectively that his kisses fell upon her neck and hair. She had to fight then to free herself.

"I thought—you were—a gentleman," she cried, in breathless anger.

Stone laughed and spread wide his hands. The heat died out of his face.

"I don't know that it matters," he said. "Here we are. It'll be fine if you kick like a lassoed jack-rabbit every time I touch you."

Ruth smoothed her dishevelled hair and garments, striving the while to hold her tongue. She had gotten herself into a dilemma from which it would take a woman's wit to extricate her.

"I'll see if I can find some wood to start a fire," he added, and strode down the canyon.

Ruth sank upon the roll of blankets, conscious of weariness and disgust, and a miserable sense of the return of the very bitterness and futility that had betrayed her to this step. Whatever she had felt for this boy had vanished, even the regret. Again, for the hundredth time, it seemed, she had mistaken something for love—love that she yearned for and which she needed so greatly. She blamed the interminable four years of fruitless life at a barren desert water-hole for the vacillation and desperation which had all but ruined her.

"I swore I'd run away from it all and never go back," she mused, broodingly. "But already I see . . . it was wicked of me to desert grandfather. He needs me. Long ago, but for me, he'd have been at the mercy of Guerd Larey and that scar-faced Collishaw. . . . It'll be best to go back, though I hate it so. . . . Oh, if I could only give up and not care. But neither mother nor I were born to stand this awful desert life. It takes peace of soul—sacrifice—strength in God—qualities, alas! I never had. And mother, she —she found an unmarked grave in Death Valley. Oh, what will become of me!"

Presently she became aware of Stone's return. He carried a scant bundle of sticks.

"Tears, eh?" he queried, with hard blue eyes on her face. "I didn't know you could cry. I sure am flattered."

"My tears are not for you," rejoined Ruth, dispiritedly.

"Nor your smiles and kisses, I gather," he flared, sullenly. "Well, we'll have it out right here, before Old Butch makes up his mind to move."

"Hal, we don't need to have it out—whatever you mean by that," returned Ruth. "For I'm not going on with it."

"What?" he demanded, harshly, throwing down the sticks.

"We'll not go any further. You can take me home."

"Like hell I will! . . . Go sneaking back to Lost Lake for Guerd Larey to make a sieve out of me with bullets. Ha, senora, I see myself taking you!"

"Guerd will believe me when I tell him I was solely to blame."

"What difference would that make to him? He'd kill me for taking you off, just the same."

Ruth reflected that it was likely Larey would not be influenced by her in the slightest, except on terms to which she would not surrender.

"I shall go back alone," she announced.

"How, may I ask?" he queried.

"I'll walk."

"Walk! When? You'd lost your way at night. And by day you'd fall on the hot sand and die. Haven't your four years of desert life—which you rave about —taught you that much? No, Ruth Larey, you'll go on with me. It's too late."

"It is never too late. That is why I have fought and fought. I shall walk back, Hal."

"Ruth, you'd risk your life rather than get out of this desert hell with me?" he asked, with poignant amaze.

"I'd lose my life before I'd go," she returned.

"Why, for God's sake?" he went on, hoarsely.

"You compel me to face the reality of such a step," she said, earnestly. "I think I have labored under a dream. I dreamed of you as a liberator whom I would come to love. You would take me far across this terrible desert to the green vineyards and the pine groves—to the cool seaside. Some day when I was free you'd marry me and make me happy. That was my dream. But you have shown me the reality, and I want none of it."

"Damn your fickleness!" he exclaimed, passionately. "You're as changeable as the shifting sands out there."

"Changeable? Why, of course. That's a woman's privilege," she retorted, with a lift of her chin.

"Ah, I see. You swore you loved me and now you don't?"

"I never swore that. I only thought I might love you some day."

He flung out his hands with a gesture which did not lack a dignity of disillusion and grief. He paled and his eyes gleamed with blue fire. Whatever his weakness, he had sincerely believed he had won her.

"Bah! You've fooled me as you have every white man who drifted into Lost Lake," he declared. "As for me—even if you'd never whispered one word it'd have been bad enough. You let me walk with you in the moonlight—and at last kiss you—though you must have known what your cursed beauty would do. . . . Your purple eyes—your golden skin—your hair like spun silk—your panther body with its softness and heat! Lord knows I wasn't an angel, but if I had been one, I'd have fallen. . . . You've done this thing before, Ruth Larey. Oh, I've heard all about you—from people who like you, as well as others who hate you. I've been warned not to lose my head over you. You were never one single day the same. Like that damned sand out there—beautiful to look at but treacherous."

"Thank you for all that, Hal Stone," replied Ruth, with a pale smile. "You have done me a good turn. I was grateful to you, sorry for you, and full of regret. But you have spared me further concern."

"I don't want your gratitude or your pity," he said. "It was your love I wanted. But I'll have you just the same. They told me you weren't in love with your husband—that he didn't care for that just so long as he——"

"*I* told you I was Guerd Larey's wife in name only," she interrupted, coldly.

"Sure you told me," he shot back at her, his face flushing hot. "But I believe you lied. You can't expect me to swallow that. I never knew anybody who could, except old Mrs. Dorn. . . . Guerd Larey to let you be his wife in name only! Why it's desert gossip that he couldn't pass by a Mexican girl, or even an Indian. . . . No, Ruth, you invented that little story to make it easier for men to want you. It sure fooled me."

"I despise you. I wonder I ever imagined otherwise," returned Ruth, scornfully.

"All the same you're out here alone in the desert with me," he rejoined, with a bitterness that held a menace. And then as he dropped to his knees to gather the firewood together he spoke as if to himself alone: "A man is what a woman makes him."

Ruth sought to conceal a dread that swiftly succeeded her scorn. Had she been wise to alienate this young man, in whom passion and violence evidently ran counterpart to his recklessness? Her situation had assumed alarming proportions. The afternoon was far spent, and despite her courage she hesitated about taking the road back. She saw that the wind was lessening and the gray haze of sand clearing. There would be early moonlight. Suddenly she decided that it would be best for her to leave Stone at once. She would take only a canteen and walk as long as she could make out the road, then rest until daylight. But next day—the sun! It would beat her down as might a savage with a club. Still, there was no alternative. It was impossible for her to stay there over night with Stone, let alone go on with him next morning. Perhaps she could keep on the road all night, and during the heat of the following day conserve her strength by resting in the shade of *palo verdes* and ironwood trees she remembered having seen. She must not ponder over the possibilities any longer, but go at once.

Stone had succeeded in starting a little fire and was now engaged in pouring water into a coffee pot.

"Open up the basket. I'll have coffee made soon," he ordered, gruffly.

Ruth arose, but instead of the basket she picked up a canteen and spread the canvas strap to sling over her shoulder. Stone stared at her until suddenly his eyes dilated and his face changed. Slowly he got to his feet.

"What dodge are you up to?" he demanded.

"I'm going back," replied Ruth, firmly, though her lips trembled. Suiting the action to the words she wheeled and started away.

She heard a muttered curse, then quick footsteps on the gravel. Stone caught her arm in a grasp that hurt. Wrenching free she turned and struck him with all her might across the mouth.

"You keep your hands off me," she cried.

A flame of fury leaped into Stone's eyes. He seized

her and flung her back. The canteen flew out of Ruth's hands and she fell upon the blankets. She struggled to her knees, slowly, because his violence had badly shaken her. It did not take a second glance at Stone to realize that he held her at his mercy and knew it. Moreover, the evil in him was in the ascendant.

"You didn't say that last night," he muttered, extending toward her the hands she had found offensive. And he clutched at her dress.

As Ruth leaped erect one of her sleeves tore, leaving her bare arm in Stone's grasp. Sight and touch of it, combined with her resistance, inflamed him to a savage degree. He jerked her into his arms and held her as if in a vise.

Suddenly over his shoulder Ruth saw two men and two burros entering the canyon at its far end. Their amazing appearance changed what had been a hopeless situation for her. Fiercely, with redoubled strength, she fought Stone, and spared breath for one piercing cry. And she gave Stone all he could do to handle her.

The moment came just when she was about to collapse. Something heavy and irresistible laid hold of Ruth from behind. She opened her eyes. Over her shoulder extended a brawny arm, half covered by a rent and ragged sleeve. At the end of that arm a great brown hand shoved Stone back yet appeared also to hold him as if he had been an empty sack. Ruth grasped then that one of the men she had seen had come up behind her. Even at the moment she felt how he towered above her.

"Young man, let go—quick!" he said in deep voice that had a curious cold ring.

But Stone did not release his hold of Ruth. His mood had been too savage to change in a twinkling. Then the brown arm flashed back and forth. Stone's face seemed suddenly obliterated behind a huge fist. With the sodden sound that followed, warm wet drops splashed over Ruth, and she felt herself freed in a violent wrench. Stone fell backward, and he rolled over and over to land against the cliff wall. There he sank down and lay still.

Ruth, almost fainting, continued to lean for support against the man she had not yet seen.

"Merryvale, I believe my long search is ended," he said, quietly.

Ruth, as one in a dream, saw the other man come round to face her. He looked stranger than any old prospector she had seen. But he had keen kindly blue eyes that fixed upon her with singular penetration.

"Wal, Adam, I reckon you're right. It's Ruth."

2

Ruth swayed back a little against her rescuer. Her head hardly reached his shoulder.

"Who are you—that call me Ruth?" she queried curiously.

The old man's worn and wrinkled visage seemed to emit a benevolent light.

"I'm Merryvale, Miss," he replied. "Adam's pard these long four years."

Ruth then became aware of a gentle pressure of two great hands on her shoulders. But almost at once the man let go his hold and strode out to confront her.

"Ruth, don't you know me?" he asked.

Ruth found herself gazing up at a very tall man, clad in the dusty weathered ragged garb of a desert wanderer. His face, dark almost as an Indian's, and strange with its deep sloping lines of sadness, she knew yet did not know. Gray eyes, clear, piercing as those of an eagle, looked down upon her with a soft and wonderful light of joy. Ruth trembled. Who was this man? It was not only that she had seen him before, but she remembered that softness of light in his eyes.

"I know you—yet I don't," she replied, tremulously.

"Surely you remember me?" he asked, gently.

"Yes—no-o," answered Ruth, gravely shaking her head.

"Have you forgotten Genie?"

"Genie? Genie who?" she asked wonderingly, with quickening currents of thought, whirling, coalescing toward revelation.

15

"Why, Genie Linwood."

"Oh!—Genie Linwood! . . . Santa Ysabel!" Ruth flashed. "Yes—yes. Oh, I remember Genie. It was to her I gave my pretty gowns when I left Santa Ysabel. She was to marry Gene, the young rancher. . . . Gene Blair, who fell in love with her—who thought her a poor desert waif when she was rich."

"Yes, Ruth—that was Genie," replied the man, in a tone not untinged by sadness.

"Now I remember *you*," cried Ruth. "You were Genie's friend—her desert man. Eagle, she called you. Oh, I remember now. . . . You had found her on the desert where she was starving with her mother. She was only a child. Then her mother died, and you took care of her for years—until she grew up. You brought her out of the desert—to civilization—to the ranch of the Blairs. You wanted to find a home for her. They took her in, loved her, believing her poor, and all the time she had riches. The gold her father had mined and which you had saved all those years. It was like a fairy story."

Ruth, warming with speech, was shaken with a disturbing and troubled memory not yet clear.

"Wal, Adam, reckon I might as well unpack the burros," spoke up Merryvale. "We aimed to camp heah anyway, an' shore now there's more reason."

"Yes, we'll camp here," replied Adam. "It's too late to find a better place before night."

"How aboot these heah mules?" inquired Merryvale.

"I'll unhitch them presently. You fetch some firewood."

Adam strode to the prostrate form of Stone and gazed down upon him. Ruth recalling her part in his predicament was filled with concern.

"Did you kill him?" she queried, aghast.

"He's just stunned," replied Adam. He returned to Ruth and regarded her with eyes she found hard to meet. "Who is this fellow and what is he to you?"

"His name is Stone. He's nothing to me," replied Ruth, shortly.

"I don't often mistake the actions of men," said Adam, thoughtfully. "Where do you live? Where were you going? What happened?"

"I'll tell you presently," rejoined Ruth. "It all comes back to me. . . . You left us at Santa Ysabel. You disappeared one night. We waited day after day. You didn't come back. Genie postponed her marriage. At last she said: 'he's gone for good. I was afraid of it. Gone back to the desert! Just like Dismukes!' I recall her very words. She was heartbroken. . . . She called you Eagle, but the others gave you a name. . . . Was it Wansfell?"

"Yes," replied Adam. "Desert men called me Wansfell. But that is not my real name. It was given me by a drunken prospector, many years ago. And somehow it stuck to me."

"Wansfell? I've heard that name more than once since grandpa and I left Santa Ysabel," mused Ruth. "But I hated the past almost as I hated the present. I cherished no memories. They hurt me so."

"Ruth, now that I've found you, tell me your story," he said, with a tone she found it difficult to resist.

"Found me! What do you mean?" she queried, catching her breath.

"Ruth, it was *you* I ran away from at Santa Ysabel four long long years ago," he answered, with deep feeling. "Not from Genie and her happiness. Not to wander back into the lonely desert. I left you in the night, without a word, because if I had stayed an hour longer my strength would have failed. I loved you so terribly that it would have betrayed me. You were only nineteen, lonely, unhappy, yearning for love. I felt that I might have made you care for me. And I had no right. I suffered under the brand of Cain. I was an outlaw. Any day I might have been caught and hanged for my crime. So I left you."

"Ah—yes—it all comes back now," she murmured. "I wondered. I was deeply—hurt. . . . You were so good—so different. . . . I remember you upbraided me for being a weak dreaming girl. And I asked you to stay."

He took her hand and held it in his. "I had my ordeal, Ruth. If it had not been for my years on the desert I would have fallen. I wandered from place to place, fighting myself. Every cloud, every stone had the contour of your face. But at last I gave you up. I went on and on, finally to the oasis where fourteen years before, as a boy I had nearly starved to death. Day after day, in the hot silent hours, and night after night, in the lonely desert starlight, I walked with my spectres. But in the end I conquered. I took the trail back to the scene of my crime. Picacho! I meant to give myself up and suffer my punishment. The law wanted me. The sheriff whom I had scarred for life had sworn to hang me for murder. I sought him to expiate my crime and so find peace for my soul. I went back to Picacho. It had been a wild rushing miners' camp, prosperous, thronged by men. I found it abandoned, but there was a settlement on the river. The surrounding ruin and decay were fresh reminder of the lapse of years. Merryvale was there. It was hard to make him recognize in me the boy he had known there fourteen years before. But at last he did. I told him I had come to accept the penalty for killing my brother. Then Merryvale explained that I had rushed off into the desert without knowing the truth. I had not killed the brother I had loved. He was alive. I was not a murderer. . . . I had become a fugitive— a wanderer of the wasteland—I had endured all the agony the desert could deal to a man—for nothing, nothing."

Ruth felt a hard constriction of her throat that made speech difficult. She had been compelled to lift her eyes to meet his gaze. His face became familiar to her again, seeing it under change and play of emotion.

"It was your brother—you thought you'd killed," she said, at last. "All those years! . . . How terrible!—

Oh, thank God, for you, Adam, that it was all a mistake!"

"I rushed back to Santa Ysabel to tell you I was free," he went on, "only to find you gone. I did not think of seeing Genie. I thought only of you. . . . Then began my search. It led me all over Southern California, over into Mexico and Arizona, and finally into the desert. You were like a grain of sand lost out there. I never knew the name of your relative— your grandfather. And not until a few days ago did I ever meet a man who I believed had seen you. He was a prospector I chanced to run across in Yuma. I had known him years before. He believed he had seen you at a waterhole we used to call Indian Well, which is now Lost Lake. . . . So I came—and I have found you."

Ruth covered her face with her hands. The moment was stingingly full of a sweet and explicable shame.

"I'm not what I was when you knew me," she whispered.

He kept silent so long that Ruth feared his next words.

"I did not expect you to be. Anything might have happened to you. I remember the tragedy of your mother."

"Oh—*that* is what I've been trying to remember," she cried out. "You knew my mother. You spoke of her. But you told me so little. Tell me now, I beg of you."

"All in good time, Ruth," he returned. "But not quite yet. . . . I felt that if I ever found you it would be reward enough. The least I expected was to tell you my story, your mother's, and then to serve you, as I tried to serve her."

Ruth felt the hot blood burn her cheeks as she gazed into the gray eyes that seemed to read her very soul with understanding and love.

"I meant the years had changed me for the worse," she explained. "You called me a dreaming, petulant

girl. I was. But even so, I had hours of hope, of desire
to be good, to help grandfather to find a happy future.
I am twenty-three now. All the four years since I met
you I've lived on this desert—at that God-forsaken
place, Lost Lake. It *is* lost. It is as false as the mirages
I see every day. This desert of shifting sands has made
me like it. I am all change, storm—burning, burning
for I know not what. Sometimes I see myself as a
woman trying to climb those stairs of sand. The
dreams and hopes of my girlhood are gone. And I
mock myself because I am a creature of terrible
moods—because I cannot grow indifferent to everything—and sink—sink to the level of an Indian
woman—as that boy Stone expected me to."

"That is because you have clung to an ideal."

"I have no ideal—and you've found me too late,"
replied Ruth, bitterly.

"Nay, it could not be too late while you live."

Ruth was used to the importunities of men. But
they, like desert hawks, were fierce and hungry. No
man had ever thought of her needs, of what it would
take to make her happy. Wansfell stirred unplumbed
depths of thought that had the strange effect of aug-
menting her antagonism to the best in her.

A movement on the part of her companion caused
Ruth to turn. Stone was struggling to a sitting posture.
His trembling hand went to his swollen and bloody
face, now almost unrecognizable. Wansfell strode over
to confront him.

"Where were you taking this girl?" he demanded.

"San Ysidro—then San Diego," replied Stone,
speaking thickly.

"But you're off the road."

"When the sand began to blow I lost my way."

"It wasn't blowing enough to hide wheel tracks. It
looks as if you deliberately turned off into this canyon."

"I didn't. I thought the road ran here. Then the
mule balked."

"Why did you attack this girl?"

"I meant no harm," he replied, sullenly. "We'd eloped. When the mule balked and she found out we'd have to spend the night here—she changed her mind. She started to walk back. I tried to hold her and she fought, that's all."

Wansfell turned slowly to the girl.

"How much of what he says is true?"

"All of it—except that he didn't mean to harm me," replied Ruth, with the heat of anger and shame rising to her face. She scorned the reluctance she felt to confess to this man. "I objected to his—his attentions. When I realized my mistake I started to walk home. Then he became violent."

"Get up," Wansfell ordered. And when Stone hastily arose he continued: "you take a canteen and some grub, and light out."

Stone lost no time in complying, and soon he was on his way toward the gateway of the canyon. Once he looked back over his shoulder.

Merryvale, returning with a bundle of firewood, passed Stone and turned to gaze after him.

"Wal, now, he shore is a pleasant nice young fellar," remarked Merryvale, as he reached the others and threw down the wood. "Heah is what he said: 'I'll get even with her'—Adam, didn't you let him off sort of easy?"

"Ruth, you really eloped with that boy?" inquired Wansfell thoughtfully.

"Yes. I was a fool. But I'd have gone with anyone," she returned, impatiently.

In the look he bent on her there was no blame, merely an immutable loyalty. Ruth's quick intuition grasped that nothing could make any difference to this man. It did not matter to him what she was. He had found her. Something vague and vast began to form around her, loom over her, baffling and disconcerting.

"Wal, the sand has settled, an' I reckon we'll be comfortable heah, soon as it's cooler," remarked Merryvale, as he knelt with active hands.

Ruth watched the band of gold sunlight fade off the canyon rim above. Long before this her absence would have been noticed, and her grandfather would be prey to alarm. She felt a pang in her breast, even though he had not had much pity for her. The desert had obsessed him, as it had her mother and father.

While she mused the shadows deepened in the canyon. The low faint moan of wind died out altogether. The camp fire crackled. Merryvale hopped back and forth in sprightly fashion from packs to his heating pots and pans. A savory fragrance made Ruth reflect that her mental state did not kill hunger. Why should a person feel tired of living yet be a victim to appetite? She watched Wansfell unroll the blankets, and make her a bed under the protecting wall of stone. Then he fetched her a pan of warm water, and her bag from the wagon.

"Adam," she said, smiling up at him, "you're very good to think of me, but what is the use?"

"Use of what?" he asked.

"Oh, of bathing my miserable face or brushing my hair—of eating—of anything."

"You ask what is the use of doing for yourself? Well—only to make yourself strong and proficient in order to help others."

"That is your religion?"

"No. It is how I saved myself."

Ruth fell silent. What kind of man was this Adam Wansfell? She remembered Genie Linwood's story, and her heart beat unwontedly, despite her mocking of any faith or hope. Too late was it for this strange desert man to help her. Wearily she opened her bag and took out the things she wanted, and then let down her hair. She brushed it slowly. The silky sound and the soft feel of her hair always seemed pleasant, soothing. Then she bathed her hands and face. The mirror pictured the same face which she had jealously watched and lovingly cared for and yet increasingly hated for so long. What would Wansfell think of it? She could not help caring. It was an ineradicable instinct. She gazed at the thick wavy dark gold hair parted from a low level brow, at the purple eyes brooding, passionate, tragic, at the red bow-shaped lips, at the golden tan of cheek and neck, at the whole contour of face which the blasting desert had no power to change; and she was aware more than ever before of its haunting loveliness. No use to deny her vanity and pride! She knew, and never before had she so despised and ridiculed this trait that she could not understand.

Meanwhile Adam was getting food and drink, which he presently set before Ruth.

"I wonder if you see in your mirror what I see when I look at you?" he asked, with a smile.

"What do you see?"

"You have changed, Ruth. I remembered you of course, but your face of a girl is now that of a woman. The desert magnifies all beauty, as well as ugliness. There are no flowers as vivid and beautiful as desert flowers, nothing in nature so hideous as some desert forms. The desert seizes upon any characteristic peculiar to person or plant or animal and develops it with an appalling intensity. It is the ferocity of life, fighting to survive."

"Adam, are you paying me a compliment?" she asked, in perplexity.

"No. I was just accounting for your beauty. You owe it to the desert and the sun you hate. You owe to it also the madness of such men as Stone. He was not to blame so much as you believe. Most men on the desert drop to the level of beasts. Many fall even lower. It is no fault of theirs, if they are born without mind and will to combat primitive instincts."

"You make me think, and I wish you wouldn't," replied Ruth. "But my primitive instinct of hunger is surely in the ascendant."

"Eat then. Merryvale is the best cook I've met on the desert."

Twilight had fallen and the heat of the day had tempered when Adam again approached Ruth.

"You must be tired after your long ride," he said. "Will you walk a while?"

"Yes, I'd like to, presently—after we've talked," she began, hurriedly. "There is so much. . . . But first, now that you've found me what do you think you're going to do with me?"

"It depends," he replied, slowly.

"On what?"

"Why, on what is best and right for your happiness."

"Would you take me out of the desert—to San Diego?"

"Anywhere, on that one condition."

"Oh, I think I'll make you take me away from Lost Lake—from this hell of changing sand dunes. . . . But I couldn't deceive you. I couldn't let you hope to. . . ."

"Ruth, I had only one hope—to find you and to help you," he interrupted. "There is a bond between you and me, which you don't realize. I will explain when I come to tell you all about your mother."

"Oh, Adam, tell me—now?" she entreated, laying a hand on his.

"It is not yet time," he replied, enigmatically. "First let me help you to get over your distress. Meeting me has upset you. But it need not. You are bound in some way that you hate to confess. Is it not so?"

"Yes, indeed I am," she murmured.

"Well then, know once for all that I love you and that my greatest wish is to serve you. I cannot hope that you might marry me—"

"Adam, I—I can't marry you," she said, brokenly.

"I gathered so much, but meant to ask you anyway," he rejoined, gravely. "Nevertheless, I can make you happy. . . . Ruth, could you care for me?"

"I *did* care. I—I shall care again. I know. I would gladly marry you. But it's too late!"

"You are already married?" he went on, a little huskily.

"Yes. But it's not only that. It's not only that I bear

a man's name. Any day I might be free of him. Life is uncertain on this desert. He is hated and feared. He is a dishonest man. Some day he will be killed. . . . But I meant, too late for another and more serious reason. I fear I have become a hopeless, miserable, half-mad woman, with no longer a belief in self or God. The desert has ruined me. I would never drag down and ruin a man whom my mother knew and trusted—cared for, perhaps."

"Your mother did care for me, Ruth."

"Oh, I guessed it. That brings me closer to you. Yet it can't change the hard facts."

"Ruth, tell me your story and let me judge of the hard facts. Trust me."

"Yes, I will. You must—think me so weak—and shallow. But it's no wonder I'm unstrung. To meet you, who knew my mother, who—But listen, I think I'd like Merryvale to hear my story. If he has wandered with you all over this terrible desert, helping you search for me, I'd like him to know about me, from my own lips."

"Merryvale, come here," called Adam, to the motionless figure beside the camp fire. "Sit down here," went on Adam. "Ruth has something to tell us."

"Wal, now, I'm shore glad," said the old man, knocking the embers out of his pipe. "I've been wonderin' a lot, an' troublin' myself. But shore, Ruth, you'll be talkin' to a friend."

Ruth drew a deep breath that was half sigh, half sob, and surrendered to some emotion beyond her ken.

"I'll begin where you left me—at Santa Ysabel," she said. "My grandfather, Caleb Hunt, about that time became interested in water rights on the desert. He had considerable money which he wanted to invest in desert holdings. And he was affected with a pulmonary disease, from which he suffered less on the desert than anywhere. Indeed he recovered from this. . . . We went first to Yuma, where he fell in with the men who figure largely in my story. Grandfather went into the freighting business with these men. Supplies from San Francisco came by sea and river round to Yuma, and were there freighted in wagons into the interior.

"Grandfather invested heavily in this business. He bought a water hole from the Indians, and here established a freighting post. Lost Lake, they call it. There was a lake there in ages past. It's now a ghastly place, on the edge of these sand dunes.

"The man who won my grandfather to this enterprise was a young handsome fellow who fascinated me. But I did not love him. He kept at me to marry him, and grandfather favored his suit. Between them they made my life wretched. The desert had begun to pall on me. I grew moody and uncertain of myself. At last grandfather told me that if I did not consent to this marriage he would be ruined. I did not know which way to turn. All my girlhood my mother had taught me never to give myself where I did not love. I told grandfather and the man who wanted me to be his wife. But their argument was that love would come. My suitor swore that if I would only marry him he would wait for love to come—before asking me to be really a wife. I didn't trust him—I feared him. Yet they finally wore me out.

"The very first night after my marriage my husband, under the influence of drink, tried to force his way into my bedroom. I learned that he considered our compact mere nonsense. At my refusal to let him in he grew violent and nearly wrecked the place. But I escaped to grandfather's house.

"Next day he approached me, sober, with all his blandishments, and begged me to overlook his action.

"I told him I loathed him, and that was the end. He tried for weeks to change me, and failing, he stood out in his true colors. He was a gambler, a dissolute adventurer who gradually gained power in Yuma. He robbed grandfather.

"That was over three years ago. Grandfather has kept his hold on the water rights at Lost Lake, and he fights still to regain something he lost in the freighting business. But this is futile. Eventually they will get the water hole from him and then he will be ruined. Lost Lake is an important post on the freighting line, and of course the water is the valuable asset there.

"All this would have been bad enough for me, without the terrible devastating maddening effect of the desert. In winter I endured. In summer the blasting sun, the moaning wind, the flying sand or the endless waste of desert, pitiless, encompassing, shutting me in, the awful heat and glare,—these at times drove me to desperation. I grew obsessed with the idea of getting away. Twice grandfather took me to Yuma. That was almost as bad. Wicked, whirling, terrible town of blood and heat and dust! Both times I had to leave on account of men who tormented me, fought over me . . . Oh, no doubt I was much to blame. I looked always for some one to free me. At first it was some man whom I could care for. But it came to mean some man who would care enough for me to take me away. Back at Lost Lake I would have weeks of awful loneliness. Then some traveler, some miner or gambler, or adventurer would see me—and the bitter lesson I learned did not seem to change me. I grew sick at my fate . . . A few weeks ago this young man I was with, Hal Stone, came to Lost Lake. He was a horse dealer and made money. His infatuation for me was welcome, I am bound to admit. But I had no sense, no judgment. He was kind, pleasant, engaging at first, and he loved me. I persuaded myself that I was attracted to him, and might some day love him. He had little trouble in getting me to run away. We left Lost Lake at daylight this morning, and not until late did I suspect Stone was off the road. Old Butch balked here in this canyon or you might—never have—met us. . . . I see no way out —I can't go back home, yet—somehow—I thank God —you found me."

3

Both Ruth's listeners maintained a profound silence. She was aware of Wansfell pressing her hand so tightly that it pained. The camp fire had burned down to ruddy embers. A lonesome desert owl hooted dismally down the darkening canyon. Ruth experienced an incomprehensible relief.

"Wal, Ruth," said Merryvale, at last breaking the silence, "I've seen forty years of desert life. An' I reckon your little time heah hasn't been so bad."

"It could have been vastly worse," added Wansfell, in voice which seemed full of relief. "I expected worse. Have you told us everything?"

"Yes, everything vital. I held back his name because I hate to speak it."

"There is no need. It doesn't matter who your——the man is. What does matter is the need for you to learn a lesson from the past." Merryvale spoke in terms of the physical. Most desert people do that. Only in rare cases does a man or woman grow spiritually on the desert. It is too hard, too fierce, too relentless, too bound by the elements. Desert creatures all, particularly human beings, concentrate on survival. A fight for life! . . . "Ruth, you have neglected your spiritual side."

"Are you preaching to me?" queried Ruth, almost mockingly.

"No. I want to wake you to facts that are outside your thinking. You imagine you've suffered terribly. But you have not—as we desert folk know suffering."

"My heart is broken," said Ruth.

"No," he contradicted, and placed his great hands on her shoulders, bending to look into her eyes. "I believe that hearts can break. And on this desert I have met many persons with broken hearts and ruined lives. But you are not one of them, Ruth."

"If I think I am, doesn't that make it so?" she asked, stubbornly.

"Yes, for the time being, until you find the truth."

"The truth? You're beyond me, Adam. I never understood you back there at Santa Ysabel. Much less can I now. You—you seem to make light of my situation."

"Indeed, I do not. It is sad enough. But the desert, for all your hatred, has not yet betrayed you. I see it has given you more wonderful health and beauty. You are not broken—lost. And now you will not be."

He drew back from her and stood erect, towering and dark. Merryvale gave her a kindly touch, as if to express something he could not voice; then he stole away into the shadow of the wall.

"Not broken—lost!" repeated Ruth. "And now I never will be . . . Why?"

"Because I have found you," he said, simply.

She could not reply to that, though it astounded and irritated, and somehow warmed her cold gratitude.

"Go to bed and rest," he said. "Tomorrow we will decide what to do."

He moved away into the gloom, his slow footfalls padding on the sand. Ruth roused herself, and groping for the blankets she sat down to remove her shoes and outer garments. Slipping down between the blankets she covered herself and lay still. It was a hard bed, yet such was her fatigue, something to be grateful for. She would rest and think, but not sleep.

As she endeavored to settle down to regulate her disordered thoughts she saw the gloom of the canyon lightening. This silvering of the shadows and the walls did not come from the cold radiant stars, for they were losing their brilliance under the influence of a stronger luminary. The moon had risen. Every moment afterward the canyon grew lighter.

What would Stone tell her husband, Guerd? He had wit enough to know that if he told the truth, Guerd would kill him. He would lie, and somehow twist the affair to Ruth's further discredit. She did not care what his machinations might be, and dismissed him with a sickening wonder at her rashness.

She lingered longer in reflection about her grandfather. Somehow the resentment she had labored under for so long had lessened. Almost, she had hated him for dragging her into the desert. But it had been a matter of life for him, and otherwise he had been most kind and loving. Remorse stirred in her. What would become of him now? Guerd Larey and Collishaw, with their hirelings, would devour him as wolves a sheep. She had been the power that had held these hardened men leashed. The irony of fate for Larey had been that the greater grew her loathing, the more he desired her. More than once he had threatened to carry her off to some lonely oasis and bend her to his will.

She knew her husband would try it. And she would kill him. That alone was enough to keep her from going back. But there were many other reasons. No, her grandfather would have to go on alone. Poor old man! The desert would claim him, as it had claimed her mother and father. But never would it destroy her!

She would not return to Lost Lake. The decision sent a tingling all over her body. To get away from the heat, the copper sky, the blazing sun, the insulating ridged waste of changing sand—what joyous prospect! How good not to be ogled by sloe-eyed Mexicans, not to be watched by silent stealthy Indians, not to live among hard men, in color and action and mood like the desert! What sweetness there could be in verdant green surroundings, by the cool seaside, in the vineyards and groves of the coast!

Ruth had clung tenaciously to the money given her by her parents when they left her. She had spent less

and less of it as time went by on the desert. Some day
she would need that money, and now the time had
come. She remembered she had confided in Stone.
Had that actuated him in any measure? More than
once he had tried to find out how much it was, and
where she kept it. Ruth, making sure she had not lost
the money, went on dreaming of travel, change, work,
a new life.

Suddenly a footstep on the sand broke her brooding
meditation. She had closed her eyes, and forgotten for
the moment the night, the canyon, and the men who
were there.

The moon stood above the gateway of the canyon,
full and resplendent, flooding the desert with silver
light. Far out there Ruth saw her stairs of sand, beautiful, illusive, mystic, climbing away to the starry
heavens. Her heart sank. She had been dreaming. The
desert was there, illimitable and encompassing. Could
she ever climb out of it?

Another footstep caused her to raise her head. A
tall dark form moved in the moonlight. Wansfell! He
walked by her, down the middle of the canyon a few
rods, his hands folded behind him. How lofty his stature! Turning back he retraced his steps, walked up the
canyon a like distance, then faced round to repeat the
performance. He passed scarcely a dozen yards from
Ruth, and in the white moonlight she could see him
distinctly. She watched him patrol this beat.

His bare head had the cast of a striking eagle. He
walked erect, with free step, though he gave an impression of a man burdened. What was on his mind
that he did not rest and sleep? Ruth knew, and she
could not control womanly emotions. A sense of protection suddenly struck her. Never a night had she
lain down in her desert home without dread! But this
night the sombre shadow of mind had not returned.
No man, not even Guerd Larey, could harm her now,
while that giant stalked out there. And the difference
became incalculable in its far-reaching influence.

Genie Linwood returned clearer than ever before

to Ruth. She recalled how Genie had talked about this man. He was like Tanquitch the mountain God of the Indians. His face was like the sun. . . . Genie's mother had prayed for someone to find them—when they were starving. And the day came when desert robbers stole Genie away. But Adam met and killed them. How terrible he was! . . . Genie's mother had said her prayer had been answered. And she died leaving Genie to him.

Ruth's heart swelled high in her breast. The thing that this desert man had done for a child could not be mistaken or underestimated. Moreover Genie had dwelt vaguely on hints she had gotten from the Indians. Had they called him Eagle only for his shape of head and gray lightning of eyes? White men had named him the Wanderer.

To think that this strange man had fallen in love with her at Genie's—four years past—had fled from her because he believed he had murdered his brother. . . . And now he had found her. What did it mean? What would it lead to?

She felt that she must flee from him before he found her to be even a shallower creature than she had confessed herself. But Adam had known her mother, loved her, no doubt, as all men had loved her. Ruth recalled the times of her girlhood that had been darkened by her father's jealousy of her mother. It was hardly possible for Ruth to go away from Wansfell without learning all he knew about her mother and the tragedy of her end in Death Valley. Yet Ruth, much as she longed to hear it, dreaded it even more. It might be a link in a chain which bound her to Wansfell.

Was there not a chain? She had been ready to fall in love with him four years ago. She wanted to now. . . . Oh, that overwhelming craving to love and be loved! To love someone! That was the awful thing the desert had magnified in Ruth. She could not deny it. . . . But she was a woman now. It would be like the raging flood or the desert sun. . . . Not Genie's Eagle! She must not love him, for he soared on the heights.

As long as Wansfell paced to and fro, Ruth lay wide awake, prey to changeful thought and emotion. At last she saw him lie down on his bed between her and the gateway of the canyon. Utter silence settled down then, brooding, inscrutable. The moon sank behind the rim of the nearer wall, and once again dark shadows encroached upon the silver. Desert night enfolded her, and the protection of these companions who had so strangely sought and found her. Closing heavy eyelids, Ruth surrendered to a drowsiness that gradually dulled her thought, and at length she fell asleep.

A voice pierced Ruth's slumbers. She awoke in a rosy cool dawn. The sun had not risen. The wall in front of her was not that of her adobe room at home, but the wall of a cliff. She remembered with a shock.

"Adam, I tell you that son-of-a-gun of a mule has stood right there in his tracks all night," Merryvale was saying. "Shore beats me for a balky beast."

"Merryvale, you know burros, but not mules," replied Adam. "Old Butch's performance is unusual, but not extraordinary."

"Old Butch? Do you know this old gray long-eared cuss?"

"I guess. I drove him eight years ago up in the Mohave. He was noted then for balking. The packers at the mine where I worked couldn't drive him. They shot him more than once."

"Wal, he shore ain't any the worse, for all I can see."

"Butch shows the wear and tear of the desert, same as we do. I wonder how he got way down here in the sand dunes. It'll be funny when he wakes up and recognizes me."

"See, heah, Adam, shore you ain't tryin' to make me believe that mule will know you after eight years?"

"You bet he will. Merryvale, I'm the only man who could fetch Butch out of a balk. I'll bet you he'll walk right out of that and lay his head on my shoulder."

"Humph! I ain't bettin' you. But I'll say he'll have to grow lots taller. An' I'm curious to know just how you handle him."

"Wait and see," replied Wansfell. "Let's rustle some wood."

"It ain't very plenty, onless my eyes are pore."

The men parted, and left camp without being aware that Ruth had awakened. She got up, dressed, and found water in one of Stone's canteens, which he had left in the wagon. Old Butch never flicked an eyelash.

"You reprobate," said Ruth, eyeing the mule. "I'm as curious as Merryvale to see how Wansfell will make you move."

Ruth took advantage of the opportunity to walk to and fro, and back into recesses of the canyon which she had not noticed yesterday. She found a nervous strain disturbing the calm in which she had awakened. Her mind had been made up and now it seemed to be wavering, to what end she had no inkling. This was another day, and it was different.

"I won't go back to Lost Lake," she announced aloud, as if to fortify herself.

Upon returning to camp, she found Merryvale there, breaking up a meager supply of wood.

"Mawnin', Ruth," he greeted her, with a smile. "Strikes me you look like the break of day."

"Good morning," replied Ruth. "I don't feel quite so bright, for all your compliment."

"Wal, I've learned things an' people are what they look like. They can't help it. Take Adam for instance. . . . Wal, heah he comes, an' I reckon I'd better wait till some other time."

"Make a time then, Merryvale, for I want to know all about him," replied Ruth, earnestly.

Adam arrived with an armful of brush and dead cactus, which he dropped upon the sand.

"It's a glorious morning, Ruth," he declared. "The sun is stepping red down over the sand dunes. Aren't you glad to be alive, young, so good to look at, with all the world before you?"

"*Buenos dias, senor,* I'd like to say I'm not glad, but I'm afraid I am a little."

"Ruth, you're not going home?" he queried, with gray flash of glance at her.

"How did you guess?"

"It came to me," he returned, simply.

"When?"

"Just now."

"Adam, you don't approve?"

"I'm afraid not. Well, let's have breakfast. Then I'll tackle the job."

"You mean changing Old Butch and me? Two mules with but a single thought!"

He laughed, the first time she had heard him do so. It was a mellow sound, ringing pleasantly upon the air. Then while he fell to helping Merryvale she watched him with studious, critical eyes. If she remembered him perfectly, there was a little more gray above his temples, but she could formulate no other change. He was so tall that his massive shoulders did not get correct estimate at first glance. Yet he was not heavy. His muscles rippled and bulged when he moved, yet appeared to sink in when he was still. He looked neither young nor middle-aged nor old. There was a lithe magnificence in his action. His hands were huge yet shapely, indicating good birth. But it was the mould of his head, the contour of his face that fascinated Ruth. Seen in profile it was clear, sharp, cruel, almost ruthless, yet singularly beautiful in its likeness to a bird of prey.

His attire was that of the desert prospector—a ragged shirt the color of sand, through rents in which gleamed the brown muscles, frayed and stained corduroys stuck in the rough heavy worn boots of a miner, his belt, one of wide dark leather, shiny and thin from long service.

While Ruth scrutinized Adam, she suddenly experienced a sensation that was familiar. It was undeniably a warmth of interest and kindness and wondering pity; and beyond that something deeper, vaguer, becoming lost in the recesses of feeling. Stone had awakened this in her, in some degree—a fact which she remembered now with disdain. Other men in the past had roused it, fleetingly. It never lasted. Here it came again, stronger than ever before, somehow changed—sweet and thrilling, until she deliberately beat it down.

Ruth strolled away then, beset again by the complexity of herself. But she did not begrudge this sentiment, or whatever it was. She thought it was singular that she would fight it, resist it, in Adam's case, when in regard to other men, she had rather encouraged it. What an ingrate she would be not to feel greatly touched at this man's regard for her.

"Wal, Ruth, come to the festal board," invited Merryvale. "What with the grub in your basket there, we'll shore make out a breakfast fit for the gods."

It was Merryvale who did all the talking during the meal. He appeared to be a loquacious old man, as spry of wit and humor as he was on his feet. His attachment for Adam showed markedly. Ruth received strengthening of the impression that Merryvale regarded her as long associated with Adam and himself. She began to like him, to feel that he could be trusted.

"Shore, you folks ain't very hungry this mawnin'," he remarked, slyly.

"Indeed I was—for me," replied Ruth, smiling.

Adam rose without comment, and his first task was to roll up Ruth's bed, which he threw into the wagon. Old Butch twitched his ears. Adam gave the mule a glance which promised much. Then he set about other tasks of packing.

"Wal, Ruth, it'll be a better day for travelin' than yesterday," said Merryvale.

"Thank goodness. I hate the sand."

"I used to, when I first took up this wanderin' life with Adam. But I got used to it, an' now it's home."

"Used to it?" queried Ruth, restlessly. "Why, this

waste of sand doesn't stay the same long enought for that."

"Wal, it's all in the way you feel," replied Merryvale, placidly. "If you loved the desert you'd understand."

"Love this hell of sand and stone and solitude!" exclaimed Ruth, shudderingly.

"Young woman, you may live to love what makes you suffer most," said the old man, nodding sagely.

Adam approached from behind.

"Merryvale, are you about cleaned up?"

"Jest about. I'm shore waitin' to see you wake up Butch."

"So am I," added Ruth, rising.

"That'll take only a minute," said Adam.

"See heah, Adam," rejoined Merryvale plaintively, "I'd shore like to see you get stuck on some job once."

"It won't be on this mule, Merryvale. But you may have your satisfaction soon," said Adam, with serious glance at Ruth. "Are you ready to talk over what you want to do?"

"Quite ready," answered Ruth, with a lightness that was not genuine.

Adam drew her back to a seat on the flat rock. "Well, then, what is it?"

"I want to go out of this desert," announced Ruth, and the expression on her yearning broke her calm.

"Where to?"

"To the coast. Or anywhere, for that matter, away from the sand and heat—this endless open space."

"What would you do?"

"Find work somewhere."

"Could you do any kind of work that would make you self-supporting?"

"I don't know. I never could keep house for grandpa, that's certain. But I'd have to work at something. I've some money to start with. But it wouldn't last forever."

"Ruth, this plan won't do," said Adam, gravely.

"I've made up my mind," she returned, stubbornly. "You can't change it."

"Yes, I can. But let me reason with you."

"I'm afraid I'm not one to listen to reason. I never was."

"Isn't it selfish of you to leave your grandfather?"

"Yes, of course it is," she replied, in impatient regret. "But I can't help that."

"You could make this a turning point in your life. To go back to him, to your obligations, to overcome your loathing of the desert, to endure and to serve—that would make you a real woman. If you run off alone, footloose and reckless and beautiful as you are, it will be only to ruin."

"Mr. Wansfell, are you suggesting that I go back to my husband?" she queried, with sarcasm.

"No. If he is truly what you say, it's right that you never go. But your grandfather—what you owe him, and more, what you owe *yourself*——"

"I owe myself freedom from this desert hell."

"Ruth, it was hell to me once," he replied, gently. "But not now. In conquering the desert I have conquered myself."

"I am a woman," she returned, bitterly. It roused her anger that already his look, his tone, his thought for her had begun to work upon her.

"Do you deny the risk you run, if you persist in going?"

"Risk—of what?"

"Of hardship, of trouble—of ruin?"

"Deny risk of all that?" she flashed. "No, I don't. But the same thing holds if I remain and at least I'd have a chance. Here I'm absolutely sure of ruin, sooner or later . . . or death!"

Adam rose perturbed and paced before her, as she had seen him in the moonlight. Yes, there was a burden upon him.

"If I let you go, I shall go too," he said, halting before her.

"Of course," replied Ruth, eagerly. "How else

could I? I expect and hope you will take me out and set me upon my feet somewhere."

"And then?"

"Why, why, you could leave me to my fate."

"No. What of my promise to your mother?" he returned, sternly.

"My—mother?" echoed Ruth, falteringly. "I—I didn't know you——"

"You shall know presently. But know now that I wouldn't leave you whether you go or stay."

Ruth vibrated to that with an emotion that held back her rising antagonism.

"You need someone just as badly as ever Genie Linwood did," went on Adam.

"God knows I do," returned Ruth, poignantly. She mastered her feeling, and continued. "Very well, then, you go with me. I can't drive you away. I—I believe I'm glad—glad, though I'm not worthy of your devotion."

"Ruth, it's not a question of my devotion," he said impatiently. "I would do this for you if I'd never heard of you until now."

"How can you expect me to believe that?" she demanded, despising herself for a doubt she could not help.

"Well, you're right. I shouldn't have expected you to. Your husband, and the desert men you've met, and this boy Stone, according to your story, if it's true—"

"Do you accuse me of lying?" interrupted Ruth, sharply.

"Ruth, look me straight in the eyes. There. . . . You have no call for fury. Tell me, have you always been truthful?"

"No. I suppose I lied to Stone—and the rest," she burst out, as if compelled. "But I told you the truth."

"I believe you, and that helps," he said. "But to get back to the main issue. . . . I don't think it womanly or right for you to abandon your grandfather."

"Right or wrong, I must," she rejoined.

"His home is your home, isn't it?"

"Yes."

"Well, I'm sorry to oppose you, but I'll have to take you back," he replied, conclusively.

Ruth felt the blood rush hot to her cheeks.

"You shall not!" she retorted, passionately. "Unless you resort to force as Stone did. In which case I shall have merely leaped out of the frying pan into the fire."

He did not seem quickly to comprehend her bitter speech. When he did it was if she had struck him.

"Forgive me, Adam," she said, cooling. "I didn't mean that last. I am a cat, you see. I fear I'm not even woman enough to appreciate you—your kindness— what you believe your duty. . . . But I did mean you are not going to take me home."

"Indeed I am."

"No!" she cried, wildly, driven to desperation by a consciousness of weakness.

"Ruth, I want to spare you pain," he said, bending over her. "At least until you're home, recovered from this mad jaunt."

"Spare me pain? You're not doing it. What do you mean?"

"Will you take my word, until some time later, that I have the power now to make you change your mind?"

"No, I won't."

"You will not trust me?"

"I can't. I don't believe. . . . There's not anyone who can change me."

"You refuse to go home?"

"Absolutely."

"You are disappointing me terribly. I hoped to find you more of a woman. At least one in whom earnestness and nobility had not wholly died."

"I don't care what you hoped for me—or have found in me," she returned, in heated bitterness, averting her gaze from the gray pitying storm of eyes she could not meet. "I'm no good. Or if I am it'll not be for long. Take me to the first settlement, and leave me."

"No. You go home," he thundered at her. Then turning his back he appeared to be fumbling at his blouse. She heard a musical clink of gold coins. Then he wheeled, strangely pale, and forced something into her hand.

"Look inside," he said, huskily.

The object was an oval locket, large and heavy, of dull gold worn smooth. With trembling fingers Ruth essayed to open it. The blood receded to her heart. Suddenly the locket flew open and lay flat in her palm, disclosing two faces done in miniature.

"Mother . . . and I!" gasped Ruth.

Adam made no reply. As she stared down, her mother's lovely face stared up at her. And opposite was the youthful portrait of herself. What a proud petulant looking child! She had been fourteen when this was painted in Philadelphia. Oh, so long ago! Her look returned to the beloved features of this mother she had lost. Her eyes dimmed so that she could not see, and at last her hot tears fell upon the open locket.

"Adam, where did you get this?" she whispered.

"Your mother gave it to me," he replied.

"When?"

"This is May. . . . It will be eight years ago in July."

"How did she—come to give it?" went on Ruth, drying her eyes, and striving for self-control.

"That is your mother's story."

"Ah! . . . Tell me now."

He dropped down beside her, so that his eyes were on a level with hers.

"Years ago an old prospector friend of mine, Dismukes by name, told me about a man and woman living in Death Valley under strange circumstances. They were gentle folk, he said, not inured to the hardship of desert life, and death surely awaited them there. It was my way to help people whom the desert had fettered one way or another. So I went to Death Valley.

"Eventually I found this couple living in a comfortless shack, under the shadow of the most terrible slope of weathered rock in all that valley of destruction. The woman was exceedingly beautiful and frail—your mother, Magdalene Virey. And the man was her husband."

"My father," murmured Ruth, with eager parting lips.

"I saw at once that I was not wanted there, but I decided to stay to try and help your mother. Virey was beyond me. He was half mad, I think. Anyway he had brought her there to the nakedest, and loneliest and most forbidding desolate spot on earth, away from the world of man. He loved her so madly that he hated her. It was jealousy of men, terrible jealousy that had brought this about. Your mother had never loved Virey and she admitted to me that she had been unfaithful to him. She had come willingly to Death Valley to suffer any privation or torture that he chose to inflict. She had a great spirit. But she was a wordly woman, with a mocking doubt of man and herself and God.

"Well, here I found the cruelest and most hopeless task the desert had ever given me. I could not persuade your mother to leave Death Valley. She vowed she would perish there as Virey wished. No woman can live through a summer in that valley of burning days and midnight blasting winds of fire. I feared she was doomed, but I fought with all my strength. She had a wonderful mind, and I interested her in Death Valley. Gradually she improved in health and strength. She came to love the grandeur and sublimity of that appalling place. Virey looked on, distrustful of me, and he listened to the falling, rolling, ringing rocks that all hours heralded the avalanche to come. I would have killed him, but for your mother.

"All that I had suffered I told your mother. All I knew of the desert. In the end it saved her soul. Then July came, with its infernal heat."

Ruth, gazing spellbound, with hands locked like a

vise, saw a sombre change pass over Adam's face. She seemed to be peering through a mask, at dim shadows and lines of torture.

"July came with its torrid sun by day and those awful winds by night. Then I had to fight death itself. One morning, after a night when for hours I believed your mother was dying, she took this locket from her bosom and gave it to me, with a sacred trust, which I will tell you last.

"The day came when I could endure her agony no longer. I decided to kill Virey, or leave him there to a worse fate, and take your mother away. So that morning I went in search of my burros. Upon my return I heard the cracking of rocks. It had an ominous sound. I ran. There was Virey high on the slope rolling rocks down. I had to dodge great boulders as I ran to get your mother from the shack. Suddenly the avalanche started with a crash. Your mother came running out. But it was too late. I could not save her. I climbed a high rock just in the nick of time. The avalanche that was carrying Virey to destruction rolled down with terrific bellowing roar. The gray mass of stones and dust, like a cloud, enveloped your mother, carried her away —buried her forever."

His deep voice, ending abruptly, released Ruth with a violent wrench of clamped emotions. She sank against Adam's shoulder, with bursting heart and blinded eyes.

"Oh, my God! How horrible!" she moaned. "Oh, mother—mother! . . . I knew something dreadful would happen to her. . . . Father was cruel to her. I came to hate him for it. . . . Mother, dear, who loved me so—dead and buried where I can never see her grave!"

"No, Ruth, you can never go there," said Adam.

"Death Valley! It has always haunted me since you talked of it at Santa Ysabel. . . . Oh, you might have saved her!"

"Yes, Ruth, but only against her will. I could not have done it except toward the end. And I meant to."

"Adam, you must—have loved mother," murmured Ruth, brokenly.

"Not at first, but at the last I did love her," returned Adam, hoarsely.

"Oh, it's come—release from that knot in my breast. The fear—the haunting fear! And now it's a pang that will kill me."

"No, Ruth. Only change you—uplift you," he replied.

"And my mother's sacred trust?" asked Ruth, with trembling lips.

"Was you, Ruth. She bade me seek you, find you, and save you from a fate such as hers had been. She said by her own love for me you would love me too. You would be like her. You would have all of her weaknesses and none of her strength. The same wild longings and passions without the desire to thwart them!"

"Oh, how true!" cried Ruth, bitterly.

"That was your mother's sacred trust. She gave me you."

"Why, oh, why didn't you tell me at Santa Ysabel?" demanded Ruth.

"I believed I'd killed my brother and was a fugitive from justice."

"What matter? I would gladly have gone with you to the very end of the world. . . . Now, too late—too late!"

"Yes, for that, but not for all the rest."

Ruth drew away from him and rose. "I yield to my mother's trust, knowing that I am more lost than ever," she replied, unsteadily. "Take me where you will."

4

Merryvale hailed Adam with a shout: "Hey. We're all packed heah, an' shore ready to move. How aboot Old Butch?"

The gray mule had been unhitched and haltered to the wagon for the night. Evidently he had moved around a little, but the moment Merryvale approached and untied him, he froze in his tracks, very like an opossum when disturbed.

"Son-of-a-gun never looks you in the eye," observed Merryvale.

Adam strode to the wagon and took off the seat a long black leather whip, the kind teamsters called a blacksnake. With this doubled in his hands Adam walked round the mule to a position about ten feet in front of him. And there he stood eyeing the stubborn brute. It was easy to see that this situation might become extraordinary, if it were possible that Old Butch would recognize the man.

Adam swung the long whip round his head, faster and faster until it fairly whistled.

"HYAR, BUTCH!"

His stentorian voice filled the canyon with its volume hard, ringing, terrifying. Then he leaped and brought down the whip with tremendous force. It cracked like a pistol.

Old Butch screamed and jumped as if he had been shot. The black whip slipped off his left front leg just above the fetlock. A huge welt bulged out as if by magic. Butch uttered another sound, not unlike a

45

groan. Then he limped up to Adam and actually laid his head against him.

"Aha, you old Mohave scoundrel. You haven't forgotten me," said Adam, pulling the gray ears.

Every line of Old Butch had seemingly softened, and he was shaking.

"Wal, I'll be doggoned!" ejaculated Merryvale, scratching his grizzled head. "That's shore a new one on me."

"There's only one place you can hurt a mule," returned Adam. "I'll bet Butch hasn't been hit there since I last drove him. Now we can hitch up."

Adam threw the whip into the wagon, and leading Butch into place beside the other mule, he threw the harness over him. In a few moments more the team was hitched up and ready.

"Come, Ruth," called Adam.

Without protest she permitted Adam to help her up to the wagon seat.

"Merryvale, you drive. I'll go ahead with the burros," he directed, and turned away.

"Wal, now, this is shore goin' to be fine," replied the old man, as he laboriously climbed to the seat and took up the reins. "I ain't no crack mule driver, but I'll rise to the occasion. Now, Ruth, let me put my coat back of you. This heah seat is hard. There. . . . Giddep, you mules!"

Adam stalked on ahead, driving the two burros.

Out of the narrow golden-walled canyon confines into the open!

The silver-ribbed desert rolled and spread away, down and down, into vast monotony. It smote Ruth mercilessly.

After a moment she shut the desert out of her consciousness and locked herself with her grief. At last she knew what had become of her mother. The mystery, the uncertainty, the dread were at an end forever. She realized the tragedy now. She had read between the lines of Adam's story. He had tried to spare her. But the truth was hers in all its stark and

naked ghastliness. She buried it deep, never to be uncovered again. And with bowed head and face hidden
in her veil she grieved for her mother. The bitterness
of loss, the sad memory of past love,—these augmented into dark hopeless misery, into cold pang of
laboring breast, into sluggish beat of heart and dead-
ened pulse.

She endured this black hour, sustained by the one
unforgettable fact of her mother's love, and prayer
that she be not victim to the heritage of blood be-
queathed her. It was this thought which pierced into
the darkness of her soul and brought the first ray of
light. By it she groped her way back, slowly dispelling
the shadows.

When again Ruth grew aware of the outside world,
she had been carried far across the sands to the rim of
the vast desert bowl of southern California.

Down the sweep of the endless gradual slope three
dark figures moved against the wavering heat veils
Wansfell and his two burros.

Farther on a green spot shone against the glaring
red and white—and that was the oasis, Lost Lake. It
lay at the foot of the stairs of sand, which in Ruth's
morbid mind, she had been destined never to climb to
the heights of freedom. Beyond the sand-bed of the
vanished lake, where pale mirages gleamed and sheets
of white dust rose, stretched the corrugated desert, disrupted at last by the weird Rio Colorado, beyond
which heaved the denuded colored hills of Arizona,
rising to dim ghostly ranges.

Above this boundless scene of desolation arched the
copper sky, with half of it a blazing blinding light, too
intense for the gaze of man. The morning was half
gone and the sun had assumed its full mastery. The
heat burned through Ruth's gloves, and the linen coat
which protected her. Yet it was nothing like the heat
of mid-summer, and the absence of blowing sand or
rising alkali dust, made the day endurable.

"Wal, we're shore gettin' along," ventured Merryvale, who had from time to time endeavored to draw

Ruth out of her stony silence. "Reckon Adam will be stoppin' to rest the burros when he gets to them *palo verde* trees. But they're far off yet from us, an' he'll aboot be movin' again when we get there."

Ruth watched the dark figure, markedly tall even at long distance. This desert man had again come into her life, and the promise of agony which had haunted her at Santa Ysabel seemed sure of its fruition.

"Tell me about him," she suddenly said to Merryvale.

"Aboot who? Adam? Wal, there's a lot to tell aboot that man, an' I reckon I don't know one hundredth of what he's done."

"How old is he?" queried Ruth.

"Wal, he was eighteen when he first come to Picacho, an' that was precisely eighteen years ago," replied Merryvale, nodding his head.

"Only thirty-six!" exclaimed Ruth in astonishment. "Why he's really young. I didn't think him old, though. . . . Picacho? Isn't that near Yuma?"

"Shore, twenty miles or more up the river. See that purple peak, all by itself, stickin' up away over heah. The little black peak is Pilot Knob, as you must know if you've been to Yuma. Wal, Picacho stands to the left."

"I see it. How far away?"

"Reckon it's over a hundred miles as a bird flies. Picacho—the Peak! The minin' camp laid right under the mountain. She was a hummer in those days— when Adam happened along. Deserted an' forgotten now."

"It was there Adam thought he'd killed his brother?" went on Ruth.

"Yep, right there at Picacho," returned the old man, dreamily, as he flicked the reins over the laboring mules.

"Why, I wonder? What was the trouble?"

"Wal, it shore wasn't no Cain an' Abel matter," rejoined Merryvale. "Listen now, Ruth, an' I'll tell you somethin' wonderful an' sad. I was the first person to

know Adam at Picacho. He had come down river
from Ehrenburg in a skiff. The minute I seen him I
knowed he'd run off from someone. He was shore a
tenderfoot, but there never was a more strappin', fine-
lookin' lad. I took to him on sight an' I reckon I
sowed in him seeds that have borne fruit. He got a
job at the mill an' lodgins at the house of a Mexican.
What was his name? Ara-Arallanes. Wal, he had a
step-daughter, Margarita, an' she was a little slip of a
greaser girl, like a mescal plant, with eyes that burned
you. She lay in wait for Adam, mawnin' an' night;
an' the lad, lonely an' hungry for companionship,
soon fell into intimacy with her. Margarita was mad
aboot men. An' Adam was too fine an' honest for her.
He reckoned it his duty to protect her—even marry
her."

Merryvale paused a moment to gaze across the
leagues of sand and stone toward the dim purple peak
in the distance.

"Wal, one day a boat stopped from up-river. There
was a lot of passengers an' one of them turned out to
be Adam's brother. He was the handsomest young
man I ever seen, a little older than Adam, an' more
of a man. He was shore a reckless devil. It was easy
to see that the wild life of the west had got him . . .
Wal, first thing he ran plumb into Margarita, an' I
reckon it didn't take him long to win her. She met
him more than half way. Arallanes told Adam aboot
it, an' Adam confronted the two on the river bank, as
I seen. I didn't miss much them days, an' I shore was
fond of Adam. Wal, the brothers had it hot an'
heavy over the pretty hussy. She shore enjoyed that.
You see Adam wanted to save Margarita from this
brother, who he knew had bad influence on women.
It was a tough hour for Adam. His brother couldn't
understand this guardianship. An' at last Adam's slip,
an' then honest intentions toward Margarita had to
come out. What shame for poor Adam! His brother
was tremendous surprised that Adam could fall for a
little greaser girl. An' next he was full of fiendish

glee. He hated Adam. I seen that plain. An' right then an' there he made Margarita jilt Adam.

"That night I went to the camp an' into the big gamblin' hall. Adam was there drinkin'. An' his brother was there gamblin' an losin. He had a friend with him, a sheriff, an' they wanted money off Adam. 'You'll get no more from me,' said Adam. An' I learned afterward that this brother had nagged and cheated Adam out of most of the money left by their mother. They had hot words an' Adam struck his brother, knockin' him over a table . . . Wal, I never seen a whiter-faced man than that brother. It all come out then, like burstin' fire—the hate he'd always had for Adam. My Gawd, but he was beautiful to look at! I'll never forget. . . . He made that gamblin' hell as quiet as a church, as he told in bitin' speech of Adam's downfall over a little greaser hussy. Adam— the Sunday School boy—the clean, sweet favorite— mama's boy—to sink to the level of a minin' camp's rag! An' he scorned Adam, shoutin', 'damn your lyin' milk-sop soul! If only your mother could be heah to know!' An' Adam, as if hurt turrible deep, answered: 'If you speak of my mother heah, I'll kill you!'

"An' that wild brother did speak, hotter an' fiercer than ever. Adam threw his gun, but the sheriff knocked it up. Then the two brothers closed in desprit fight over the gun. In the stuggle it went off . . . An' that handsome devil fell over the table with a great widenin' spot of red on his white shirt. He looked as if death was near. The sheriff yelled: 'You'll hang for this!' . . . An' Adam fled."

The narrative, broken here by Merryvale, gave Ruth a moment free of suspense, in which she took a deep breath.

Merryvale raised a brown hand and pointed.

"You see that crinkly brown range? Wal, it's the Chocolate Mountains. Somewhere between Yuma an' the Chocolates, Adam fell on the desert. He'd run miles. He'd gone thirst mad. A prospector named Dismukes found him an' saved his life. Adam had lost seventy pounds in one day! Fact. The desert—but you know how the desert dries up anythin'. Dismukes was a great man. He saw Adam's trouble, told him what the desert was—how it made beast or god of man— gave him a burro an' food an' set him on the trail he had to follow. . . . Now look farther along the range —half way. Do you see a green spot?"

"Yes, I do," replied Ruth, as she sighted faint color on that sinister background of red.

"Wal, there's the first camp Adam made. His burro set fire to his pack an' then ran off. Adam's supplies all burned. He was left to perish. He could not go back. He went on. There is an oasis at the west end of the range, an' Indians live there at certain seasons. Adam reached it. But the Indians were gone. Heah began his fight for life. Slowly he starved. Rabbits an' birds were scarce an' finally there was no more. He ate lizards an' snakes. He grew so weak he could scarcely crawl. Last, he was trying to kill a rattlesnake to eat, when he fell an' the reptile bit him. Indians came an' saved his life. He stayed with them a long time, learnin' the ways of desert life.

"That was the beginnin' of Adam's wanderin'. He grew an' the desert changed him. Made him like it— like the Eagle. In years to come he got another name. Wansfell, the Wanderer. He knew where there was gold on the desert, but he did not want it. He kept to the lonely waste, seldom visitin' the mines an' camps, an' towns on the border. Evil men—of which there are many on the desert—learned to fear him. He was ever on the side of the weak, the lost—of which, too, there's many in the desert—an' he had a turrible avengin' hand. It has dealt death to many—an' always, so I've heard, they've been bad men, such as stole Genie Linwood from her mother. An' so at last he came down the trails to Santa Ysabel."

"Oh, what a life! All for nothing," murmured Ruth.

"Wal, I used to think so myself, but I'm changin'. Adam's life heah in this wasteland has been beyond words of human to tell, even if he knew. I've jest given you a few threads to piece together. It don't take no pains to see he's great. He told you why he ran away from you at Santa Ysabel. But he didn't tell you the months of torture out heah, fightin' to give you up, an' then fightin' to surrender to the law. It was right over there in that oasis where he nearly starved eighteen years ago. There he fought such a battle as I reckon no other man ever fought. . . . I was in Picacho when he came to sacrifice himself. I was the one to tell him aboot his awful mistake—that he hadn't killed his brother at all. An' I've been with him ever since. An' it's since then that I've learned Adam's life when a boy—how he loved this brother who from childhood up robbed him of everything. . . . By Gawd, that's the dastard part of it, an' why I was always sorry he didn't kill his brother!"

"Merryvale! What a harsh—a cruel—thing to say!" exclaimed Ruth, aghast at his sudden passion.

"No matter. Adam was a gentle, kindly boy, favorite of his mother. He loved his brother as I never knew any brother to be loved. An' in turn he was hated. Always everythin' he had or wanted went to his brother. Toys, sweets, clothes, girls, money—and finally honor. The mother died. Adam gave half his little heritage to save his brother. He fetched him out west, always hopin'. An' he saw him go the way of the gamblin' hells. The split came at Ehrenberg an' then the bitter fight at Picacho. . . . An' there goes Adam now, ploddin' along after eighteen years of hellsfire."

After that Merryvale maintained a long silence. And Ruth was absorbing something strange and new about a man's attitude toward life.

Meanwhile they reached the *palo verdes,* pale green trees with shiny truck and branches and twigs, and a few yellow blossoms. Wansfell had unpacked his burros and was sitting in the shade.

"Rest here a while," he said, as Merryvale drove in; and he rose to help Ruth out.

"How did you stand the ride?" he asked.

"Quite well, except that I'm tired," she replied.

"Walk a little, then sit here. I will fix something comfortable. The worst of the day is still before us, and we had better spend it here."

"I remember those *palo verdes*. Aren't we near Lost Lake?"

"Ten miles, perhaps. We will get there in three hours."

Ruth threw off hat and coat and walked among the trees. Beside the *palo verdes* there were numbers of the beautiful and forbidding crucifixion thorn trees, or smoke trees, as the prospectors called them, because at a distance they resembled soft clouds of rising blue smoke. The place was a sandy wash, dry as tinder, from which the heat rose in filmy sheets. There was not a living thing to be seen, not even an ant or a buzzing fly or a passing bee. Yet there seemed to be a faint hum of something in and about the trees.

Soon Ruth returned to the men. The burros cropped at the brittle weeds; the mules stood motionless, heads low. Merryvale lay on the sand. Adam motioned Ruth to a comfortable place he had arranged with packs and blankets. She was glad to recline there. Face and hands were moist; an oppression of her breast hindered breathing; and her head hurt. What relief to stretch a little and close her eyes! Dull thought faded into blackness and she slept.

Upon awakening from her *siesta* Ruth felt free of the headache and the oppression, though she seemed as uncomfortably warm as before. The great blaze of sun had slanted far to the west. Adam called Merryvale to bring the burros for repacking.

"Ruth," he said, coming to her side. "I know how you feel. It's hard. I hated to make you come back. I wanted to take you far away. I love you the same as any other man. Yet I think I have a higher love than that. I'll find happiness in making your burden easier —in keeping my word to your mother."

"You shame me," she replied, with lowered eyes. "I

—I wish I could repeat what I said to you in Santa Ysabel. I would if you were any other man. But you'll never regard me as free."

Once more Merryvale drove out upon the glaring desert, this time with a slight wind blowing from behind. It whipped up thin streaks of dust. Adam, stalking ahead, did not gain this time, for the road was freer of sand and had more of a descent. Far across the basin gleamed a wide bar of pale blue water and beyond it loomed dark mountains. There were beauty and sublimity in the grand sweep of this desert, in the range of jagged hills and peaks, glimpses of which Ruth had now and then through her parted veil. What had happened to her that she could see anything but the ghastliness of the desert all around? She pondered over that. It had to do with Adam Wansfell. He began to loom in her thought.

The hours slipped by and towards sunset the dust ceased to blow and the heat lessened. Ruth removed her veil. The green trees and squat adobe huts of the Indians and Mexicans showed plainly now, a mile or more distant. They clustered below the heavy dark patch of verdant foliage which marked the water-hole owned by Caleb Hunt, Ruth's grandfather. This clump of green hid the house where Ruth lived. Soon the square whitewashed freighting post showed below the green.

Sight of it reminded Ruth of what lay in wait for her. She experience a relief at the thought of returning to her grandfather. He would be so overjoyed to see her that he would forget her dereliction. She was stirred then by thought of Stone, and her husband, Guerd Larey. But it was merely curiosity, gratification, excitement. The last twenty-four hours had removed her immeasurably from these men—a consciousness of which dawned vaguely upon her remembrance of them.

Adam halted his burros just short of the post and waited for Merryvale to come up. They then proceeded under Ruth's direction. The wide space, rather

than street, in front of the post, was deserted. It and
the long low white structure had a tinge of faint red
from the setting sun. Ruth was glad there did not appear to be anyone to see her return. Assuredly no one
had remarked her departure the previous morning
with Stone, as it had occurred before daylight.

What from a distance had resembled an oasis was
only a thick hedge of *palo verdes,* cactus and brush
that surrounded a bed of green rushes, and stood
somewhat higher than the freighting post. Water from
the spring flowed through a pipe to a stone trough.

"My home is there," announced Ruth, pointing to
an earth-colored adobe structure, visible through the
trees, above the spring.

"What shall we do with the wagon and mules?"
asked Adam, as he deposited her baggage on the
ground.

"I don't know. Perhaps you had better look after
them, until we see. Come with me."

Adam followed, carrying her bags, while Merryvale
led the mules to the watering-trough, where the
thirsty burros already had their noses submerged.

Once inside the hedge Ruth slackened her pace.
The dank warm smell of the rush-pond below the
spring assailed her nostrils. Bees hummed in the *palo
verdes;* rabbits scurried into the thicket of green
rushes. She espied the dark stolid visage of her grandfather's Indian servant. There was no sound except a
tinkle of running water. The adobe house was long
and low, with a porch running its length.

"Here—we are—Adam," announced Ruth, breath-
lessly. "Look what you've brought me back to—for all
my life."

Adam's keen eyes surveyed the scene, lingering
upon the little pond with its green moss and rushes.
Then his gaze swept out over the hedge upon the tremendous vista of desert.

"I'm afraid you don't see truly," he replied, with a
smile. "This is an oasis. And I would never tire of the
view."

"Gracious!" exclaimed Ruth, impatiently. "I don't see grandfather," she called walking along the porch. "He must be at the post, unless he's gone off to Yuma in search of me. . . . Sit down, Adam. This porch was not made for your height. My room is at this end of the house."

Ruth walked down and pushed open the gray weathered door.

"Oh, dear," she sighed. Had it been only thirty-six hours since she left? It seemed so long. Evidently the little room had not been entered during her absence. Her bed was as she had hastily left it, with coverlet and sheet half on the floor. This room had the only window in the house. Ruth gazed around at the colored walls, the Indian blankets, the spare furniture, the curtained niche where her few dresses hung; and a sickening leaden sensation momentarily weighed upon her. Then she saw the letter she had left for her grandfather. It had not been found. She took it and went outside.

"Adam, this letter I left has not been opened," she said. "Grandfather must be greatly alarmed. He would not know what has become of me."

"Let me go find him," replied Adam.

"Yes. I'll go with you."

But they had scarcely started when Ruth caught sight of the old man entering the hedge gate.

"Wait, Adam. Here he comes."

Upon nearing the porch her grandfather looked up to disclose a worn troubled face, which instantly lightened with amaze and gladness. He hurried forward —a slight man, gray of hair, and rather stoop-shouldered.

"Ruth!" he burst out, quaveringly. "Where in the world have you been?"

"Hello, Grandad," she returned, kissing his cheek. "Don't you know where I've been?"

"No. At lunch yesterday Marta said you were not in your room. I began to worry then. Last night I feared you'd run off to Yuma, as you've threatened

STAIRS OF SAND   57

often. Where have you been, and who is this stranger?"

Adam had arisen, to stand with head bent under the low ceiling.

"Grandad, this is an old friend, Adam Wansfell. . . . Adam, my grandfather, Caleb Hunt."

The men shook hands and exchanged greetings.

"Wansfell? . . . Wansfell," added the elder, reflectively. "Well, sir, I never saw you before. I'd never forget such a man as you. But I've heard your name."

"No doubt. It's pretty well known on the desert. I've traveled far and wide," replied Adam.

"Grandad, what did Hal Stone tell you?" interrupted Ruth, eager to have explanations over.

"Ruth, I haven't seen Stone," returned Hunt, in surprise. "Some one saw him just a little while ago, limping by the post."

"I ran off with Stone yesterday," went on Ruth, hurriedly.

"Good heavens! You ran off—eloped with Hal Stone?" ejaculated her grandfather. "Your husband will shoot him!"

"Not when I explain. It was all my fault, grandad. —Well, we got within ten miles of the mountains, when the gray mule, Old Butch, balked. We could not go on. Stone said we must camp there. Then, when I repulsed his—his advances he got ugly. Adam happened along with Merryvale, and rescued me. He sent Stone away last night. We made camp there and this morning started back."

"Sir, I thank you indeed," said Hunt, courteously and warmly to Adam, extending a nervous hand. "Perhaps this will be a lesson to my granddaughter."

"Grandad, I'll never run off again," murmured Ruth, mournfully.

"Well! Something has come over my lass," declared Hunt, affectionately placing an arm around Ruth. "It is very welcome, but rather perplexing. How did you bring about this change? Ruth is as hard to change as

Old Butch. And, by the way, how'd you ever move *him?*"

"Butch and I are old pards," answered Adam. "I drove him eight years ago, up the Mohave."

"Grandad—listen," interrupted Ruth, tremulously. "Adam had no trouble changing me. . . . He knew mother. He was with her—and father—the last weeks of their lives. . . . In Death Valley! . . . Oh! such a terrible story—but you must hear it."

"What—what is this? Ruth! . . ." he burst out, in great emotion. "Wansfell, did you know my daughter Magdalene—this girl's mother?"

"Yes, Mr. Hunt. I knew her—during the last tragic weeks of her life in Death Valley," replied Adam, sombrely.

"This is most extraordinary. After all these years! Thank God, we have come to know at last. . . . Did Magdalene give you any message for us?"

"The locket, Adam. Let him see that," said Ruth, eagerly.

Adam's big brown hand slipped inside his worn blouse and appeared to jerk to a stop.

"Who is that man?" he whispered in so low and tense a voice that Ruth gazed in startled change of feeling up at him. His eagle eyes, fixed upon the path, held a quivering steely light.

Ruth's swift glance following their direction, saw a man striding up the walk. She laughed outright.

"That is my husband," she said, and rose, conscious of a sudden tingling heat along her veins.

She heard Adam utter a husky stifled exclamation, incoherent; and out of the corner of her eyes she saw him rise and step quickly into the open door. His voice and action gave her a queer feeling. Her grandfather likewise stepped into the room.

Ruth had awaited Guerd Larey's approach many a time with mingled emotions, but never with the poise and certainty of this moment. Fear had left her. She watched him come—a magnificent man, tall and stalwart, booted and belted, without coat or hat, the sunset light glinting on his thick fair hair and his handsome dissolute face.

"Ruth!" he exclaimed, and he strode to the very edge of the porch where she stood, and bent to search her face with his great hungry green eyes. Joy, relief, suspicion, anger all strove there.

"You're back," he asserted, offering his hand, which she appeared not to notice.

"So you see," she replied.

"Where the hell have you been?" he demanded.

"None of your business," she returned, coldly. "Guerd, don't speak to me in that tone. You have nothing whatever to do with my actions, nor can you bully me."

"But I've been frightened. I can't help but love you," he replied, harshly.

"That's your misfortune, if it's true," said Ruth. "But you never really loved *me*. Please let us have an end of that. You nag me to death with your protestations of love—when all the time I know what your life is."

"You'll never believe that you could have changed my life?" he queried, with bitter passion.

"Never. You are a slave to your selfish desires," she returned scornfully. "In love—in business—in everything. You were a gambler and a cheat even when you married me."

"Ruth, I swear to God I'll—I'll mend my ways—if you'll be my wife, really," he implored, with a pathos that was almost savage. "I'll give the freight business back to Hunt. We'll leave this cursed desert."

"It's impossible, Guerd," she replied, wondering why she could not feel pity for him. Surely he believed himself. "And if that's what you came to say, please—"

"Hell, that only came out when I saw you," he flashed, with passionate gesture. Then the eloquence and dark radiance of him faded. "This young Stone is bragging around he eloped with you. I want to hear what you've got to say before I—"

"Guerd, don't kill Stone," interrupted Ruth, in distress. "Don't even strike him. He's been punished enough. It was all my fault."

"It's true, then?"

"Yes. I ran off with him. I encouraged him—let him make love to me—let him think. . . . Oh, there's no excuse for me, Guerd. It seemed lately I couldn't stand this place any longer. I just had to get out."

"Damn you!" he retorted, white to the lips. "You'd go with anyone—even a Mexican—rather than with me. . . . Well, what happened? Stone's face is all smashed. He said Old Butch kicked him. But that's a lie. Some man's fist did it. Who was he—and what for?"

Ruth divined the imminence of peril for the boy she had led to such extremes. "Guerd, we couldn't reach the Indian settlement," she began, impulsively. "Old Butch balked. There was nothing to do but camp. Stone wanted to make love to me. I wouldn't let him. He had a perfect right to expect that—and more. . . . To my shame I confess it. He grew violent then, and during a struggle between us two men came up—and ended it."

"One of them struck Stone?"

"Yes, indeed he did. But——"

"Who did it?"

"Adam Wansfell, an old friend whom I knew from years ago at Santa Ysabel."

"Wansfell! I know that name. I've heard about one Wansfell. Was he a big man—as big as I am?"

"Taller, I think, but not so heavy," replied Ruth.

"He's a desert tramp," returned Larey, reflectively. "Wanders around doing all kinds of queer tricks. And you knew him in Santa Ysabel? . . . Well, he can hardly be the Wansfell I mean."

"He brought me back home. You may learn for yourself who and what he is."

"That doesn't matter. Did you tell me this young Stone had a perfect right to expect love from you—and *more?*"

"Guerd, it's only fair to him to confess that," returned Ruth, feeling her face burn. "I didn't realize till today how—how wild and irresponsible I've been."

"You let Stone kiss you?" he queried, darkly.

She averted her face from the jealous blaze of his eyes. How earnestly she wanted to meet them and lie! But she could not do it.

"And you never let *me* kiss you!" he rasped.

Ruth had likewise no reply to that poignant accusation. But when he wheeled away she found voice to call him back. He paid no attention. Rapidly he stalked down the path and through the hedge gate.

Then Ruth's grandfather came out of the house, his worn face working, his hands trembling.

"Ruth, he'll kill that poor boy or horsewhip him within an inch of his life."

"I'm afraid, grandad," replied Ruth, fearfully. "Won't you go after him—fetch him back?"

"I'll go, but it won't be any use."

Suddenly Ruth remembered Adam and there was strong shift of alarm and remorse on behalf of Stone, to an unaccountable curiosity and distress for Adam.

"Adam, did—did you hear it all? Why did you go in? You'll have to meet him some time."

Receiving no response Ruth went hurriedly into the room. At first glance she did not locate Adam. Could he have gone out the back door? Then she heard a long shuddering breath. Adam lay on her grandfather's couch, his face buried, his great hands clutching the pillows. The wide shoulders strained as if in convulsion. With contracting heart Ruth ran to the couch.

"Why—why—Adam!" she called, and put a faltering hand on his shoulder. "What in the world. . . . Oh, what could make you this way? It was only my husband. You must have heard. . . . ."

"It's not dead—it'll never die," interrupted Adam, in a smothered voice.

"What?" cried Ruth.

"My love."

"For me?—Oh, Adam, I'm glad it'll never die. Glad! I want you to love me."

"No, Ruth, not for you. But for him."

He lifted a face of agony that made Ruth sink to her knees in front of him.

"No—not *him!* Not Guerd Larey!" she gasped wildly.

"Yes, Ruth."

"Oh, my God!—Don't tell me—don't tell me what —I fear—what I feel. . . . Adam, I am bound to love you. My mother did. . . . I do *now*. It comes tearing my heart. Oh, don't tell me he is the vile brother who ruined your life. I couldn't bear it, Adam. I couldn't bear for you to find me his— his——"

"Ruth, it is true," he replied, brokenly. "He is my brother. My right name is not Wansfell. I am Adam Larey."

5

Lost Lake slumbered at noontide under a June sun. The vast desert sky, like a copper lid, shut down close, hiding the limits of the wasteland in the haze of obscurity. The heat veils waved up from the sand like transparent smoke. An Indian stood motionless in the shade of an adobe wall. The wind whipped puffs of sand across the open square before the post. The desert brooded, as if forbidding life and movement.

Merryvale awoke from his *siesta*. He had taken up lodgings in an abandoned Indian shack, which was no more than a shed of *ocatilla* poles, open on two sides, and sheltered by *palo verdes*. It was situated on the outskirts of the post, and suited Merryvale well. Adam had taken the burros that first night and gone into the rocky recesses of the canyons above Lost Lake. Ruth had implored him to go—not to meet Guerd Larey—for reasons Merryvale guessed easily enough. Adam had returned once, at night, for a meeting with him and Ruth, and he was due again on the night of this day.

Merryvale pondered while he folded his bed neatly on the brush mattress. He was always in a brown study these days, absorbed in his loyalty to Adam and Ruth, and the fateful tangle of their lives. Merryvale had been forty years on the desert. He loved it even as Adam, but he did not dwell on the heights. It was the people of the desert that interested Merryvale and he saw them clearly, in the raw, elemental, physical—answering to the law of this barren, hot, lonely, and fierce environment.

While he sat there thinking he heard the freighting wagons lumber by. It reminded him that the stages were due, one from Yuma going north and the other coming south. Lost Lake was an important post, because it possessed the only abundant water on a hundred mile stretch of desert, the whole northern fifty miles of which was below sea level.

Merryvale went out and encountered Indian Jim, a native with whom he had taken pains to make friends. This Coalmila Indian had once owned the waterhole, which had long been familiar to prospectors under the name of Indian Wells. Jim and his people had been prosperous before they sold the spring which was a mecca for all desert travelers. But they had squandered their fortune and now eked out a beggarly existence, bitter against the owners of the freighting-post and especially Hunt.

"How many wagons come?" asked Merryvale, of the Indian.

He held up eight fingers, then pointed out into the sandy void.

"Ugh. Stage come," he said.

Far down on the mottled gray expanse moved a black object under a cloud of dust.

"Hot day, Jim."

"No," replied the Indian.

Merryvale sauntered on toward the post where the freighters had hauled up. Passing under the *palo verdes* to an adobe house, Merryvale halted to address a Mexican woman, who sat in the shade, busy with bright colored clothes. A half naked child, dusky-haired and with skin like brown ivory, played in the sand at her feet.

"Buenas tardes, Senora," Merryvale greeted her. "May I look in?" And he indicated the open door.

"Si, Senor," she replied, showing her white teeth.

Merryvale entered. Upon a bed under the window lay a young man, haggard of face, with uncut beard and hollowed eyes.

"Wal, Stone, how are you today?" inquired Merryvale.

"Oh, God, it's hell lyin' here," returned Stone, wearily, as he rolled his head from side to side.

"Are you still in pain?"

"No. That's most gone, I guess. It's just the infernal heat. My face and hands sweat. And the damned flies stick."

"Wal, boy, you're gettin' better fast," said Merryvale, cheerfully. "Say, when I dropped in heah first your eyelids were fly-blown. I wiped out the eggs myself, an' you didn't know it."

"Yes, I must be," replied Stone, hopefully. "Ruth was here this mornin'. She said so."

"Ahuh! An' Ruth was down? Wal, that was shore good of her."

"Oh, she's kind. She took all the blame for Larey's shooting me. But I don't want her kindness."

"Reckon she wasn't all to blame, Stone. You talked aboot Ruth, so I'm told. Larey shore meant to kill you for that an' not for runnin' off with her. He damn near done for you, too. Lucky that doctor was passin' through on the stage or you'd been fodder for the vultures."

"I'm not thankin' anybody, Merryvale," returned the young man, sullenly.

"So I see," drawled Merryvale, with a little coldness creeping into his voice. "What's you goin' to do when you get on your feet again?"

"What'd I do before I stopped these bullets?" snapped Stone.

"Wal, you sold hosses an' gambled some an' looked at red liquor more'n you ought, an' you ran after a young woman heah," replied Merryvale, in his lazy drawl.

"Yes, and that's what I'll do again."

"Not as regards the last, Stone," said Merryvale, with some sharpness. "You'd show sense to leave Lost Lake. But if you won't, then take advice an' leave Ruth alone. She may have led you on, flirtin', even bein'

soft an' sweet to you, as women always did an' always
will. But she couldn't go through with the deal as you
wanted, an' when she got back heah she took the
blame. She squared you with everyone, and tried to
with Guerd Larey. At that, hard as Larey is, he
wouldn't have shot you if you'd kept your mouth shut.
Ruth did a big thing throwin' shame upon herself to
save you. An' you ought to appreciate it by leavin' her
alone."

"Bah! You're an old fool, Merryvale," retorted
Stone. "You don't know women, much less Ruth
Larey. She's like this desert. She has as many moods as
the wind. She'd purr at me one minute and the next
scratch my eyes out. Like as not she'll want me back."

"I reckon not, young man," returned Merryvale,
shortly. "But find it out for yourself. An' if you caint
take advice from a man who knows the desert an' who
meant kindly, wal, go on your wild way."

Merryvale left the bedside and went out, satisfied
that Stone's love for Ruth would turn to hate, and that
he would be an enemy whom it would be well to
watch. The passions of men know no curb in this sun-
blasted waste. Every element of nature worked to aug-
ment the primitive; and hate, greed, envy, jealousy,
lust—all the dark and evil traits of humanity seemed
unleashed and rampant. Merryvale reflected that, as
often before in his desert experience, he had fallen
upon an intricate and baffling drama, which, if indeed it did not end tragically, must grow terrible before there could be any light for the principals.

At the post there was a break in the day's drowsy
lull. Bustle and dust and noise attended the unhitch-
ing of the sweaty mule teams, three to a wagon, and
the unloading of boxes and bales and barrels into the
freight house. This was a busy hour for the Mexican
and Indian laborers. Caleb Hunt stood at the wide door,
directing the disposition of supplies, and making en-
tries in a book.

Merryvale lounged in the shade of the porch, which
ran along the front of the post, and played the part he

had chosen—that of an idle old man, past labor or activity, and not particularly interested in anything save rest. But as a matter of fact he was keenly alert to see what went on, to note the ever-increasing amount of freight—which in itself was a significant matter—to listen to the teamsters and the handlers of stores, to watch Hunt and his man, the crafty-faced Dabb, and especially, if possible, to get a glimpse of Guerd Larey.

One of the grimy drivers halted near Merryvale to catch his breath and wipe his dripping face.

"Warm day, old timer," he remarked.

"Reckon so, for you. It's only fair to middlin' warm for me. Lots of freight you're handlin'."

"More comin' all the time," he replied, nodding vigorously. "We left the dock stacked full. You see, freight is comin' to Yuma on the railroad now."

"You don't say. Wal, that's news. So the railroad's built far as Yuma?"

"Yep, an' she's headed north."

"Wal, then, there was somethin' in the talk we've been heahin' for years. Where do they aim to build this way?"

"Don't know for sure," replied the teamster. "But course the rails will have to go between the Chocolate Range an' the sand dunes. They couldn't run no railroad over them."

"Shore couldn't. It'd be buried every day. Reckon they'll lay tracks round the west end of the dunes, an' mebbe cut north across the valley this heah way."

"I heard a railroad man say Lost Lake was in line," replied the freighter, and went his way.

Here was extraordinary news. A railroad north through the valley meant an enormous increase in value of property, Merryvale saw that the water rights on the land belonging to Hunt would be worth a fortune. Guerd Larey had long been trying to buy Hunt out; and of late, according to Ruth, had been offering more, and nagging Hunt to sell.

Then the stage came rolling up with its six horses

caked with dust and lather, and the driver looking like a snow man.

"Hyar we air, boys," he shouted, flinging the reins. "Lost Lake or bust! Howdy Bill—howdy Tim. We come hell bent fer election, with twelve passengers an' one devil aboard. . . . Hi, Tony, have a care of the hosses."

Dust flew in clouds as the stage door opened to emit, first, a tall man in a long frock coat. He had a hard gray face, grim, lined, square-jawed, more striking for a hideous scar that blotted out his left eye.

Merryvale controlled the start with which he recognized Collishaw, the sheriff who had been Guerd Larey's ally at Picacho years before. Collishaw had not changed much, except to grow grayer. Merryvale's mind flashed back, bringing a picture of the fight between Guerd and Adam. Again he saw Adam fall back from the ghastly brother and fling the gun with terrific force in Collishaw's face. He would carry that mark, that loss to his grave. His one eye burned with the spirit of an implacable and ruthless man.

One by one the other passengers descended from the stage, weary and begrimed, and mostly silent. They were all men, most of them rough-garbed, and from their appearance, intimately associated with the desert. They filed into the lodging house that adjoined the post.

Merryvale remembered well indeed the part Collishaw had played in Ruth's narrative. He and Guerd Larey had indentical interests, if they were not hand and glove. Moreover Collishaw conducted one of the many gambling saloons in Yuma. Merryvale saw Collishaw met by Larey with outstretched hand, and led toward the bar. Merryvale decided to follow. In the crowded saloon he contrived to edge close to the couple.

"Guerd, heah's to luck," Collishaw was saying, low-voiced, holding up his glass. "The S.P. is shore goin' to take in Lost Lake!"

"The hell you say!" whispered Larey, hoarsely, lifting his glass; and a light brightened the heat from his face.

"Shore. I got inside information," replied Collishaw. "For reasons of their own the directors have let it go they were runnin' the railroad up the east side of the valley. But it's comin' on this side."

"We want Lost Lake, Salton Spring and Twenty Nine Palms. . . . Drink!" returned Larey.

Merryvale edged away from behind the tall Texan, not wishing to take the risk of being recognized in such suspicious proximity. But once outside in the lobby, he waited to place himself where the ex-sheriff could not fail to see him. The two men emerged, evidently in high spirits, and encountered Merryvale apparently bent on going into the bar.

"Hullo. Wher'd I ever see you?" Collishaw queried, gruffly, his eye boring at Merryvale.

"Wal, I'm shore I don't know," replied Merryvale.

"You're a Texan."

"Bettja. I'd never disown the old Lone Star State."

"I never forget a face," went on Collishaw. "What's your name?"

"Wal, it might be Jones, only it ain't," returned Merryvale, with asperity.

Well pleased with himself and Collishaw's failure to recognize him, Merryvale hurried out and into the storeroom of the post, where Hunt was still receiving and recording freight.

"Hunt, I've a bit of news for your ear," said Merryvale.

"Ah! Merryvale. How do. Thank you, I'll be at your service presently," rejoined Hunt.

Merryvale waited in the gathering shadow, watching the piling up of tier after tier of freight. It was a large storehouse and now almost half full. When at length the work was done darkness had intervened.

"It's supper time. Come with me, Merryvale. Ruth will be glad to see you," invited Hunt.

Merryvale did not choose to speak while they were walking along in front of the post, where there were passers-by, and dark figures of Indians leaning against the railing. But when they turned the corner to pass on toward the hedge he said: "Mr. Hunt, shore there's a lot of freight comin' in."

"Indeed there is. We're handling twice the volume of business we used to."

"Who's it all billed to?" asked Merryvale, curiously.

"Most of this lot today is billed to names I don't know. Struck me queer. And now I have time to think, I see it is most unusual."

"Wal, I reckon it is. Mebbe I can give you a hunch aboot it."

"Ah, that's your bit of news," replied Hunt.

It was dark inside the hedge, so that Merryvale had to peer down to locate the narrow path. The tinkle of running water fell pleasantly on the sultry air. Far to the north sheet lightning flared along a dark battlemented horizon. They reached the porch, where a slender white figure stood out from the gloom.

"Who's with you, grandad?" came the query in Ruth's soft voice.

"Merryvale, my lass, I've asked him to supper."

"Oh—I've looked for you all day, Merryvale," she said, taking his arm and squeezing it. "I'm lonelier than ever. I used to go down to the post. But now I stay in the yard."

"Ruth, lass, go tell Marta to hurry supper," requested Hunt, taking a seat. Opening his shirt at the neck and brushing back his hair, he met the faint breeze with evident gratitude. "Now tell me the hunch and the bit of news."

"Wal, I reckon that excess freight is for railroad men," replied Merryvale.

Hunt leaned forward in his chair so abruptly that Ruth, returning from the house, marked it and stopped short.

"Your faith is this water-hole is justified," went on Merryvale, impressively. "The S. P. is goin' to run the railroad through heah."

"Oh, how wonderful!" exclaimed Ruth, slipping to the arm of Hunt's chair.

He gave vent to a hard expulsion of breath. "Merryvale, how do you know?"

"Collishaw came on the stage. An' I overheard him tell Larey that he had inside information."

"Well, well! I always believed it'd come. . . . And what did Larey say?"

Merryvale leaned forward to whisper: "He said 'We want Lost Lake, Salton Spring an' Twenty-nine Palms.'"

Hunt uttered an imprecation that was unintelligible and sank back in his chair. "He named the three best water holes in the valley. These will be important railroad stations and eventually towns. For the valley above here has rich soil. All it needs is water. I can see it green over and blossom like the land of Canaan."

"Wal, Hunt, I reckon you had better vision than most desert prospectors. For you bought Lost Lake."

"Yes, and I have a clear title. I took the Indians to Yuma. I own this water and when I die it'll go to Ruth. She'll be rich some day."

"Hush, grandad. You are full of life and energy," said Ruth. "Oh, I am so glad. . . . Yet it troubles me. If Guerd Larey said he wanted Lost Lake, and those other places, he meant something."

"Ruth, he has always wanted it. You see the post was built on my land. He always disputed this, but the Indians can verify it. These six acres I own constitute the value of Lost Lake."

"Wal, all I say is you're goin' to hang on to it," interposed Merryvale, doggedly.

"My friend, as yet the only law on this desert is the law of might," replied Hunt.

"Shore. An' that's where Wansfell will come in."

Merryvale saw the girl's face flash at him and her eyes widen and gleam in the gloom. She put out an entreating hand.

"I don't understand you, Merryvale," said Hunt.

"Never mind. My temper was up. Shore I talk too

much anyhow. But I jest had to tell you the news
—good an' bad," returned Merryvale, apologetically.

At this juncture the Indian woman called them to
supper. As Merryvale rose to follow his host Ruth took
his hand and clasped it, whispering: "You mustn't
frighten me. Remember, I've heard Genie Linwood
tell how terrible Adam can be."

They went into the little dining room where, in the
light of the lamps, Merryvale looked across the table
at this girl who had begun to twine herself about his
heart. His friendship for Adam and the long search to
find Ruth had engendered his interest in her. He was
old and he had traveled, but never had he seen so
lovely and so disturbing a creature as Ruth. The pliant
form, slender yet full, the beautiful lines of her golden
throat, the oval face with its curved red lips, drooping and sweet, the delicate nostrils, the wide purple
eyes and the rippling hair of gold—these he felt stir
his pulse and gladden his sight; but it was not only her
beauty that had called to the depths of him. Adam
loved her, but it was not wholly that which had inspired him to chivalry. He wondered at himself, at the
capacity for fight there seemed still to abide in him.
Ruth had not painted herself in glowing colors. And
what he had learned from the Indians and Mexicans,
and the several white women of Lost Lake, was not
calculated to change for him the estimate she had given
of herself. Yet Merryvale was forming his own opinion, and seemed to divine how the desert might take a
girl's wild potentialities and mould them into noble
womanhood.

After the meal they again repaired to the porch
where Hunt talked a few moments, then went down to
his work at the post.

"Let us go," said Ruth. "Some one might come."
And she led him beyond the house, up a path to the
dark hedge, where in the shadow of *palo verdes* there
was a bench.

"I can hear him—when he comes," whispered Ruth,
panting a little.

"Ruth, I dropped in to see Stone today," said Merryvale, low-voiced. "He told me you had been there."

"Yes, I went to see him, and took him some fruit. I felt sorry for him. Sight of him so pale, hollow-eyed, with those bloody bandages on him, stung me with remorse."

"Wal, it's to your credit, but you musn't go again. An' you must avoid him heahafter. He's bad medicine, Ruth, an' doesn't deserve your pity."

"I have two task masters now," she replied, with a little laugh. "But oh, if you only knew how I need and want to be guided and helped."

"Wal, I'll shore try to live up to that," returned Merryvale.

"God knows it's hard enough to stay here," she said, twisting her hands in her dress. "I resigned myself. I let Adam dominate me. But I didn't realize. I'm shut in, walled up by the desert. I try to work, read, sleep, but I can't do any for any length of time. By day the sun glares down—the monotony of endless barren ground ever mets my eyes. By night I hear the tinkle of this spring that means so much to grandad. It haunts me. Then the dead silence and after that the wind. You know the wind—how mournful—how it seeps the sand—how it rustles the leaves! I am alone—alone. And I feel I'll go mad. Then the night turns gray and then—that awful rose of dawn."

Merryvale racked by his mind for a suggestion that might lend some ray of comfort.

"But, Ruth, heah are those who love you," he said, feelingly. "Your grandfather an' Adam. . . . An' wal, I reckon me."

"You, Merryvale," she replied in soft surprise. "Oh, you are good. And I feel so worthless, useless, helpless. I don't fit here. Just today I've had a thousand thoughts, all faithless to you who care for me. It would be better if I didn't know it. I used not to know or I didn't care. But now I have other kinds of discontent. I—"

"Listen," interrupted Merryvale, in a husky whisper. "I heah a step."

In the silence which ensued Merryvale felt her hands trembling on his. They had a clinging quality of which she seemed unaware. A soft footfall sounded outside the hedge.

"It is Adam," she whispered.

"Reckon so. I know that step."

Merryvale slipped along the hedge to an aperture, which let him out into the desert. A lofty figure took shape against the opaque gloom. Merryvale advanced and silently meeting his friend led him back through the hedge and under the shadow to where the white form of Ruth gleamed wanly like marble in the starlight.

"Adam?" she whispered, rising to meet him.

"Yes, Ruth," he answered.

They clasped hands. And Merryvale, standing close, saw with his nighthawk eyes, that they forgot him.

"Ruth, dear, I do not like this," said Adam very low.

"What? Seeing me again?"

"No. Meeting you in secret."

"But you must. I'm afraid—if you meet your—my —Guerd Larey. You couldn't avoid it. And the thought frightens me."

"I understand. I don't want to meet Guerd and I don't want him or anyone to—know I see you. Still—"

"You must meet me here. Adam, I'd never have gotten through this day but for you."

It needed no word from Merryvale to bind Adam to the inevitable, yet Merryvale chose to speak it, proving to himself how far, that night, he had gone on the road of friendship.

"Adam, shore there's no way out of meetin' Ruth heah, even if you wanted one, which you don't. There's hell ahatchin' down at the post. Collishaw is heah, drinkin' with Larey."

"Collishaw?" muttered Adam. He drew Ruth out into the starlight close to Merryvale.

"Shore. Listen, pard," began Merryvale, and in forceful whisper he told what little he had seen and heard, and how much he suspected. "I'm an old hand at figerin' such men. An' you know, Adam, how I feel toward you an' Ruth. I seen through Guerd Larey! I read his mind. When he said 'Drink!' he meant to the possession of Lost Lake Spring, an' of the lass whose hand you're holdin' now."

"I can't speak for the water-hole, but he shall never have Ruth," returned Adam.

"If he did get me, it'd be only my dead body," said Ruth, her face pale, and her great eyes mirroring the brilliance and mystery of the stars as she gazed up at Adam.

"Wal, I'll walk up an' down outside the hedge," said Merryvale.

"You needn't leave us alone," objected Adam. "If anyone did surprise us I'd rather you'd be here."

"No one is goin' to surprise you, I'll swear to that," rejoined Merryvale. "Not with my eyes an' ears peeled."

Merryvale slipped away noiselessly along the hedge to the opening. Here he paused. The moment seemed exhilarating, and revived long dormant emotions. In his youth he had loved romance, adventure, women, and the feelings they had aroused in him seemed somehow linked with the present. He worshipped Adam. He, who knew the desert, saw in Adam all it exemplified. Adam was his hero. And now he felt himself finally committed to Ruth.

Merryvale stood in the shadow, peering forth, listening while his thoughts revolved round his friends. There was no light now in the Hunt house. Evidently the Indian woman had gone down to visit her people, as was her habit. Hunt, no doubt, was at work at the post. The usual silence characteristic of Lost Lake was disrupted this night. The sound of footsteps, the hum of voices, broken occasionally by a discordant laugh, the lights that threw a glow on the *palo verdes,* somehow seemed unfitting to this lonesome water-hole.

Merryvale heard the gurgle and tinkle and a murmur of running water. Hunt's spring! The waterhole which the Indians claimed had never gone dry! It had turned out to be a well-spring of gold, a treasure mine.

Merryvale saw trouble hovering over this water-hole. In his day he had known of countless feuds over water rights. The desert recorded more bloodshed over water than over all its other treasures. Larey and Collishaw would stop at nothing to gain their ends. Hunt would refuse to sell. And these men would involve him in some plot of debt or former claim, and failing that they would resort to harsher methods. The Indians hated Hunt, though he kept them from starving. There were degenerate Mexicans in Lost Lake, and always the nameless desert rats, the tramps of the wasteland, were passing through. Collishaw had a foothold in Yuma, and Larey held a controlling interest in the freighting business. Merryvale saw clearly that the situation was hopeless for Hunt.

With this conviction settled in his mind, Merryvale sought to decide how he would meet the issue. He could never influence Adam without facts. Ruth was an unknown quantity, a creature all fire and moods, unstable as water, yet he believed he could influence her. He could play upon her emotions. It was written that she would love Adam. Already Merryvale felt her dependence upon Adam, her thought and feeling centering round him, her sorrow over the tragedy of his lonely life, and her horror at the blow a cruel fate had dealt him—in finding her his brother's wife. Merryvale had sensed her torture over this. Out of it surely would grow love—such a love as might save Ruth Larey's soul.

Merryvale had likewise divined Ruth's fear. She had not betrayed the all of Guerd Larey's villainy. She knew that Adam still loved this brother and playmate of his childhood—loved him because in his great heart love was ineradicable. And if, through her, Adam should really kill this brother, for whose supposed murder he had been an outcast for fourteen years, he must go on to a lonelier, more terrible wandering, the misery of which even God could not assuage.

But Merryvale did not hold with what he considered Ruth's point of view, which was actuated by emotion, and the birth of unconscious love. Secretly Merryvale had always regretted that Adam had not killed this green-eyed snake of a brother; and also that one-eyed, gun-packing, hangman sheriff, Collishaw.

The early frontier had developed Merryvale. This later day was lawless enough, in remote districts, but he despised the bloodless wrangles. Unknown to Adam he had acquired from every source possible on the desert, knowledge of Adam's fame as Wansfell the Wanderer. To save his own bitter soul from sinking to the beastly, Adam had sought out all the unfortunates he could find on the desert. And these, whom the desert had wrecked, and the desperate dogs of men who plundered and ravaged the weak, somehow had fatefully gravitated across Wansfell's trail. Merryvale kept this knowledge warm in his heart. Had he not been the first to set Adam toward the greatness of the desert—eighteen years before?

So Merryvale, pacing to and fro in the shadow, alert to outside things, formulated a plot of his own, matched his wits against the craft of Collishaw and Larey, dedicated the last service of his waning years to the happiness of his friends.

The night wind rose and moaned through the hedge —desert wind with its mystery, its voice, its latent power, its breath of sand. The stars brightened. And the running water tinkled on. Out there the desert slept, black, unfathomable, brooding, accomplishing its inscrutable design.

Merryvale heard soft steps. A towering dark figure with a slight white one close beside it, moved toward him.

"We must go. It grows late," said Adam.

Ruth had her arm through Adam's, holding herself

close to him, and her face was turned upward to his, mute, yet exquisitely eloquent under the starlight.

After a moment she withdrew from him and turned to Merryvale:

"Goodnight, my friend," she whispered, and with light hold upon his arm she raised herself to kiss his cheek with soft cool lips. Then she glided down the path, disappearing like a pale spectre, in the gloom of the trees.

"My Gawd, I wish I was young again," ejaculated Merryvale, fervently.

"If wishes were horses. . . . you know," answered Adam, sadly.

"You'd have a rival, Adam," went on Merryvale.

"Come," replied his companion. They went noiselessly along the hedge to the desert. Adam did not speak. And Merryvale kept pace with him until, far from the post, they found seats upon a rock.

"Wal, Adam, what're you thinkin'?" began Merryvale, with a sense of pleasure in the moment.

"Thinking! My mind's in a whirl," muttered Adam.

"What're you goin' to do?"

"*Quien sabe?*" replied his friend, breathing deeply of the cool air.

"Ahuh. Wal, pard, I confess to bein' some flabbergasted myself," returned Merryvale. "But we've got to tackle it. When're you comin' in again?"

"Tomorrow night," returned Adam.

"Good," blurted out Merryvale.

"I ought not. Yet how could I refuse? How *could* I when I wander out there all day in the canyons, hunting rabbits, gathering firewood, trying to keep active, cursing my loneliness—fighting the longing to see her."

"Ha, pard, you're shore comin' around. I reckon I'm downright glad to see it."

"Coming round to what, man?" demanded Adam, as if suddenly conscious of himself.

"Why, to thinkin' of *her,* an' not so much of her troubles an' frailties. Reckon helpin' her is all right, an' shore savin' her soul might be important. But what she needs worse is to be loved—the way a woman wants to be loved."

Adam relaxed from his sudden rigidity. "Good heavens, pardner, have you no idea of the awful fix I'm in?" he exclaimed, with hopeless importunity.

"Shore. I'm figurin' on it all the time. An' I'm askin' you—do you know Ruth loves you?"

Adam's eyes blazed at him in the starlight. He made a ponderous gesture, as if thrusting a mighty thing from him.

"Wal, she does," went on Merryvale, mercilessly. "She doesn't know it yet, an' that's how I found out aboot it. But she loves you. An' pard Adam, when she finds it out—wal, I reckon you'll be the luckiest an' distractedest man in this whole world."

"Merryvale, old friend—don't—don't make me believe that," implored Adam, huskily. "It's hard enough . . . She's Guerd's wife. . . . I couldn't be strong to—"

"Hell, man!" burst out Merryvale, torn by his friend's pain. "Get that Guerd's wife idee out of your haid. Ruth's *not* his wife. She never *was*. . . . I swear to you she loves you. Wal, now, when you see her again take her in your arms."

Adam towered to his lofty height, shaken as an oak in storm.

"My love is greater than that. . . . Could *I* make of Ruth what her mother feared other men might make?"

Merryvale laid a pitying reverent hand upon his friend. "Wal, let's not quarrel. It's a hell of a mess. But we cain't leave that girl alone for one single day. I wish now the S. P. wasn't comin' to Lost Lake. We might have persuaded Hunt to sell the water-hole. But not now. So we must meet what comes—anticipate it, if we're keen enough."

"Yes—yes," returned Adam, hurriedly. "I must go now. My part is to wait—and pray, if that were any use. . . . You must get the drift of things, and watch over Ruth."

Merryvale bade his friend goodnight and watched

the tall figure merge into the blackness. Then, deep in thought, he took a roundabout course toward his lodgings. Far out on a ridge wailed up the desolately lonely mourn of a wolf. It suited the desert and the hour. It struck Merryvale with the implacability of nature. Man was only an animal, too, subject to the same physical laws—hunger, fear, instinct to preserve life and reproduce it. Yet what of the beating of that collossal heart—the spirit which enveloped the desert and the night, and reached to the whirling stars and into the void beyond?

6

Merryvale, in staying up late at night, had departed radically from his regular habits. He slept late the morning after his talk with Adam. A ray of sunshine, creeping between the poles of the wall behind his bed, fell hot upon his face, awakening him.

He got up, laced his worn boots, and made ready for what he felt would be a day of moment. His food had about petered out, as he had insisted on Adam's taking most of their supplies. It was necessary, now, that he eat at the inn, or the little restaurant kept by a Mexican. This would further his plan of mingling with the natives of Lost Lake, and of watching, listening, peering, of becoming an idler at the store and the post, a habitue of the saloon, all in the driving interest of his friends. These water-holes of the desert were hot-beds of intrigue, of sordid greed, of sinister motive. There were no petty or little things. The desert did not develop human beings any different from its few surviving wild creatures. Even Adam, gentlest of men, had at times the swoop and ruthlessness of an eagle.

As Merryvale sauntered toward the post he espied Stone sitting outdoors in the Mexican's yard, propped in a chair. Merryvale passed, with a nod, which was not acknowledged. Stone would be well soon, he reflected, to further complicate Ruth's situation.

In front of the post, the northbound stage was about ready to depart, with passengers climbing aboard. There was only half the number Merryvale had seen arrive, and Collishaw was not among them. Merryvale approached the stage driver, who stood waiting, long whip doubled in hand. The driver was loquacious. It served Merryvale's turn to make his acquaintance, and to hold him in conversation until it was time to depart.

"Adios, old timer, hope you strike it rich out in the hills," were the driver's parting words.

Then Merryvale found his way to the Mexican's place for breakfast. Here again he made himself agreeable, and was not long in discovering that the Mexican, Jose Garcia by name, had lived at Lost Lake when it was known as Indian Wells, and could add considerably to his store of information.

When he had finished his morning meal he wandered into the post. Mr. Hunt was dealing with the freighters, four of whom were to start back that day to Yuma. The others were bound north. It was not lost upon Merryvale that four wagonloads of freight had gotten no farther than Lost Lake.

Merryvale ventured to approach Dabb, whom he had distrusted at first glance.

"Reckon this heah freight business is boomin'," he remarked presently. "Shore, I've a notion to give up prospectin' an' go in for hoss-dealin'."

"What's your name?" inquired Dabb, pricking up his jack-rabbit ears. He had deep-set eyes, and his forehead was knotted with wrinkles.

"Merryvale. My pardner an' me dropped in some days ago. He's out in the hills workin' a lead. Reckon he likes it better outside. But I've got some money banked in Yuma. An' I've a darn good notion to go into hoss-dealin', if not freightin' outright. What's your idee aboot it?"

"It's something you're not the only one who's thought of," replied Dabb, meaningly.

"Ahuh? Wal, I'm not so doggone smart, after all," returned Merryvale, with apparent disappointment.

"It takes more than being smart. You've got to have money," said Dabb, with intensity. "That's what keeps me back. I'd been talking some to Hal Stone about throwing in with him. But he got shot up bad. . . . Say, Merryvale, what money could you invest?"

"Wal, I reckon ten thousand," replied Merryvale, thoughtfully. "But I'm gettin' along in years, an' shore I'd want to go slow, so's not to make a bad deal."

"Man, with that much capital the horse-dealing would be only a side issue," returned Dabb, with a sharp crushing of the paper he held in his hand. Then he fastened his deep-set eyes on Merryvale. "Lost Lake is not the place to begin operations."

"Wal, you don't say. An' why?"

"There's going to be a change here soon. Besides it's on the edge of the sand dunes. Never will be anything but a water station. Important, yes, and a gold mine for somebody. But there'll never be any development of the land here. A man wants to look ahead. There's a big future for this old prospector's trail through the valley."

"Shore. I know the railroad's comin'," ventured Merryvale, sagely. "That's one reason for my idee."

"How'd you find that out?" queried Dabb, surprised.

"Wal, I'm posted from Yuma."

"So. . . . You're on the right track, Merryvale. Suppose you meet me tonight, for supper. We'll have a little talk. Maybe I'll take you in with me. Keep mum about your idea," he said, and bending nearer to Merryvale he whispered. "It'd never do for Larey to get wind of this."

"Ahuh. Wal, I'll meet you aboot sundown," returned Merryvale, and went out, to find a seat in one of the windows in front of the post. Already the heat of the day had set in, and under this long wide stone porch, with its archways, Indians were lounging, and Mexicans passing to and fro.

Merryvale knew that Dabb was employed by Hunt, and he suspected that he was dominated by Larey. What had Dabb meant by a change at the post? The answer was not difficult to find. Dabb's whispered words, however, were not so easily analyzed to their exact purport. Recalling Dabb's air of mystery, his crafty look and assurance, Merryvale arrived at the conclusion that Dabb knew of a prospect of gain which Larey would be quick to snap up. In his own interest Dabb evidently would not hesitate at anything short of jeopardizing his skin. And Merryvale, shrewdly weighing the consequences, concluded he had found a way to get conversant with Larey's plans, if not direct knowledge of his machinations.

Whereupon Merryvale went on his way to see Ruth. The sun beat down. The heat waved up. There was again a gray haze over the desert, hiding the reach of sand. A hot wind blew in from the open, dry, fragrant, bearing its almost invisible burden of dust. A row of buzzards perched upon the end wall of the post. But inside the hedge which enclosed Hunt's property there was relief for the eyes, if not from the heat. The green flags rustled, the pond rippled gently, the water ran on with its musical tinkle.

Before Merryvale was half way up the winding green-bordered path he espied Ruth on the porch. She had seen him. No doubt she kept sharp lookout for visitors, some of whom she might not want to meet.

Ruth was standing when he reached her. She wore a simple gray dress, rather short, which made her look like a girl. She gave him her hand with a smile he had not seen before. The intensity he always felt in her seemed absent. She must have had pleasant dreams, which the day had not wholly dispelled.

"Wal, lass, I told Adam last night if I was younger he'd shore have a rival. An' this mawnin' you look like a desert lily—the white an' gold kind that grows in deep canyons," drawled Merryvale, as he took the chair she pulled forward for him, and laid his hat down.

"Flatterer! I'll bet you were a gay gallant back in those old Texas days," she replied.

"Yes, I reckon. Gay an' wild," he said, with pathos. "Some day I'll tell you my story. . . . You shore look different this mawnin', Ruth. I don't know jest how."

"Merryvale, I slept and I dreamed—and awoke almost happy," she replied, resting her elbows on her knees and her chin on her hands, while she looked gravely into his eyes.

"I'm glad, lass. An' so you should after last night," returned Merryvale. "Shore Adam was out of his haid."

"Oh! What—how?" she queried, startled out of her reverie.

"Wal, I went off on the desert with him for a while," replied Merryvale, watching her with a little twinge. But he could not depart from the deliberate course he had set. "I wanted to talk aboot your grandpa an' trouble impendin' heah. But Adam never ketched a word. He was like a man in a trance."

"Why—what was the matter?" asked Ruth, her eyes opening wide.

"Wal, he jest loves you so turrible, Ruth."

She was startled. A great wave of scarlet spread under the golden tan, and she covered her face a moment. "Merryvale—I—you—" she faltered. Then she looked up, trying to meet his gaze to laugh something away. Merryvale thought he had never seen anything so lovely. Where now were the discontent, the passion, the wayward emotions of a woman fighting herself and a hateful environment? This perhaps was just another phase of her marvellous capacity for change, but it was beautiful, and Merryvale thought he would give his life to make it permanent in her.

"Ruth, lass," he began, very seriously. "I'm a blunt old desert rat. You mustn't mind my way. I'm Adam's pard, an' I'm heah to plan an' work an' spy for you. . . . An' as I was sayin', Adam loves you turrible. It almost struck me dumb to see him. An' if I hadn't got mad, I'd shore been tongue-tied. Wal, we talked then, of course, aboot you an' your bein' together. An' presently I got a hunch that the darn fool didn't even *tell* you he loved you."

"Not last night," murmured Ruth. "We talked of— of the trouble brewing here. How to meet it—to help grandfather—and I guess that's about all. The time flew by."

"Wal! An' he never made you kiss him?" queried Merryvale, in pretended amaze.

Ruth shook her head and again the blood dyed her cheek. His rude query had more than embarrassed her.

"Adam's a strange man," went on Merryvale, in apparent wonder and disdain. "After four years of huntin' for you all over the Southwest he caint tell you the truth. An' he caint demand even a kiss from you. Wal, I would. Of course, you're married—even if it is only a name—an' you couldn't belong to Adam till you're free. But jest the same you do belong to him. Not only because your mother gave you to him. But because of the agony he has lived an' the mighty love for you that's come out of it. Why, Gawd will make you love Adam, if you don't already. It's written. It's the law of this desert. Adam has spent the best of his youth on this desert, searchin' for tasks no other man would dare. An' now the desert has fetched him to you, his best an' last an' greatest opportunity. He will *save* you. This Lost Lake is hell for a woman, let alone such as you. Some day he'll take you away from it—when he can do so without hurtin' your good name. He's foolish aboot that. But it's because of your mother. That's why he caint make love to you an' be like other men."

"Oh, I don't want him to be," she cried, bowing her head.

"It's love you need, Ruth," went on Merryvale, without mercy. "Wal, make Adam love you—in the little tender ways a woman craves. Make him. Make him give in to love. Then you can fight this battle heah to beat Larey, to save your grandfather."

"What can I do?" cried Ruth. "All you say, and more, has filled my mind, shaming me. . . . I have trifled with man after man. Oh, if only I had not! . . . How could I sink to such miserable guile—to move and hold *him?*"

"Wal, forget that past triflin'," returned Merryvale,

sternly. "An' be earnest. Be shore of yourself. An' for Adam, be all a woman can be. Be for him all this desert has made you. You cain't escape your destiny any more than change your beauty. You have the purple eyes of a cactus flower. Your skin an' hair are gold. You're sweet an' wayward, like a girl, but you have the mystery of a woman. You can make your weakness into strength, your discontent into loyalty. . . . This man you love is a desert eagle. *Be* his fit mate!"

"Merryvale! you—you torture me," she returned, passionately.

"Ruth, love is torture. Life is torture," he said, relaxing back into his chair. "You must give one an' endure the other."

"You hurt—yet you uplift me," she replied, with effort at composure. "I have stagnated here. No one made me think. If I hadn't loathed the desert it might have taught me."

It satisfied Merryvale, while it caused him regret that his brutality had struck fire from Ruth. He had not dared to hope so much. What strange elements mingled in her! How at the mercy was she of an unstable emotional nature! She had potentialities for evil, and many grave faults, but she was honest, she was loving, she was still, by some saving grace of blood and breeding, an untainted woman.

"Look! Two men coming in the gate," she exclaimed, pointing. "Guerd Larey!"

"Yes, an' the other is Collishaw," returned Merryvale, rising. "If you don't mind I'll jest step inside the door." He suited words to quick action. "Don't let them upset you, Ruth."

"I'm not in the least afraid to face them," she replied, calmly.

Merryvale took a seat on the couch where he could not be seen unless some one entered the door. Perhaps it was Larey's plan to approach Ruth before going to her grandfather. Footsteps and low voices sounded without, and then:

"Howdy, Ruth," said her husband, genially. "You know Collishaw. I've fetched him up to see you."

"Good morning," replied Ruth, coldly, with a hint of interrogation in her tone.

"Mawnin', Mrs. Larey," replied Collishaw, blandly. "Reckon I haven't seen you for weeks. An' shore I'm the loser for that. If it were possible, you grow handsomer all the time."

"Thank you, Mr. Collishaw. But surely you didn't call upon me to pay compliments," returned Ruth, with faint sarcasm.

"Wal, no. It's business, an' I'll take your hint an' get to it.—We've had a talk with your grandfather aboot buyin' him out. He won't listen to no reasonable offers."

"Why should he?" queried Ruth. "He has slaved here for years. And now when the property has suddenly increased a hundred percent in value he would be a fool to sacrifice it."

"You know aboot the railroad comin'?" inquired Collishaw.

"Yes."

"Wal, there's no gainsayin' the sense in your agreement. But you don't know every angle to this deal. This heah water-hole belonged first to an old Spanish grant. Indian Jim an' his family didn't have a clear title. Fact is they didn't have anythin' in writin'. I've looked it up in Yuma. That Spanish grant has gone to the state, an' I've staked a claim for Larey. Wal, if Larey throws your grandfather off this land, nothin' could be done aboot it. It's like a minin' claim. If you let someone jump it, you lose."

"I don't believe you," retorted Ruth.

"Naturally. But all the same I'm speakin' gospel."

"Ruth, it's news to me, and I believe it's a fact," spoke up Larey, with conviction. "I know Hunt hasn't a patent to this land. He can't get one short of another year, if he can at all."

"Please come to the point," said Ruth, impatiently.

"You can't scare me with your arguments. Why do you approach me?"

"Wal, the whole deal hangs on you, Mrs. Larey," continued Collishaw.

"Ruth, that's true, but he doesn't put it very nicely," said Larey, suavely. "Hunt and I did not get along well, as you know. I have not pressed claims against him for the simple reason that I've not despaired of a reconciliation with you. But this railroad proposition forces my hand. The freighting business will be killed, eventually, but the water right is worth a fortune. Now I'll agree, if you'll come back to me, not to drive Hunt off this property."

A moment of tense silence ensued, during which Merryvale felt the blood boil in his veins.

Collishaw cleared his throat: "There you are, Mrs. Larey. You see how the deal hangs on your going back to your husband."

"*Back* to him," retorted Ruth, in ringing scorn. "I never was his wife."

"Wal, he gave me a different notion aboot that."

"I've heard so from other sources. He lied."

"Aw now, Ruth," interposed Larey, "don't get riled. I didn't mean what—"

"I know what you meant. When I ran out of your house on your wedding night you lied to save your face. You lied to save your vanity. You lied to make me out what I was not."

"Mrs. Larey, I shore apologize," returned Collishaw, gruffly, as if aggrieved. "I'm from Texas where a woman's word an' a woman's honor mean somethin'. If Larey lied aboot—"

"Look at his face!"

"Damn you, Ruth Virey!" ground out Larey. "Of course I lied. What could you expect? You ran off from me two hours after you married me. You made me the laughing-stock of gamblers, greasers, freighters, all the riff-raff of this desert. And I've never forgiven you. And what's more I'll drag you back by the hair—if you—"

"See heah, Larey," interrupted Collishaw, heatedly. "I caint stand heah an' listen to you talk to a woman that way. Reckon I belong to the gamblin' riff-raff myself. But I know what's due a lady. You'd get shot in Texas—"

"To hell with Texas," rasped out Larey. "We're in California, and on the desert. You get out and leave this *lady* to me. I didn't want you to come. I knew your soft talk would queer me. After this, you stick to the business end of our relation. Leave this cat to me. What she needs is to be tamed."

"Wal, Guerd, you'll excuse me for interferin'," came Collishaw's stiff reply. "But I'll have one word. I'm not surprised at the regard this lady has for you. An' I'll bet you a million you'll never tame her."

Quick firm footfalls of heavy boots broke the ensuing silence, and died away down the path. Collishaw had gone; and if Merryvale knew anything about Texans the choleric Mr. Larey had not strengthened friendship.

"Now, Mrs. Larey, we'll have it out," began Larey, with a change of tone.

"As far as *I* am concerned, Mr. Larey, we're already out," returned Ruth, in weary indifference.

"Listen. I'm not going to quarrel with you again. I'm through. My patience is gone. For three years I've begged. I've accepted your insults. I've watched you flirt with this and that man, and swallowed my jealousy—when I wanted to kill. I took my medicine. I'd have hated you if I could. But the rottener you were to me the more I loved you. That's what brought me to your feet. All my life women have been like ripe grapes to me. I had only to reach. But you—you made me love you until it has nearly killed me. . . . Do you understand that? I could be as noble and good as I am base and crooked—if you loved me. I have that in me. You couldn't believe me. I see the ridicule in your eyes. Guerd Larey to change his spots! That's the cursed paradox of my miserable state. I *could* do it. But all that is of no avail. . . . I'm at the end of my rope. Will you give in to me to save your grand-father?"

"No. Not to save his life or mine!"

"Very well. I'm answered. Now answer this. Here we are on the desert. What is to prevent me from dragging you to my house and holding you prisoner there? At least long enough to drag you down to my level. Every man in this wretched hole would laugh and up-hold my action."

"Not quite *every* man," replied Ruth, mockingly.

"The majority would. But answer—what's to prevent me from doing it?"

"I'd kill you!"

"Maybe you would. It's not so easy for a woman to kill a man who knows her. And the more of a tigress you'd be, the sweeter I'd find it to break you."

"The desert has certainly found the beast in you, Guerd Larey."

"I can't see that the desert has made an angel of you, my lady. Take, for instance, your affair with Stone. If that boy hadn't been a jackass he could have won you. I saw you hanging on to him. Aw—you needn't blaze at me with your damned eyes! You don't know *what* you are—*what* you're capable of. Like as not you'll get sweet on Stone again."

"Surely. And perhaps many another man. But *never* you!"

Larey cursed mutteringly and his heels savagely crunched the gravel. Ruth came stumbling into the room, to slam the door, and sink upon the couch be-side Merryvale. Then she slipped to her knees on the floor, quivering all over, with eyes tight shut yet streaming tears, and her face drawn by conflicting passions.

"Ruth, lass," said Merryvale, drawing her head to his shoulder and holding her with tender hand. But in the stress of his own feeling he could not think of any word of comfort. So he just held her closely and that moment grew marvelously sweet to him. Merryvale did not blind himself to Ruth's imperfections, but he loved her because it was impossible not to love her. There was a woman now and then, he believed, who exacted this from men. Perhaps it was her beauty alone—perhaps the indescribable charm that haunted her voice, her look, her action—perhaps the very unattainableness which deceived and allured. Larey had betrayed his reason for loving her.

The silent storm subsided at length, and she raised her wet face from his shoulder.

"You heard it all?" she asked.

"Every word, Ruth."

"I wasn't afraid, but I couldn't control myself. The very look of that man infuriates me. His green-toad eyes! They seem to—to strip me."

"Wal, Ruth lass, you shore gave him a flayin' with your tongue. It frightened me for you. Larey is dangerous. He has laid his cairds on the table. Now how are we goin' to play against him?"

"I don't know. We must think. But this I beg of you," she replied, passionately eloquent. "Don't tell Adam about this. Promise me, Merryvale."

"Ruth, I'm afraid I caint promise that," rejoined Merryvale, feeling troubled.

"I can only stand so much," she persisted. "I couldn't bear for Adam to know of Larey's brutal threats—of his vile lie."

"Why couldn't you, Ruth? I reckon sooner or later Adam is goin' to find out for himself."

"Oh, I pray to God he doesn't. I must see that he never does."

"You're afraid he might—"

"I know, Merryvale. I *know*," she cried, wildly. "Adam would kill this brother he still loves!"

Merryvale weakened. "Wal, then, I promise I'll not say a word to Adam aboot what jest happened heah."

"Thank you," she replied gratefully.

"I'll go now an' see what's doin' at the post," said Merryvale. "Keep careful lookout from now on. Don't meet Larey again when you're alone. Lock yourself in, if anyone you don't know comes. I'll be heah at dark to take you to meet Adam."

Before Merryvale entered the freighting post he heard Guerd Larey's voice raised in loud angry tones.

Merryvale hastened in. Dabb was there, standing stock-still, in the attitude of one so intent on listening that he did not note Merryvale's entrance. The office, from whence the voice emanated, was a partitioned-off little room, open at the top. Larey was in there, evidently with Hunt, and no doubt also Collishaw.

"—— —— —— anyhow," Larry was cursing. "You held up a big deal for me with the steamboat company, —— —— —— you're not going to do it here."

"I refuse to be partner to dishonest business," declared Hunt, forcibly, and he struck a table with his fist. "I'll not accept supplies, especially liquor, smuggled across the border."

"Hell, man. You wouldn't need to know what those cases contained," fumed Larey.

"I would know, and that's enough."

"Once more, you tight-fisted old geezer, will you go in with us on this new deal?"

"No. Moreover I'm about through with you, Larey."

"You *are* through. I'll throw you out of this office in a minute," shouted Larey. "But first listen to Collishaw."

Thereupon the Texan began to hold forth rapidly, forcibly, in speech of which the content was not always distinguishable. There was enough, however, for Merryvale to gather that it concerned Hunt's invalid title to the water rights on the former Spanish land grant.

"It's a devilish scheme to ruin me," declared Hunt, shrilly. But his voice rang with shock and alarm.

"Shore it's only your poor haid for business," returned Collishaw, speaking freely now. "I advise you to accept Larey's offer. If you don't you'll get put off the property without anythin'."

"How—how could you put me off? asked Hunt, quaveringly.

"Wal, didn't I jest tell you that Larey had the claim now? An' besides, you owe him money."

"It's a lie," rejoined Hunt, hoarsely. "I owe him nothing. He has cheated me out of thousands. He is worse than a bandit."

Larey laughed coarsely. "Prove it, Caleb. Now you get out of here."

A chair scraped the floor, a shuffling of feet and an exclamation followed. The door flew open and Hunt catapulted out. His face was red, his white hair ruffled, his demeanor one of mingled fury and alarm.

Merryvale had slipped behind a pile of bales, from which vantage point he saw Larey make good his threat. Hunt was shoved out, if not thrown, and with violence.

"Caleb, you can tell Ruth you've got one chance to keep your land," said Larey, sharply, standing in the doorway. "That's for her to come back to me!"

Larey wheeled then to espy Dabb, who had begun making pretence of searching on a shelf.

"Didn't I tell you to get out?" demanded Larey.

"Yes, sir, but I came back. You didn't say—"

"How much did you hear?"

"Only your last words, sir."

"Well, you leave us alone for an hour. When you come back I'll talk to you about taking Hunt's job."

Dabb hurried into the ware-room and shut the door. Then Larey and Collishaw returned to the office.

"That's done, and it's a damn good riddance," said Larey, with a clap of his hands. "Do you think we can trust Dabb?"

"No. You caint trust any man if you are not straight yourself," replied Collishaw.

"Say, are you giving me a hunch?" snarled Larey.

"Dabb was listenin', you can bet on that."

"What do I care for these two-bit hang-dog fellows? I'll give Dabb a chance."

"Guerd, I'm shore afraid you're crackin'," said Collishaw, with gravity. "You never used to fly off the handle like this. You're reckless an' sort of desperate. It's the woman!"

"Ha! Look for the woman, when every man breaks!"

"Wal, I don't like the way the cairds show," went on Collishaw. "An' shore that goes without your drinkin' hard an' your mind bein' cluttered up aboot Ruth."

"Leave her out of our business," returned Larey, with passion.

"Wal, all right, for the present. But later I'll tell you aboot an idee I have, concernin' her, that'll fetch you. . . . Now aboot Hunt. You've got rid of him heah, an' he caint prove nothin'. But go slow with the Spanish grant bluff. It might work in the end. But don't you throw him off his land like you did out of this place. He might have friends. An' your sweet little wife is no damn fool, let me tell you that. If she'd ever wake up an' forget herself long enough to think, she'd raise more hell than ten men. Fact is, Larey, I'm afraid of her."

"Will you shut up harping on Ruth?" demanded Larey, in extreme irritation. "Let's find Hunt's books and go over them."

Merryvale glided stealthily from his post and gained the door without betraying his presence.

"Whew!" he muttered, moving leisurely away. At first he meant to find Hunt, but on second thought he went on toward the Indian shack, where he lodged, and seated himself on his bed to ponder over what he had learned.

The Spanish grant claim as set forth by Collishaw was evidently a ruse to discourage Hunt and render Larey's scheme easier of accomplishment.

Indeed it had worried Merryvale, for it might well have been true. Hunt had showed himself vulnerable in this regard. Nevertheless even if it was false, the very idea itself had powerful advantages for an unscrupulous man. Sooner or later Larey would act upon it, despite Collishaw's advice. Then, all depended on what happened to Ruth, whether or not Adam would stalk into the scene. A leap of Merryvale's pulse attended the thought of seeing Adam meet his brother. To Merryvale there did not seem to be anything more desirable, outside of Ruth's happiness, than the death of this treacherous Guerd Larey. The thought again seized Merryvale's imagination and this time took root in fertile soil.

What was the idea concocted by Collishaw and calculated to find favor with Larey? It concerned Ruth. It could have only one angle—that of breaking Ruth's will. How impossible! Yet that seemed Merryvale's loyalty to her, what he wanted to see, rather than what might actually happen. Away from the enchantment of her voice and face, Merryvale did not wholly trust Ruth. He never had trusted any women. Yet Merryvale's doubt of Ruth seemed pierced by reproach. She had the passion in her to be great. But no matter, Merryvale reflected, he had divided his love and allegiance, and he would fight and die for Ruth.

7

Merryvale kept his appointment that night, but it was almost sundown when Dabb joined him, and led him hurriedly to the Mexican's restaurant, where they occupied a table in a corner.

"You happened in on somethin' today," began Dabb.

"Wal, yes, reckon I did," returned Merryvale, casually.

"How much more did you hear?" went on Dabb, his devouring eyes on Merryvale.

"Nothin'. I jest slipped out the minute their backs was turned."

"Larey gave me charge of the post."

"Ahuh. Wal, Dabb, that means you fell in with his idee of the freightin' business," asserted Merryvale, shrewdly.

"You heard Larey ravin' at Hunt."

"Shore, an' I'm smart enough to savvy he wouldn't hire you unless —— ——."

Merryvale allowed a meaning look to conclude his speech.

"You're an old fox. Well, that's one reason I'd like to go in with you on somethin' that's been eatin' me."

"You didn't tell me what."

"It's this. Larey an' Collishaw are goin' to get hold of Lost Lake. You seen a sample of their methods today. Then same with Salton Spring up the valley an' Twenty Nine Palms. I'm not sure about Salton bein' easy to get, but I know Twenty Nine Palms could be bought cheap. Coachella Indians, poor as Job's turkeys, an' no whites there at all. Lots of water, an' a hot spring that alone will be worth a fortune when the railroad fetches the people. What d'ye think?"

"Shore, I think what you say, if it's true, is plumb interestin'," replied Merryvale, guardedly.

"True enough. Larey said so. He was there only a month ago."

"Wal, go on."

"Let's get there first," returned Dabb, brightly, spreading his hands with a gesture of finality.

"Ahuh. Would you be double-crossin' Larey?"

"Yes, but he doesn't know I know about this chance. Suppose you go up to Twenty Nine Palms an' look the ground over. Make friends of the Indians. You can prospect a little on the side."

"Dabb, it's a good idee. I'll take you up," returned Merryvale, heartily.

"But we shore don't want to buy out the Indians until we know more. Larey will jump this water right here. He's got Collishaw, an' all the Indians on his side. Then I've heard that Collishaw controls some bad hombres in Yuma. So Larey will be safe takin' over a claim like this one, anyway he can get it. But we wouldn't be strong enough to hold Twenty Nine Palms, if it falls under the old Spanish grant."

"Ha, I see. Wal, the idee then is for us to find out."

"Yes. You go to Yuma pretty soon an' look it up. Meanwhile I'll be working out another scheme just as big. So we'll have it to fall back on. Savvy, Merryvale? My brains an' your money!"

"You're sure a brainy one," said Merryvale, admiringly. "Now tell me. Does this other scheme touch on Larey?"

"I should smile. It's easier to work, but riskier."

"Larey is a dangerous man. Look at the way he shot that boy, Stone."

"Yes, Larey is a bad hombre all right," conceded Dabb. "But this Lost Lake is his dunghill."

"Wal, I'll shake hands on hopes," returned Merryvale. "An' take one hunch from me. You've got a chance now to pry into all Larey's doings. Savvy?"

Dabb uttered a short laugh, stronger than any affirmative he could have made in words. They concluded their meal and talk, and parted at the door in the gathering dusk.

Merryvale bent his steps toward Ruth's home, and halted in the gloom beyond the dim yellow lights of the post.

The early night hour was sultry, almost sulphurous, with the heat of the day lying like a blanket over the desert. Not a sound broke the ominous silence. Far out over the black void lightning flared across the ranges of Arizona, showing them for a fleeting instant, bold, wild, desolate. What mystery out there in the open space! This oasis seemed marked for extinction, as centuries before the desert had decreed against the lake, which the Indian legends had located.

Merryvale found a subtle potency of the wasteland fastening upon his thought, as had always been the case when he took up an abode with people living in such a lonely and remote place as Lost Lake. How well he remembered Picacho! Then there had been a like period, spent with Adam at a waning gold camp, Tecopah. The desert weaned men from the law and order that they observed in civilized communities. It worked worse havoc upon women.

In the darkness, standing there, peering away down the starlit aisles which ended in obscurity, Merryvale seemed to encounter a stifling oppression. The heat not only hindered his breathing and movement. It weighed upon his brain. He never could forget the forbidding, insulating, fascinating presence of the desert. Most wayfarers and natives regarded it as a physical obstacle to all that might be striven for. To Merryvale, particularly since he had wandered over it with Wansfell, whom the desert had christened Wanderer, it was a Collosus of natural elements in process of decay, dying through the ages, destructive, terrible, dominated by the spirit of the sun. At this melancholy hour of dusk Merryvale felt hope only for the present, and for these fortunates who could abandon the abode of the shifting sands.

At length he made his thoughtful way up through the dark yard to Ruth's home. The tinkle of water fell upon his ear with strong relief. He endeavored to shake off the oppression. Under the porch the gloom was thick, streaked by a thin light from a crack in Hunt's door.

Merryvale knocked, and spoke his name. The door opened and Ruth came out, again in white. The flash of light showed her bare neck and arms. The glimpse he had of her face reassured him.

"Evenin', Ruth, you shore look like the moon an' stars. Where's your grandpa?"

"Gone to bed. He feels poorly tonight."

"Did he tell you aboot Larey puttin' him out?"

"Yes. I think he's glad of it. I know I am. It's not that. He's upset over Collishaw's claim."

"Wal, you tell him I was hid in the post when Larey threw him out, an' I was there after. I heard Collishaw speak of the Spanish grant bluff, an' advise strong against any rash move."

"It was all a lie. I knew, Merryvale, yet I didn't feel that we could do anything."

She went back into the room, leaving the door ajar. Merryvale heard her low eager voice and Hunt's tremulous one in answer. Presently she returned.

"He was overjoyed," she said, happily. "I think he was wavering. But he'll stand firm now. He called you a friend in need and thanked God that I had you and Adam to rely upon. And, Merryvale, he asked me something very strange."

"He did. Wal, now?"

" 'Ruth,' he said, 'if anything happens to me, this property will be yours. You will be rich. What will you do?' I asked him what he'd want me to do? He asked if I'd ever be Larey's wife. I told him I'd die first. Then he replied he'd like me to hold the property."

"An' what did you say?"

"I didn't commit myself. But I'm afraid I wouldn't want the place."

"Wal, let's look on the bright side. Come, I reckon it's time for us to meet Adam."

They took the pale path, winding among the trees, with Merryvale leading and Ruth gradually hanging back.

"Wal, what's the matter, lass?" he asked, drawing her close, so that he could see her face in the starlight. Had those stars ever before been mirrored in such eyes? Merryvale thought of the starlit Arabian waste and of the woman at the lonely well.

"Merryvale, I'm weak as water," she whispered. "I've surrendered. What you told me has been—too much—for me."

"You mean aboot makin' Adam love you?" he whispered, low and eager, bending to her.

Ruth bowed her head.

"I've fought all day. I've tried to kill my old self. Perhaps I did. . . . But I want more than anything ever before in my life—that he may find a little joy in me."

Merryvale drew her arm within his and led her on, mute for once, one instant stricken with remorse, and the next tingling with rapture for his friend.

They reached the hedge, and then the wide spreading *palo verde*. Adam stepped out of the gloom.

"Heah she is, pard," said Merryvale, huskily, giving Ruth a little shove.

"Oh—it's—so dark!" she whispered, as Adam caught her.

"Ruth!"

"Adam!"

"Child, this Merryvale is a devil in the disguise of a friend. He will ruin us."

"No—no. He is good, Adam. Not blind like you and me."

"Blind! What then is it I see now?"

"A happy girl one moment—in dreams. . . . A wretched woman—the next—when I think."

Merryvale started to glide away, savage in his glee, yet conscious of that blade in his heart.

"Don't go," called Adam, softly. "Stay close by, Merryvale."

So Merryvale paced a short beat between the hedge and the tree. Upon his return Adam and Ruth were sitting on the bench, faintly discernible to eyes growing accustomed to the darkness. He heard their low whispers, and once Ruth's sweet contralto laughter, suddenly hushed. Now and then Adam's voice struck a deep note, above a whisper. They forgot Merryvale pacing more and more slowly. They forgot, or did not care, while his ears and eyes grew keener. Strange deep happiness stirred in Merryvale's breast. He had a vicarious pleasure in Adam's situation.

The time came when Merryvale saw the pale gleam of Ruth's face upon Adam's shoulder. He did not go near again. He paused on the brow of the slope, half way between tree and hedge, and spent the strength of his vision upon the immense starlit expanse of desert.

It was, perhaps, the greatest and most clarifying moment of his life. Something beyond him justified his cunning, his implacability. He seemed to see into the future. There was a whisper at his ear, come on the faint night wind. Merryvale worshipped no God but nature, but it was certain that he trembled. His friendship for Adam, his love for Ruth—were they but mundane moods, to die when his day was done? Ruth would win this lonely fierce eagle of the desert, and in the end he would fall like a thunderbolt upon her enemies and destroy them. Life held no more for Merryvale than this.

But this wonderful exaltation did not last. The old materialistic physical grip of the desert returned to clutch Merryvale's heart. Were they but climbing stairs of sand, these lovers? The desert was immutable. How ghastly the stark and naked truth—the desert would not abide tenderness!

Midnight, when Adam parted from Ruth! If the

hours had sped fleetly even for Merryvale, they must have been but moments for these two.

Merryvale found himself unable to engage Adam's attention to any extent.

"Say, pard, suppose I'd need to find you any time. Where'd I come?"

Adam might as well have been walking alone. In fact, he was not of the earth. Merryvale repeated his query, louder, and accompanied it by a tug at Adam's arm.

"Follow the wash to where it runs out of the canyon," replied Adam. "Go up the canyon till it forks. Take the left fork."

"Ahuh. All right. Reckon we'll see you tomorrow eve?"

Merryvale tarried as he spoke, but he got no answer. Adam strode on, like a blind giant, to be swallowed up by the black mantle of night.

"Wal, I'll be doggoned!" muttered Merryvale. "Adam's clean gone. Not a word for me. An' if he only knew it, I'm the hombre who threw Ruth into his arms. But Lord—no wonder!"

He turned back, muttering to himself, and feeling his way carefully over the dark uneven ground, he reached his shack and went to bed.

Four days passed swiftly by. Merryvale saw Adam only once, the second night. Ruth reacted bewilderingly to her conquest of Adam. She was wildly gay and eloquently silent and passionately gloomy by turns. Merryvale spent hours with her, some of which were dismaying.

For the rest, Merryvale employed his time in the idling, watching, listening and inquisitively strategic way which he had chosen to adopt. Nothing escaped him except what went on behind closed doors, and even some of that he acquired.

Larey did not attempt to gain audience with Ruth, though he sent messages by Indians for Hunt to come out and confer with him. These were ignored. On the fifth day of that week Collishaw left Lost Lake in a light canvas-covered wagon, drawn by four horses, and driven by a taciturn Mexican who Merryvale had observed was devoted to Larey. They headed north, a circumstance Merryvale at once connected with Larey's scheme to get hold of important water rights up the valley. Dabb was not cast down by this circumstance; he informed Merryvale that he had more than one string to his bow.

Stone was up and about again, very pale and handsome after his narrow escape, and a subject of considerable interest around the post, which he evidently had no compunctions whatever about visiting. Dabb, who was a taciturn fellow and did not waste his time on anyone for nothing, grew friendly with Stone. It roused Merryvale's curiosity. Another rather peculiar circumstance was a meeting between Larey and Stone, at which Merryvale was present.

Larey, passing along the hard-packed sandy road before the post, encountered Stone talking to bystanders.

"Hello, you out? How are you?" queried Larey, halting.

"Gettin' along fine, Larey," replied Stone, coolly.

"Somebody said you were still packing a bullet."

"Yes. The doctor couldn't dig it out."

"Well, Stone, I'm glad you recovered. But if you deal the same trick again, I'll do a better job on you," returned Larey, with grim humor, and went his way.

That very day Merryvale espied Stone walking with his slow labored steps into Ruth's yard, and up the path toward the house. Merryvale was not surprised. He watched for Stone's return, which did not occur short of half an hour. Later in the day Merryvale met Hunt, who told him Stone had called, but had seen Ruth only in his presence. She was kind, solicitous, plainly sorry for him. This, Merryvale conceived, was Hunt's opinion. It might well be and very probably was the truth.

That evening at twilight Merryvale, finding Ruth in

her accustomed seat on the porch, took her rather severely to task about it.

"We were sitting here," she retorted. "Why should I run and hide? It was hot in my room. And what do I care? I was only civil to the fool. He looked pretty bad."

"Wal, I haven't no more to say aboot him," returned Merryvale.

Ruth seemed petulant, restless, sombre, the first time for days. She was pale, too, and had deep shadows under her eyes. Merryvale attributed her mood to the fact that Adam was not to come this evening; and after talking a little while to Hunt he said goodnight to Ruth and started to leave.

She caught up with him, and clung to his arm, and walked with him down the path to the hedge gate.

"You're angry with me?" she asked.

"Me? Shore not. But I reckon you're not yourself tonight, an' I know why, so I'm takin' myself off."

"You know more then than I do, Merryvale," she returned, leaning over the gate, "I'm cross. I want to go somewhere—do something. I'm cooped up all day long. Oh, not in the house. But this hedge is like a pen. That damn restlessness of mind and body has come back."

Merryvale could see her eyes gleaming large and dark from her pale face. They were as deep as the desert night, and held infinite mystery. She was at the mercy of a complexity of emotion increasing day by day. Merryvale's disappointment merged into pity.

"If I knew the way out to Adam's camp I'd go," she went on, dreamily.

"Aw, no, lass. Don't say that."

"I would, and right now," she flashed, awakening to his antagonism.

"But, my dear, that would be folly," rejoined Merryvale, trying to control both alarm and temper.

"No woman should be left alone, much less I," she said, somberly.

"Shore, I agree. I told Adam so," replied Merryvale, earnestly. "But he's mad aboot you, Ruth. An' I reckon the trouble is he's afraid he'll disgrace you."

"How, in heavens name?"

"Wal, Adam's afraid Guerd Larey will find out your friend Wansfell is really Adam Larey. Then nothin' on earth or in heaven could prevent catastrophe. Guerd would never believe in your innocence. An' he would blacken your name heah an' everywhere."

"Merryvale, Guerd *will* find out," declared Ruth. "And sometimes—when I'm like this—I don't hate the terrible thought."

"Natural. Reckon you're a woman," said Merryvale, betraying bitterness.

It did not touch her.

"Merryvale, you never told me why Guerd hated Adam. You've spoken often of Adam's love from childhood for this brother—how it survived the bitter fury at Picacho—how it lived and grew all those awful years on the desert. But why Guerd's hate? It seems unnatural. I've wondered and wondered. Surely it couldn't have been jealousy."

"Wal, I reckon yes. You know the Bible says: 'Who can stand before jealousy?' "

"But why so terrible a jealousy? Why something that drove Guerd from earliest childhood to hate Adam—to fight him—to rob him of everything?"

"Ruth, I've often worried aboot tellin' you," pondered Merryvale, slowly surrendering to the inevitable.

"But I should know," she went on, earnestly, lending her hands in persuasion. "Surely I can find out from Adam?"

"No. Never in this world," asserted Merryvale, positively.

"Is it something that will hurt Adam in my estimation?" she asked hesitatingly.

"Shore not, Ruth."

"Would it make me loathe Guerd more?"

"I reckon you'd feel somethin' you never did for him."

"What is it?"

"Pity."

"Pity?" she echoed, in amaze. "Me pity Guerd Larey!"

"Shore you would. For you're big in heart, Ruth."

"Then tell me," she demanded.

"Guerd Larey is a bastard," replied Merryvale, in suppressed voice, as if the hedge had ears to hear. "All his mother's love was lavished on Adam. As a child Guerd knew it. But Adam never found out until they grew to manhood."

Merryvale, lying awake in his bed, felt that something of Ruth's mood had communicated itself to him. It was unusual for him not to go to sleep at once.

The night was cool. The wind rustled the brush roof of his shack and whipped between the poles of the wall, laden with the dry taint of dust. It moaned out there on the desert, continuously and monotonously low.

Merryvale covered his head to shut out the mournful sound, as well as the sifting sand.

Suddenly he heard a cry. Was it wolf, or woman, or just a freak of the wind under the eaves of his shelter. He threw back the coverlet and listened. But the cry was not repeated. What illusions his imagination sometimes created!

Again he composed himself to try to sleep. But he was at once disturbed by the rattle of wheels over gravel and the thud of rapid hoofs. A vehicle of some kind was passing his shack. What could it be? Not a freighter! He listened. The sound quickly died away with the wind. Sometimes travelers preferred night to day, but owing to the danger of losing the road and getting off into the sand dunes, it was rather an unusual proceeding. Merryvale collected his wits. Four horses had passed his shack at a brisk trot toward the Yuma road. He had no way to tell now whether that vehicle had come through or around Lost Lake. Merryvale made a mental reservation to find out when daylight came. Wheels and hoofs left tracks, even on hard desert, to such experienced eyes as his.

He lay back again. But sleep would not come. He began to associate the woman's imagined cry with this mysterious night driver. Then he thought of Ruth, to become prey to all kinds of conjectures. Night in the desert always worked treacherously upon his mind. He convinced himself that he had heard the weird staccato cry of a coyote—that a party of railroad men, not wanting their presence known, had gone by under cover of the darkness.

That was Merryvale's reason. But it did not wholly allay misgivings. He felt what he could not explain. His mind revolved all that had happened at Lost Lake and manufactured a thousand things that might happen. Not until late in the night did he fall asleep. When he awoke the sun had long been up.

Daylight did not dispel the misgivings of the night. They had augmented in his slumbers. Merryvale hurriedly dressed and went out. The red sun, the glare of desert, smote him like a blow. He crossed the road. Narrow wheel tracks! Four well-shod horses! To Merryvale's relief they led straight down the road to the post. Whoever had driven that double team had manifestly no fear of being seen, for he had come down the stage road. Merryvale's concern lessened somewhat. He went to breakfast.

Upon his return he met Larey coming out of the inn, clean shaven, immaculate in white soft shirt, open at the neck, with sleeves rolled up. He wore as usual a gun in his belt, dark trousers and high boots. Larey always attracted the eye. He was magnificent to look at. He appeared a man whom it would not be safe to cross. But he seemed vastly more than that this morning—different to the crafty Merryvale.

"Hullo, old timer, you here yet?" he asked, as he came abreast of Merryvale.

"Mawnin', Mr. Larey. Shore I'm heah."

"What're you doing?"

"Wal, mostly restin'."

"Where's the man who was with you when you met Stone and my wife?"

"My pard? He's out in the hills prospectin'," returned Merryvale, concealing his intense interest in his questioner.

"Is he the man they call Wansfell?" went on Larey.

"Who's they?" drawled Merryvale, deliberating.

"They? Why, you blockhead, I mean men of the desert. Anybody inside?"

"Shore, his name's Wansfell," returned Merryvale.

"The hell you say!" ejaculated Larey, blankly. Then his great green eyes dilated and fixed. They had the same quality as Adam's only they were green, and therefore less piercing than the clear gray of his brother.

"Wansfell?" went on Larey. "It's not a common name. But I've heard it here and there. . . . And this Wansfell knew my wife?"

"I think he met her once, years ago, over in Santa Ysabel."

"What was he doing there?"

"Workin' on a ranch, if I recollect."

"Well, he can't be the Wansfell I'm thinking of. Still —Stone swore he might as well have been hit by a giant. . . . Damn funny!"

"Sorry, Mr. Larey, I caint help you out," drawled Merryvale. "Fact is, I don't know much aboot Wansfell, myself."

When Larey jerked aside and went on, Merryvale had food for reflection. Upon first sight, Larey had been glowing, whistling, vibrant with a physical ecstasy of life, with something impossible to define, through which, to the deep-visioned Merryvale, showed a dark secretive powerful flash of the man. The difference that had struck Merryvale was not this last, but the signs of spirits heightened extraordinarily. What now had happened to Mr. Larey?

Merryvale had quickened his steps. The atmosphere seemed charged. Only one thing could happen in Lost Lake that would be a calamity to him—misfortune for Ruth. He must put an end to uncertainty.

The hedge gate hung open. Merryvale, with the

instinct of the old tracker, peered down into the dust of the path. Heavy boot-tracks with imprints of hobnails had obliterated his own tracks, made early last evening. He bent down to scrutinize them. Two men, and a third and smaller footprint. These tracks came down the path. He followed them back to the gate and out; then, careful to avoid attracting attention, he returned and hastened up the path.

Hunt came out of the door of Ruth's room, his face and movement expressing extreme agitation.

"Merryvale! Ruth's gone!" he ejaculated.

"What?" cried Merryvale, aghast.

"Gone! Ruth! She's gone again!"

"Where?"

"I don't know. She didn't wake me this morning as usual. I called her to breakfast. She didn't come. Then I went to her door. Unlocked! . . . Come, look. Her bed hasn't been slept in."

Strung hard as Merryvale was he felt a tremor when he crossed Ruth's threshold and saw the neat little bed, with its white smooth pillow.

"Hunt, when did you see or hear Ruth last?" queried Merryvale.

"At nine o'clock she came in to say goodnight. Then, when she went out, she spoke to someone. I recognized that Stone's voice."

"Stone!" exclaimed Merryvale.

"Yes. I heard her ask him what he wanted. He answered something. Then he seemed to be appealing to her. I couldn't understand what she said, but I'd heard that tone often. Ruth answered him sharply. Then they had hot words. I caught enough to gather that Stone wanted her to intercede for him in some way, or get something for him from Larey. He was most persistent and begging. I called to Ruth once, wanting them to know I was awake. After that they talked lower. Presently I heard Ruth's footsteps on the porch. She went to her room. After a little I heard her in there. That was the last, for I went to sleep."

"Wal, I'm shore stumped," pondered Merryvale. "There's some tall thinkin' ahaid."

"Merryvale, she's run off again with Stone," declared Hunt, in anger and distress.

"Aw, no!" fiercely returned Merryvale.

"I remember more, as I think," went on Hunt. "Stone said something about 'money' and 'Larey' and 'being shot.' "

"Ahuh! Wal, Stone'd have to say more'n that before—"

"Ruth has had another bad spell," interrupted Hunt. "I saw it coming yesterday. She's hardly responsible when she's that way. Stone has persuaded her to leave."

"Hunt, it shore looks bad—but no—no! It caint be that."

"Merryvale, you run down and see if Stone is gone. If he is—"

"Easy enough, I'll go pronto," replied Merryvale, hurrying off.

"I'll look for Ruth's traveling bag and things," Hunt called after him.

Merryvale's mind outpaced his rapid steps. So long as he was uncertain of facts he could not think logically. His love for Ruth rose up to clamour in her defense. The voice of his bitter knowledge of life on the desert could not make itself heard. Anything might happen, but not treachery in Ruth. At that moment of stress he would have staked his soul on her honor.

When he reached the pretty little adobe house where Stone had his lodgings, Merryvale was out of breath. The bright-eyed senora could not understand him at first. When she comprehended his breathless query she replied:

"Senor Stone go las night an' no come back."

The unexpectedness of this news and its significance staggered Merryvale, and shocked him back into the stable character which had been overwhelmed by Ruth Virey's charm. He would withhold final judgment upon her until the facts of her disappearance were clear; but he stifled all the beautiful illusions and dreams under which he had smothered his wits for Adam's sake and her.

Merryvale retraced his steps, but now he lagged, suddenly feeling old and hopeless and heartbroken. Who was to tell Adam? The thought made him writhe. Shaking off a deadly weakness he faced what he felt he owed himself and Adam and the girl. Poor Ruth! Alas, she was right! She should never have been left alone. Adam and he must again take up the search for her.

An uproar in the post halted him before the wide open door. He heard the thud of blows, then a crash. Striding in, Merryvale was in time to see Dabb sink down at the foot of the wall, against which he evidently had been knocked. Larey moved forward, towered over him, his fist doubled.

"Maybe that'll loosen your jaw," he shouted.

"You didn't give—me a chance—to talk," replied Dabb, haltingly, raising himself on his elbow.

"Get up, then, and talk."

Dabb gathered himself up with effort and rose, his hand to his face. It was livid, and beads of sweat stood upon his brow.

"Where's that money?" demanded Larey.

"I don't know. I swear I didn't take it."

"Why didn't you miss it last night?"

"I never looked. You always lock the desk."

"I forgot it. Were you alone here last night, when you closed up?"

"No, sir. Stone was here for a while—till nearly nine o'clock."

"Ha! Young Stone. Did you go out any time while he was here?"

"Yes. I went into the store-room several times."

"Go fetch Stone," thundered Larey.

Dabb, hastily starting at this command, almost bumped into Merryvale.

"Gentlemen, your man left sometime last night," announced Merryvale coolly.

Larey, to the keen eyes fastened upon him, betrayed amaze at Merryvale's presence rather than at the content of his words. A deep frown disfigured his broad brow.

"How'd you get in this?"

"I was happenin' along, an' hearin' the racket I come in," returned Merryvale.

"Strikes me you're pretty nosey, old man," said Larey, stridently.

"Not at all. Anybody would run in to see a fight—or somebody gettin' murdered," replied Merryvale.

"Who told you Stone was gone?"

"The Senora where he lives."

"What business was it of yours?" queried Larey, now sharply, forgetting his fury.

"Wal, I had reasons of my own, Mr. Larey," he drawled.

"Are you meddling in my affairs?" demanded Larey angrily.

"I didn't steal your money, if that's what you mean," returned Merryvale, with dry sarcasm.

"Merryvale, you've got something up your sleeve," said Larey, hotly.

"Wal, Mr. Larey, if I have you can bet your life it's a stack of aces," replied Merryvale.

Larey fumed in angry speculation, unable to match this old man in wits, yet suspicious of an undercurrent of meaning. At last, remembering Dabb's presence, he waved Merryvale out with a curse that had its menace.

Merryvale had sustained a strong check to the direction of his thoughts. Larey did not ring true even in his villany. Merryvale had known innumerable bad characters. He had worked in mining camps with gamblers, bandits, outcasts, gun-men, all kind of hard characters which the West had developed, and this vast desert had finished in its fierce evolution. But in the main they were real men. Larey struck Merryvale as being one of those Easterners who had not the fibre to withstand the dry rot of the desert. In any case he could never last long in such a country as this. It was only an accident that he had dominated this out-of-the-way water-hole. Merryvale smiled grimly when he thought he knew why Larey's trips to Yuma were growing fewer and farther between.

While reflecting thus Merryvale was hurrying up to see Hunt. He found him, crouched on the porch, pale and downcast.

"Wal, what did you find out?" queried Merryvale.

"Ruth did not take her bag, or any of her toilet things. Not even a coat! She had only the clothes on her back."

"Wal, I'll be —— ——!" swore Merryvale, abruptly sitting down.

"Not even her mirror! Now, if you know Ruth, you'd be mighty sure that is a strange omission."

"I reckon. Ruth was the tidiest lass. . . . Wal, Hunt, shore this heah deal thickens."

"I'm more bewildered than ever," replied Hunt. "But I don't believe Ruth would run off with *any* man without clothes and things to keep her pretty."

"I savvy. But you caint never tell aboot a woman. She's gone."

"But, man, she couldn't go alone," expostulated Hunt.

"She shore could if she wanted to. Last night she told me if she knew how to find Adam, she'd go—right then. Wal, she might have gone anyhow. She'd heard Adam an' me speak of the canyon up heah, where he camps. She might have tried to find it."

"She might indeed. Ruth was always roaming around at night. She'd gaze at the moon and the stars as one possessed. She loved the darkness, the night that hid the sun and the desert from her. . . . Perhaps she tried to find Wansfell and got lost."

"Shore. I hope so. Because I can find her easy enough. I'll track her. But, I reckon, Hunt, it's a forlorn hope."

"Did you find Stone?" queried Hunt.

"No. He's gone."

"I knew it. I felt it."

"An' he's not all that's gone. Larey has been robbed of considerable money," said Merryvale, and went on to narrate the incident at the post. He kept to himself, however, his own deductions and speculations.

"Worse!" gasped Hunt. "Stone's a thief. I *heard* him speak of money and Larey. . . . Ruth has gone with a thief. My God!"

"Wal, whatever she's done we've got to fetch her back," replied Merryvale, sharply. "Now, Hunt, you spend the next few hours down at the post, watchin' an' listenin'. But keep your mouth shet. Heah that! . . . Wal, I'll take a circle round Lost Lake an' look for tracks. I'll get an Indian I know to go with me. Reckon I knew somethin' when I made friends with them Indians. . . . The stage from up north is due to-day. Reckon it'll be late gettin' in. But if it comes you see who's in it. Then I'll make a bee-line to find Wansfell. An' you can shore bet your life there's goin' to be hell!"

8

Merryvale located the Indian in the saloon. Hindfoot, as they called him, locally, was one of the many tragic derelicts of the desert, ruined by contact with the whites. He understood English, though he could speak only a little; he was capable in many ways, but so addicted to drink that he could not get work. When the saloon was open, from morning until late at night, Hindfoot could be counted upon to be there.

His dark sombre eyes gleamed from the gold coin in his palm to Merryvale's face.

"Come, follow me, but keep far behind," whispered Merryvale, and went out. He did not want to run the risk of being seen making for the desert with Hindfoot. There appeared small chance of that, however, for all of Lost Lake was in the freighting-post.

Merryvale went north along the road. He met Mrs. Dorn, a dark little woman, wife of a freighter. She was wiping her hands on her apron.

"You hear the news?" she asked, excitedly.

"Wal, Mrs. Dorn, reckon there's a lot of news flyin' around," replied Merryvale.

"Ruth Larey has run off again," she babbled, her eyes rolling. "With that young horse-dealer, Stone. It's the second time with him. Larey is crazy they say. . . . Isn't it dreadful? Poor Mr. Hunt! I've been a good friend to Ruth. But she's got worse an' worse. I think I saw it coming."

"Mrs. Dorn, it looks pretty bad, I'm bound to say," replied Merryvale. "But I'd wait a while before callin' Ruth an out an' out hussy."

"Oh, I didn't," protested Mrs. Dorn. "But I'm frightened. You *know* she ran off with Stone once, because you an' that desert man stopped her. This time it's worse. They robbed Larey's office. Stole money to go away on."

Merryvale passed her without further comment. The inhabitants of Lost Lake were what the desert had made them, with Ruth and Caleb Hunt no exceptions. Merryvale extended the symbolism to himself— a lean desert fox, sharp of fang, without issue, lonely, hungry, warped. Had not all the human in him gone out to Adam, and through that strange love, hard and tenacious as cactus, to the woman Adam loved?

Once on the outskirts of the post Merryvale turned to see the Indian following at a goodly distance. Merryvale went on as far as some smoke trees where he waited.

"Huh! What you want?" queried Hindfoot.

"We go all round post," replied Merryvale, getting up. "Look for tracks made last night."

"What kind tracks?"

"Any kind."

"Come?" asked the Indian, pointing north, and then turning to the south with brown hand outstretched he went on: "Go?"

"Shore. Hoss an' wheel tracks," rejoined Merryvale, eagerly. "Then I want to know if any man or woman tracks came in last night or left."

"Me savvy," said the Indian, and stepping back into the road he put his toe against a narrow wheel track, identical with that which Merryvale had trailed on the other side of the post.

"Come an' go last night. Me see um," continued Hindfoot, cautiously, his sombre gaze hard on his listener.

Merryvale, with hand that shook, gave the Indian another gold coin.

"Tell me—who?" demanded Merryvale.

"You no make bad?" asked Hindfoot, tapping his breast with forefinger.

"No. I'll not give you away," answered Merryvale, in deadly earnest. "No make you trouble."

Hindfoot covered his right eye, hiding it with one hand, while with his other hand he pointed to his uncovered eye.

"One-eye man come."

Merryvale's frame leaped as if it had been galvanized.

"By Gawd, it was Collishaw!"

"Four hoss. Wagon come. Me see um." He held up two fingers. "Mex and one eye man. No stop post. Stop way. Long time. Go fast!"

"Hindfoot, you're an Indian," replied Merryvale, wiping his wet face. "Whew! . . . Did you see these men get out, or meet anybody?"

"No. All dark there."

"Did you heah a woman scream?" went on Merryvale, breathing hard.

"No. All quiet."

"Did you see Larey, then?"

"No. He drink like fish. Go way soon."

"All right, Hindfoot. Now we'll look for tracks. You go far round. Meet me Indian Jim's. I go this side."

They separated. Merryvale had chosen the upper half of Lost Lake to circle, and he strode off with searching eyes bent on the ground. In some sandy patches and likewise on hard-packed gravel, tracks would have been difficult to find. On the other hand, there were stretches of adobe clay which would have betrayed the imprint of the lightest foot. Merryvale did not sight any fresh tracks. Back of Ruth's yard he passed his own and Adam's footprints made several days previous. From that point down and round to Indian Jim's there was no sign to be detected.

Hindfoot was waiting for Merryvale, though that fact would not have been evident to anyone else.

"No see more tracks," said the Indian.

"Where me get hoss to ride?" asked Merryvale, his mind leaping on to the next issue.

"Jim got mule."

"Saddle?"

"Injun saddle. Heap good."

"Hindfoot, go get Jim's mule an' saddle. Fetch over there," said Merryvale, pointing to his shack through the *palo verdes*.

"Huh!" replied the Indian.

Upon arriving at the shed, the shade of which was markedly welcome, Merryvale threw off his coat, surprised to find his shirt wet and his body burning.

"Wal, think of me gettin' het up," he soliloquized. "These heah June days are comin' on hot. Reckon I mustn't forget water."

He searched among his effects for his canteen, and finding it he sat down to rest and wait. His mind was full, though no longer whirling. It was imperative that he get to Adam that day, in time for them to return to Lost Lake and catch the stage in the morning. Adam, once in possession of all Merryvale had heard and seen and thought in connection with Ruth's disappearance, would act with the eagle-like swiftness for which he was famed. Merryvale did not know just what direction this action would take, beyond getting to Yuma with all possible speed, but he began to feel the old revelry in peril and mystery that the desert had bred in him.

Hindfoot arrived with the mule, a dilapidated antediluvian beast that Merryvale eyed askance. He despatched the Indian to fill his canteen at the post watering-trough, while he lengthened the stirrups. Soon, then, he was mounted and riding in a detour through the trees, to avoid being seen.

A mile above the post, Merryvale struck the wash, along the margin of which Adam's tracks showed plainly in the sand. Merryvale kept to them, yet he had eye for the sweep of the slope, the broken horizon line, and sometimes he seemed pulled around to gaze at the awful desolation behind.

Lost Lake, shrunken to a spot of green, then dropped under the ridge, out of sight. The desert changed as if by magic and seemed to come into its own. That spot of verdure was inimical to the purpose of the weathering rock, the shifting sand.

Heat and glare and silence, the great openness without life, the silver sand, the red outcropping ledges, the copper sky—these closed in upon Merryvale, gradually to color his thought, and to alienate him from all that was in contrast to them.

Five miles or more up the slow heave of desert there was a break in the monotony. It was the mouth of a canyon. Merryvale entered and rode along a winding ditch of sand, where water ran in times of flood. He had come into the region of rock. The walls grew higher until they towered above, stained and seamed.

He rode at almost a level. The canyon cut its way back into a rising bulge of plateau. A few scant weeds, an occasional *ocatilla* and a rarer stunted specimen of the *bisnagi,* barrel cactus, a clump of blue smoke trees, emphasized the lifelessness of the scene.

As he progressed, the canyon grew wider, darker; weird, and full of a silence that did not seem of earth. Yet there was life to give the lie to the morbid imagination of the traveler. He saw a green lizard, beautiful as a strip of gems, scurry across the sand, leaving a tiny trail. A rat, the color of the sand, scurried among the rocks. Across the streak of sky above, swept an eagle, with bowed wings, swift and grand in its flight. These ceatures knew how to defeat the desert, at least for a brief span of days.

The canyon forked in an amphitheatre of ruined cliffs, of vast sections of wall, and slopes of weathered sandstone. Merryvale found Adam's trail, well defined now, leading up the left fork. This was a dismal crack between two overhanging precipices. It might have been a gateway to an inferno.

Farther on there was a widening of the canyon, lighter, with less frightfully leaning rims and balancing crags and split shafts. Riding around a corner Merry-

vale came suddenly upon one of those amazing surprises to which the desert wilfully treated its faithful
adherents upon rare occasions. The great walls formed
an oval bowl, gold in hue, with magnificent blank
faces, sheering down to a beautiful floor of lucent sand
and amber rock fringed by green growths. The glittering sun struck white light from a pool of water, set in
solid rock.

As Merryvale rode into this paradise, guiding the
mule towards the shady side, Adam suddenly stepped
from behind a huge rock, gun in hand.

"Hello, Merryvale. I heard you a long way off," he
said, advancing.

"Wal, you skeered me. Reckon I'm nervous, an' I
shore come through an arm of Hades to get heah,"
returned Merryvale, and reaching the shade he dis-
mounted. "Howdy, pard."

"I'm well, Merryvale, but seldom have I felt the
loneliness and terror of the desert as I have here.
There's nothing to do but wait for the hours to pass."

"Reckon it shore must be hell," replied Merryvale.
"But it was your fault you had to wait *so long*. I told
you it'd be better to see Ruth often. Every night anyhow. If you'd only come last night—"

Merryvale broke off huskily, as if he were guilty,
and afraid to meet the lightning of those gray eyes
that pierced him.

"You've bad news. I knew that when I first saw
you."

"Pard, it couldn't be no worse. Ruth is gone again!"

In one stride Adam reached Merryvale, to lay those
talon-like hands upon him.

"Yes, Adam. *Gone!* Gone again with Stone or—"

"NO!" Adam's voice, high, ringing like a sonorous
bell, clapped in echo from wall to wall.

There was a streak of cruelty in Merryvale, a twist
of his nature, that came out now in his sorrow for
Adam, his anger at Ruth, and in his conception of the
fateful situation.

"Wal, if she didn't go with Stone it's a damn sight

wuss," he declared, throwing off his hat and flipping the sweat from his forehead.

"Merryvale, you're old and crabbed sometimes—when you're worn out or discouraged. But, friend, I can't be patient with you now."

"Adam, I ain't wore out, but I'm shore blue."

"Talk! Facts I want! Not what you think," commanded Adam, shaking Merryvale as if he were a limp sack.

Whereupon Merryvale poured out the story of Ruth's disappearance confining himself sternly to what he had heard and seen and done.

"She never accompanied Stone—willingly," replied Adam, with such tremendous weight that Merryvale felt his slow sluggish blood quicken.

"It does seem impossible—now I see you, Adam," he said. "I hope to Gawd I wasn't traitor to Ruth."

"You were, unfortunately. But you named my brother only in connection with his attack on Dabb—the lost money—and Stone?"

"Wal, you yelled for facts only," replied Merryvale, conscious of an obstacle that had strangely arisen to his opportunity to set the destroying angels loose upon Guerd Larey. Ruth's face—her look—her whisper! Merryvale could not voice what his sagacity had evolved.

"I'd rather it would be Ruth's dishonor than Guerd's crime," Adam wrung out.

Merryvale sprang up as if lashed by a whip. "Gawd Almighty! What're you sayin', Adam?—That girl, still good, fightin' the devil that was born in her an' the beasts of men who want her body! I'd die for her an' sell my soul to save her honor. . . . Adam, you are mad."

"No, not yet," said Adam, lifting a face like ice. "I would love her the same—even more. I could save her. . . . But if Guerd laid his lustful hand on her—so help me God . . . *I'd tear out his heart!*"

The great horny desert-talon hands gripped the air with appalling intensity.

"An' that'd be good!" choked Merryvale, overcome by passion. He walked away and paced under the wall until he had gained a semblance to composure.

"Merryvale, time is flying," spoke up Adam, gravely, as he approached.

"Wal, I was thinkin' of that," responded Merryvale.

"How soon can we get to Yuma?"

"Down stage due today," replied Merryvale. "It leaves in the mawnin'."

"You go on that stage," said Adam, swiftly. "I'll pack my burros and leave here before dark. By sunup tomorrow I'll be out by Bitter Seeps. I'll wait there. If my brother Guerd is on that stage you throw a paper or a bottle or anything out upon the road. If he's not I'll stop the stage and go with you."

"So far, so good. Suppose Guerd's on the stage?" queried Merryvale.

"Would he recognize me?" asked Adam, a spasm of agony crossing his face. "Do you remember the boy who came to Picacho—eighteen years ago? . . . It seems a life time. Have I not changed terribly? Who would know in Wansfell the boy Adam Larey? . . . Merryvale, would he know me?"

"Never in the world!" ejaculated Merryvale, shrilly. "You could face him for an hour an' he'd not see anythin' familiar in you. Adam, pard, you forget the transformin' power of the desert."

"But I could not trust myself," went on Adam, his tragic supplicating gaze on Merryvale. "I will never confront Guerd—or let him confront me—unless it is to be the end!"

Mournful words! Merryvale suffered anew in the trial of his friend. Adam shook his frame like a rousing lion.

"Enough. If Guerd's on the stage, I will walk to Yuma," he decided. "Hide my packs and leave the burros at Bitter Seeps. Travel by night. Get to Yuma only twelve hours behind you. Meet you at Augustine's. You know his place. I befriended him. He owes me much. Augustine can find Ruth for us—no matter where they hide her."

"Wal, pard, I'm on my way pronto," replied Merryvale.

Neither heat nor rough travel, nor sinister desert had place in Merryvale's consciousness. He was lifted above himself, inspired by something, the greatness of which he began to divine but which ever held aloof from perfect understanding. The miles and hours were as if they were not.

It was after dark when he rode into Lost Lake, unaware of fatigue or hunger. After returning the mule, Merryvale hurried up to see Hunt, whom he found at supper, and who bade him sit and eat. Then Hunt plied him with queries.

"Wal, Ruth will probably be sittin' heah at your table again in less than a week," replied Merryvale, answering all questions at once.

"If I could be sure of that, I'd be relieved of a burden," returned Hunt, grateful, yet full of doubt.

"You can be shore, providin' Ruth is alive. No one can tell what's in store on this desert."

"Larey came up to see me," announced Hunt.

"You don't say? Surprises me. What did he want?" exclaimed Merryvale, powerfully interested.

"I was astonished myself," went on Hunt. "He seemed to have forgotten the scurvy way he'd treated me. He asked many questions about Ruth. He was curious, bitter, but evidently had gotten over his fury."

"Humph! How'd you know Larey was furious?" asked Merryvale, bluntly.

"I met Mrs. Dorn. You know what a gossip she is. Well, she had been to the post. According to her story Larey nearly tore the place down. He was like a madman. Indoors and outdoors he raved and cursed. The Indians ran away. The Mexicans were afraid of him, too."

"Ahuh, I savvy. Shoutin' it out to the skies, hey? His wife run off again with Stone?"

"Yes. Mrs. Dorn said as much. But here with me he

was composed. He said Stone wasn't much to blame. A beautiful woman played hell with a man. Last he told me he'd go north on the stage to meet Collishaw at Salton Springs—that he would require Collishaw in Yuma, where he must hurry to catch Stone and Ruth. He would fetch Ruth back, and this time make her live with him."

"Wal, I'm a son-of-a-gun!" burst out Merryvale.

"It's clear enough to me," went on Hunt. "And if Ruth would only care enough for Larey to go back to him, and make a decent man of him, it'd remove our burdens."

"It shore would, Mr. Hunt," returned Merryvale, with sarcasm.

"The up stage arrived early this afternoon and left very soon afterward," said Hunt. "I suppose Larey in his hurry was responsible for this unusual proceeding."

"The down stage in yet?" asked Merryvale, ponderingly, forgetting the cup of coffee he held.

"I haven't heard it. But it's overdue."

"Wal, I'll go see," said Merryvale, rising. "Don't worry too much, Mr. Hunt. It mightn't turn out so bad. Goodnight."

Merryvale strode out into the darkness, down the winding path, out toward the dim yellow lights of the post, reiterating one muttered exclamation. "What next? What next?"

Larey's move, at first flush, perplexed Merryvale. If Collishaw had already gone on to Yuma, Larey certainly was aware of it; and if so why did Larey go north to meet him? If Stone had been party to some underhand game of abducting Ruth, why would Larey trust him for longer than seemed necessary? Could it be possible that Larey was not in the secret? Merryvale did not credit this supposition. He would have staked anything on his belief thet he saw Larey under his mask. It must be that Larey in his extremity, or under powerful suggestion from Collishaw, had resorted to more finesse, more cunning.

In front of the saloon, where the yellow light flared, Merryvale encountered Dabb.

"Hello. Where you been?" greeted the latter, curiously, and yet with welcome.

"Off in the hills to see my pard," replied Merryvale. "Where'd you get the double chin?"

"Don't be funny," growled Dabb. "You saw that— hit me."

"Wal, I shore did. An' I've been wonderin' ever since why you didn't respond like a Westerner."

"Because I'm a damned coward. But I couldn't fight Larey with my fists or meet him with a gun. All the same I'll—"

"Where is he?" interrupted Merryvale.

"Gone north. Took the stage off ahead of time today. An' that cooks our little deal up the Valley."

"Mebbe not. You're in too big a hurry, Dabb. I'd like to bet Larey never thinks of water rights on this trip."

"I had that hunch, too," said Dabb.

"Wal, we'll talk again," replied Merryvale, and went into the saloon. It was noisy, full of smoke and smell of rum. As Merryvale had expected he found the stage driver with whom he had previously scraped acquaintance.

"Come an' have a drink," invited Merryvale.

"Don't care if I do," responded the driver with alacrity.

"How aboot a seat to Yuma in the mawnin'?" asked Merryvale, over his glass.

"Plenty room, old timer. Only three aboard this trip down."

"Good. An' bein' a desert man who loves the open I'd like to set with you up on top. How aboot it?"

"You're welcome. You'll have fifteen hours of open, all right, 'specially if it's blowin'. I'm startin' early— at six."

"All the same to me. Have a good trip down?"

"Fair, only hotter'n hell over that below-sea-level stretch."

"Is Collishaw one of your passengers?" asked Merryvale, with apparently casual interest.

"No. I asked about him at Twenty Nine. But he hadn't been there."

"Wal, reckon I'd better turn in. See you in the mawnin'."

"What's your name, old timer? Mine is Hank Day."

"Mine's Merryvale, when I'm home," answered Merryvale with a grin.

Merryvale, once he lay down on his bed, realized the mental and physical strain exacted from him that day. His brain throbbed and his body ached. He was on the eve of great events. The desert voice whispered that to him. Broodingly the silence lay upon that desert world, thick as the starless night; and it weighed down to oblivion.

Merryvale was stirring at dawn, packing the few belongings he chose to take on the journey. His money was about gone, but that did not worry him, for he could get some from Adam. There was gold in Adam's belt—gold coins he had heard clink less and less as the years had passed.

Merryvale went out to breakfast and did not forget to get some food packed and his canteen filled. The stagecoach, with its six fresh horses champing their bits, stood in front of the post. Hank Day had a cheerful word for Merryvale. "Up with you," he directed. "Say, you're spry for an old timer. We'll be leavin' pronto."

There was another passenger besides himself already aboard, but Merryvale could not get a good look at him. Presently two more emerged from the inn with their baggage, and entered the stage. After a glance at them, Merryvale felt assured they would not have any interest in him or Adam.

Day climbed to the driver's seat beside Merryvale, and untied the reins. He was loquacious and merry.

"Say, old timer, if I get shot off by bandits can you drive the six in?"

"Wal, I could make a stab at it."

"Soon as the mail comes out we're off. Dabb's slow this mornin'. He's carryin' extra weight on his jaw. Haw! Haw!"

Presently Dabb arrived with a mail bag and parcel, which he deposited inside the stage.

"Where you goin'?" he asked, with speculative glint of eyes on Merryvale.

"Yuma. I shore got to see my banker an' buy a new outfit," drawled Merryvale.

"I'll bet your bank's in your pocket an' that's got a hole in it," declared Dabb, half in jest, half in earnest.

Hank Day cracked his whip and called cheerily to his horses: "Out of hyar—on the way—while it's cool —an' we can see!"

Merryvale's ride to Yuma had begun. He leaned back, as if in unconscious relief that he had not been halted. Wansfell would be out there on the desert, waiting, as surely as the red sun burned the sea of sand into waves of rose. If only no harm had befallen Ruth! Merryvale tingled to the adventure now at hand, but he checked his fears, his insistent and profitless conjectures, his unformed plans. They all could be left in abeyance.

"Goin' to Yuma, eh?" inquired the driver, genially. "When was you there last?"

"Reckon aboot the first of April," replied Merryvale, reflectively.

"Yuma's a boomin' town now. She always was a hummer, but she's aroarin' these days."

"Wal, you don't say? Yuma always was the liveliest place I ever struck. What's the difference now?"

"All she used to be an' a dinged sight more," replied Day, emphatically. "Course the railroad buildin' has fetched the darndest lot of greasers, niggers, redskins, chinks, gamblers an' robbers an' bad wimmin you ever seen in your life. But there's a lot of honest bizness goin' on an' comin'."

"Ahuh! Plenty of money in sight an' a wide open town?"

"You bet. What law there is amounts to nothin'.

Leastways it's Arizona law, an' don't go far on the California side. Some time ago Jim Henshall, the only sheriff who was any good, got killed in a fight. An' nobody's took his place. I heard nobody was keen to take it except Collishaw, an' he's not very well liked by the solid citizens."

"Collishaw? He was an old time Texas sheriff, a hanger. What's agin him in Yuma?"

"For one thing, Collishaw has an interest in the hardest place there," answered the driver. "Old three story Spanish buildin' called Del Toro. Saloon, gamblin'-hell, lodgin'-house, an' that's not all. It's owned by a Mexican named Sanchez, an' Collishaw is in with him. Sanchez is pretty well heeled, an' he's been able to smooth over some of the hard deals credited to the Del Toro."

"I recollect bein' in the Del Toro," said Merryvale. "An' shore it didn't strike me no wuss than some of the other places."

"Wait till you see Yuma now, old timer," vociferated Day, cracking his whip. "She's speeded up, an' it's a safe bet she'll go faster before she slows down."

"Wal, come to think aboot it, I've no love for a wide-open town any more. . . . Will you have a smoke?"

"Don't care if I do," replied Day.

The stage rolled on down the winding desert road. It was a hard gravel road, slightly down hill, over which the horses traveled at a brisk trot, covering distance rapidly. Merryvale enjoyed the rhythmic beat of hoofs, the clinking of the chains and creaking of harness, and the rattle of the wheels; and especially the sweet dry fragrance of the desert air, still cool at that early hour.

Clumps of bright green greasewood grew at regular distances apart, as if they had been planted by a gardener. Mounds of silver sand, glistening almost white, heaved up here and there, held from blowing away by thick massed roots of the mesquites. And beautifully red and gold against the light lacy green of these mesquites were the knots and balls of the parasitic mistletoe, which by some strange chance lived off the harsh desert trees. In the gray sandy washes the smoke trees appeared like soft blue clouds rising from a campfire. At long intervals of distance a *palo verde*, exquisitely delicate and green, dotted with its yellow blossoms, stood out against the pale desert background.

A jack rabbit, rangy and wild, with his enormous ears grotesquely erect, bounced away to disappear among the mounds. A little speckled hawk poised, fluttering its wings over one certain spot where no doubt some luckless desert rodent was hiding. Then the rarest of desert birds, a chapparel cock, ran with remarkable swiftness across the road, his long slender tail spread, his mottled gray back shining, his tufted crest erect showing the red, like flame. His cruel beak held a lizard.

Always there seemed to be beautiful life on the desert—creatures that were fleet and sure and destructive.

Merryvale did not know how far down the road Bitter Seeps lay, and he did not care to excite the stage-driver's curiosity by asking. So he contented himself with watching. He could not see the vast range and sweep of the desert from this winding course of low country.

In the distance the green heightened and thickened. Then a palm tree lifted its graceful head. A patch of darker green gave relief to the eye. The road wound along a deepening wash, where desert growths multiplied and flourished. Merryvale sighted two gray burros grazing out toward the hill. They might be Adam's, but were too far away to recognize. Next an Indian shelter of poles and palms greeted Merryvale's seeking eyes and beyond that a small adobe house, squatting under *palo verdes*.

From behind this house a tall man stepped, to gaze toward the stage. Merryvale's heart gave a great leap. Wansfell!

"Driver, what place is this?" inquired Merryvale.

"Bitter Seeps. There's enough water to keep a few Indians alive."

"Reckon you're goin' to pick up a passenger," remarked Merryvale. "Looks familiar to me. Yep, he's a prospector."

"Tall hombre, ain't he?. . . . Whoa, Bill! Whoa thar Iron-Jaw!"

Day brought the six horses gradually to a stop opposite the adobe house, in front of which Wansfell stood waiting, with a small bundle tied in a red scarf.

"Howdy. Want a lift?" called Day, leaning over.

"Yes. To Yuma," replied Wansfell.

"Twenty dollars from here," he said, and then caught the bright gold coin Wansfell flipped up to him. "Climb in."

"Wal, hello there, prospector," greeted Merryvale. "Thought I'd seen you somewheres before."

"Howdy, Merryvale. I saw you first," replied Wansfell, as he stepped to enter the stage.

"I'll bet you did—me settin' up heah like a buzzard on a daid cottonwood."

The stage door closed upon Wansfell, the horses took to their eager trot; and Merryvale leaned back in his seat, conscious of a grim and exalted emotion. Now! Wansfell had joined him. What a terrible reckoning for some man or men was rolling toward them in this stagecoach.

That was the break in Merryvale's strained mentality. The next hour he talked Hank Day to the limit of that individual's knowledge of Yuma. Meanwhile the miles slipped by under the rolling stage. It progressed through the last of Lost Lake basin and began to climb. The horses slowed and sweat, the driver dozed on his seat, the sun burned so that Merryvale hid his hands.

Out on top at last—and Merryvale seemed to feel something magnificent flung in his face. The silver sea of sand, the vast rising, heaving billows barred the way to the south. Ruth Virey's stairs of sand.

Merryvale caught the symbol; and all his old deep mystic fear of the desert mocked at his hope for Ruth. Who could surmount that sliding stairway? Up and up, toiling, dragging, panting, fighting, only to find it false!

There was no wind to blind the eyes. The barrier was a mountain range of shifting sand dunes, curved, scalloped, rounded, rippled, in a million beautiful shapes, silver and gold and gray. It stretched across the desert ninety miles, a strange phenomenon of nature, unsurmounted except for one wide pass, through which the road ascended and wound.

Here the horses toiled, the hours lagged, the miles magnified. Merryvale succumbed to the heat, the weary climb, the glaring sky, the encompassing slopes of sand, and he dozed until the stage at last emerged from the silver inferno upon the level hard desert.

Merryvale awoke to have his drowsy senses electrified. There gleamed Black Pilot Knob, the prospectors' landmark, and on the left the crinkled Chocolate Mountains, and above the desert floor to the fore, the grand purple mass of Picacho.

Again the scene changed. The sand lay behind, and all forward and on each side spread the desert, flat and hard, with *ocatilla* and *mesquite* and ironwood green against the drab, and the red Chocolates looming closer, and dim in the distance hazy ghost shapes of mountain peaks, ragged and wild and unattainable.

The sun set over a scene that, for Merryvale, could not be equalled in all the West. From the stagecoach, at the last height of the long plateau, he gazed down into the Colorado Basin. There wound the red river of the desert, fringed by vast borders of bright green cottonwood and arrowweed; and above the bends of the stream, and heaving on all sides, rose the banks and benches, the mesas and mountains, the corrugated mosaic of this wasteland gulf, at once beautiful in its wonderful coloring and ghastly in its jagged and barren wildness. A yellow pall of dust rose from the point where Yuma lay.

The coach rolled down gravelly hills, down and down for miles, until the far-flung scene of beauty was lost in the intimacy of the lowland, and dust that rose like smoke from a prairie fire. The sun shone magenta through the pall. Twilight and dusk! The coach rolled on, round bends, and always between walls of dusty arrowweed. And at last night fell, so black that Merryvale's tired eyes could not see a rod ahead. The weary horses plodded on.

The last turn of the road Merryvale saw the lights of Yuma.

9

Merryvale had to lengthen his stride to keep up with Adam down the wide dark main street of Yuma.

Lights were many, but their yellow flare did not extend beyond the pavement. Dark figures showed back under the arches; tall Indians with great coils of hair on the tops of their heads moved like shadows. Mexicans, small of stature, with their huge sombreros and colored scarves lounged before the shops, jabbering like so many monkeys. Miners and other white men in rough garb were sprinkled here and there in the throng.

"Ain't this heah the Del Toro?" asked Merryvale, as they came to a three story structure of Spanish design, on the corner of an intersecting street.

Adam nodded and pointed to the figure painted on the wall between the arches. Bulls and *matadors* and mounted *bandilleros,* executed in colors on the white background, symbolized the name of this notorious resort.

A wide dark hallway opened to the right, and led upward, suggestive of the secretiveness of the Mexicans. The doors of the saloon were painted in fantastic designs, permitting light from inside to show them in silhouette. Adam and Merryvale halted on the corner. The place was humming inside. The doors swung continuously with the passage of a motley file of men. Adam drew Merryvale across the street to an opposite corner. From this vantage point they studied the Del Toro. The second story had a line of arched openings down the side street, and these gave upon a veranda that evidently extended the same length. On this hot night no lights shone. Here and there the red glow of a cigarette emphasized the gloom. Low voices and laughter, the wail of a guitar, the melody of a Spanish song, the light sound of footsteps, and then the trill of a woman's laughter—these lent some of the romance and atmosphere of the past to the mystery of Sanchez's Del Toro.

The third story was low, with dark eye-like windows, not one of which showed a light. Adam gazed up at them as a man who would pierce their gloom and learn what was inside.

Presently, in silence, he led Merryvale down the street, towards the less pretentious section, where the lights grew fewer. At length he entered a narrow areaway that led into a *patio,* dark, smelling of smoke and *mescal,* where figures moved like shadows.

"This is Augustine's place," explained Adam, as they mounted some stone steps to a stone porch, and from there entered what appeared to be a kind of marketplace. A robust, black-browed Mexican stared with sloe eyes at Adam, got up and threw away his cigarette. His swarthy face suddenly beamed, and he leaped at Adam.

"Santa Maria! It is my *grande senor,*" he said, embracing Adam. Merryvale did not need to be told that somewhere and sometime this Mexican had run across Wansfell, the Wanderer.

"Si, Augustine," returned Adam, pushing the man back to wring his hand. "My pard Merryvale. We're starved, thirsty—and in trouble."

Augustine's gladness and gaiety changed into serious solicitude. "Come in," he said, abruptly, and led into a large bare stone room. It had few articles of furniture—a table and two benches, a lighted lamp smelling of oil, and a long hammock that curved from a ring in one wall to a ring in the opposite wall. He clapped his hands and when a fat dark woman, and two slender little girls came running in, he talked swiftly in Mexican. Then, as they departed to fulfill his orders he turned to the white men.

"Senor Adam, my house, my people, my friends are at your service."

Without wasting words Adam told him the particulars of Ruth's disappearance from Lost Lake, according to Merryvale's information and deductions.

"Senor Collishaw is in Yuma. I saw him today," said Augustine.

"Let me describe Stone to you," returned Adam, and gave minute particulars of Stone's appearance.

"No," said the Mexican, decidedly. "Senor, be seated. Eat and drink. I will go see."

"Collishaw had a Mexican driver with him. Can you locate that man?" went on Adam, as he disposed of his long legs under the table.

"Senor Adam, there could be nothing hid long from Augustine." he replied, his sloe-black eyes glittering.

"Find out from that driver if Collishaw had the girl, and if so where they took her."

"Senor, if Collishaw brought the senorita to Yuma for himself. she will not be at the Del Toro," said the Mexican, with a subtle smile. "But it is nothing for a white girl to be taken there. Sanchez brings women from Guaymas, from Frisco, Sacramento—from everywhere. Yuma is a town where women do not last long."

"Augustine, I served you once. The time has come when you can serve me," rejoined Adam, with deep feeling.

"Ah! Is the senorita daughter or sweetheart?" he asked, softly, with his hand going to Adam's shoulder.

"She is the woman I love, Augustine," returned Adam.

"Senor, if she is in Yuma we shall find her. I go now. You will lodge here with me?"

"Yes."

"Eat and drink. My women will serve you and show you rooms. Do not leave here. Augustine works slowly. But you may be sure."

He bowed with ceremonious assurance and left the room. Adam and Merryvale turned in silence to appease their hunger and thirst. One of Augustine's household, a daughter, probably, came in and stood near, a slender girl clad in a dark loose gown. She had a small oval face, olive in hue, red lips, and eyes large and dusky and beautiful. Her hair was a black mass. Merryvale looked at her again and again, and each time something more was added to a ghost of resemblance, until a clear image stood forth.

"Pard, look at that girl," whispered Merryvale, in Adam's ear.

"I did, old friend. Once was enough," replied Adam, sadly.

"The ghost of Margarita Arallanes!" exclaimed Merryvale.

"Yes. She is like Margarita—without the devil in her eyes."

"Wal! Queer things do happen," muttered Merryvale.

They finished the meal and drew the benches away from the table.

"Adam, I reckon waitin' around will go hard on us," said Merryvale.

"Patience. We are lucky to find Augustine here. Sometimes he is at his rancho across the border. He knows every Mexican in this country. As he said, he can find anything. If Ruth was brought to Yuma by Collishaw, we'll soon know."

"Why would Collishaw fetch Ruth heah?" whispered Merryvale, huskily.

"Have you forgotten what Augustine told us about Sanchez's place?"

"But Collishaw is a Texan," replied Merryvale. "It is born in him to respect women."

"Is he not hand and glove with my brother?" queried Adam, the gray storm of his gaze on Merryvale.

"Shore. But even so. . . . why I heard him snap up Larey for talkin' so low-down to Ruth."

"Friend Merryvale, my brother Guerd never deals

with men he can't control. Besides, Collishaw, for all his Texas breeding, is a desert blackguard. He was the worst kind of criminal on the border. A man, once backed by the law, who affects honesty, when under his mask he is desperate, base. Collishaw has had his day."

After that Adam lapsed into a silence Merryvale did not care to intrude upon. The minutes dragged along. The stealthy shadows of women passed the doors. Outside there were faint sounds—voices and steps, laughter and far-off music. A hot wind sometimes waved in, redolent of dry dust and over-ripe fruit and the sweet smell of flowers and a faint hint of smoke. The house hung oppressively over Adam. He longed for the open, for the stars, for the desert wind, that was pure, if it did burn and blast, and bring the ever-present melancholy tidings of the wasteland.

A long hour passed by, and time wore on toward a second. Adam stretched his long frame in the hammock, spreading it and lying diagonally across, so that his body rested on a level, after the custom of the Mexicans. But Merryvale grew restless. He sat and walked and sat again, only to rise and pace the stone floor, always listening for footsteps.

The clip-clop of horses' hoofs passed faintly on the outside; the distant bray of a burro rang into the growing silence; the murmur of unseen life lulled at intervals.

At length quick steps on the stones! Augustine entered, blowing cigarette smoke, his dark face heated, his eyes like black daggers.

"Ah, Senor. I have kept you waiting," he said, and drew a bench close to Adam, who lurched up.

Merryvale came near, warming to this friend in need, marveling at the loyalty of a Mexican. But he knew that if a Mexican's heart was touched he had not treachery.

"Senor Adam, Collishaw's driver is Manuel Gomez, distant kin of mine. We are long acquainted."

"That is well. But tell me, Augustine," replied Adam, leaning forward.

"Has Senor Adam's sweetheart a face like the Virgin—hair like the Lluvia d'oro of the Spaniards—eyes deep and purple like the canyon gates at sunset?"

Adam stared at his questioner, checked by that verbose eloquence. But Merryvale filled in the breach.

"Augustine, the woman he seeks has the face of an angel. Shore her hair is like the Spaniards' Shower of Gold, an' her eyes are the shadows of the desert."

"She is here," he replied, and flicked the ashes from his cigarette.

"At the Del Toro?" queried Adam, with deep agitation.

"Gomez does not know," returned Augustine. "Sit down, Senor . . . He told me this, knowing I would protect him."

Collishaw, according to Gomez, had left Lost Lake to travel north, but when night fell he had turned back and waited till late. Then he had gone on past the post to stop by the water-trough. Here Collishaw left the wagon and went off into the darkness. He came back with another man, and they were carrying a woman wrapped in a blanket. They got in the wagon, where Collishaw held the woman. Gomez drove rapidly out upon the desert, taking, as directed, the Yuma road. Then they removed the blanket from the woman, who appeared half smothered. They laid her down upon the hay in the bed of the wagon. At length she came to, and screamed and fought the two men like a she-panther. They handled her brutally until she fell back, spent and half naked. Both men then seemed affected at once and in the same degree by her allurement and helplessness. Each protected her from the other.

They drove all night. No one slept. At dawn they turned off into a canyon, well back from the road. Water and food, feed for the horses, had been provided for this occasion. The woman drank, but refused to eat. They tied her hands. All day she lay in the wagon, sometimes moaning, sometimes asleep. The men watched and slept by turns.

When night came they resumed their journey, and reached Yuma long after midnight, halting at the edge of the town. The younger man lifted the woman out of the wagon. Then Collishaw took her away from him. They cursed each other and disappeared in the darkness.

"Senor, that is all," concluded Augustine, dropping his burnt-out cigarette.

"Did your Gomez hear word of another man involved in this deal?" queried Adam, his mien dark and terrible.

"No, Senor."

"You think Collishaw took her to the Del Toro?"

"If he wanted her for himself—no. If for some one else—yes."

"How can we find out?"

"Senor, it is hardly possible tonight," returned the Mexican, spreading wide his hands.

"I could take a sledge and wreck the Del Toro in short order."

"Si, Senor. It would be one grand bull-fight. But if the senorita was not there?"

"Augustine, you are my friend," returned Adam, hoarsely.

"Wait. Tomorrow I can find out where the Senorita is hidden. Then we will make plans. It is well to go slow—be sure. Your Lluvia d'oro is in a sad plight. *Quien sabe?* . . . . Perhaps—but you must think of her life."

Adam acquiesced with a bend of head, and stood looking at the blank stone wall, with eyes that saw through it.

"My friend—Augustine will want to see the *grande senor* kill that one-eyed Gringo," said the Mexican, with the softness of a woman.

Merryvale jumped out of his rigidity shot through and through with a bursting hot sensation along his veins. But Adam, if he heard the Mexican's deliberate speech, gave no heed to it.

"Senors, come, you must sleep," said their host, rising.

They were conducted to a room with American couches, for which Merryvale was grateful, because he never could get straightened out in the Mexican hammocks. Not that he expected to sleep! The look of Adam caused him great concern. Merryvale removed his boots and outer garments, but Adam stood gazing out of a window.

"Pard, ohore the chances are that Ruth ain't been harmed yet," said Merryvale, with strong solicitude.

"Her body may not be," replied Adam, heavily.

"Wal, what else matters?" exclaimed Merryvale, irritated and impatient with his friend. "My Gawd, this heah is the southwest an' Yuma to boot. What could you expect? The men are few, I tell you, who think of anythin' in this heah desert but their flesh. An' I'll bet there's not one woman who thinks of anythin' else. So if Ruth ain't been hurt—or—or wuss—I'll swear we're lucky."

"Blow out the lamp, friend, and sleep. Not the least of my griefs comes from the suffering you endure for me."

Merryvale had no reply for that. With the room black, except where wan moonlight fell upon the motionless Adam at the window, he lay down to rest and compose himself. Yes—he was old. He felt it in the ache of his bones, in the dull pang of his heart. Not so very many more journeys could he take out into the wearing wasteland that he loved and feared. If he could only help Adam and Ruth to their freedom, to the fruition of their love, to know before he lay down for the last time that they were gone from the blasting sand realm, to a home among sweet-scented clover fields and green pastures and murmuring streams!

He found that sleep would not hold aloof. His eyelids seemed weighted. Despite his efforts to keep them open they would close and stick for moments, until by sheer will power he could lift them again. The time came when Adam no longer kept his vigil at the window. Had he lain down to rest? A shaft of moonlight shone in to fall upon Adam's bed. Merryvale saw the long dark form. That persuaded him to succumb to the all-pervading need for sleep. The last thing he heard was a low hum of Yuma's night life.

Merryvale was awakened by a call from the door of his room. "Come pard, the day's broken."

Augustine did not appear while they were at breakfast, but later he came in with new clothing and boots for Adam.

"Wal, I'm most as ragged as you," said Merryvale. "We'd shore make good scare-crows for a Texas cornfield."

Adam gave Merryvale some money. "We look worse than that, and old clothes can't hang on forever. Buy what you need. Get a gun—a forty-five like mine, and some shells. Also razors, towels, soap and things we need so much."

"Fine. But how aboot the risk of bein' seen?" returned Merryvale.

"No one but Collishaw or Stone would know you. See them first and dodge."

"Wal, I'll go pronto. Anythin' more, Adam?"

"Wait. I must not forget Ruth."

Merryvale remembered then the story of the driver, Gomez, and that Ruth's clothes had been torn.

"It's not likely these men would get clothes for Ruth," went on Adam. "When we leave Yuma she may be exposed to cold at night—the sun and wind by day. . . . Merryvale, buy a veil for Ruth and one of those long linen coats—the kind she had on that day."

"Adam, I reckon Ruth had on them light things she wears hot evenin's at Lost Lake. Thin little slippers an' stockin's. I'd better buy shoes an' stockin's."

"Yes, anything you think you can pick out—that would—"

"Wal," interrupted Merryvale. "It's been long since I bought clothes for a lady, but I can shore make a stab at it. When do you aim to leave Yuma?"

"Tomorrow morning. Augustine will arrange to have the stage stop here in front of his place."

"Huh. That depends on gettin' Ruth?"

"We are going to get her today," returned Adam.

"Si, Senor," verified Augustine.

Merryvale eyed the Mexican skeptically. There was such a thing as being worse than too swift, and that was too sure. Assuredly if Ruth could be located, Adam would rescue her, if he had to level the Del Toro.

Merryvale wound his way out of the patio and corridors through the arches to the street. The blinding white light of the sun struck him by surprise. It had been shady and cool inside those thick stone and adobe walls. The pavement and street were hot stifling with dust, colorful and noisy as the main thoroughfare of a country town on circus day.

He turned to the right, favoring the shade when there was any, and found himself indeed amazed at the activity and increase of life in Yuma.

A motley and picturesque stream of human beings thronged the pavement, passing up and down. Mexicans predominated, of all sizes and ages, with more female than male. Most of the men and boys wore big sombreros, white cotton shirts, trousers held by a sash or belt, where a knife or machete hung, and bare feet in sandals. Some Mexicans were adorned by the boots, huge spurs, chaps, and the braided vestments of the *vaquero*. The women were clad in loose flowing gowns, mantillas and scarves, mostly in bright colors. Interspersed among these towered occasional Yuma Indians, very tall in stature, none under six feet in height. They were striking to observe—so wonderful in physique, clad in slovenly white man's garments, with their large faces, almost black, wrinkled like dried leather, and with the coils of black hair on their heads and the flat lumps of damp mud on top of the coils. This queer headdress of the Yumas always amused Merryvale. But they knew how to keep their heads cool, if not clean. The Papago Indians, of whom he saw several, were smaller, clad more like savages of the desert, and remarkable for their inscrutable faces, handsome, impassive, with eyes that seemed not to meet those of a white man. Merryvale encountered one Yaqui, a short powerful man, in *vaquero* costume, broad and brown of face, with fierce eyes.

White men—miners, ranchers, cowboys, teamsters, moved in the throng, adding their attractive garb to the scene. Merryvale, with his wide slouch hat pulled well down over his face, to conceal it partly, peered out from the brim with the eyes of a hawk. He saw every person moving toward him.

He entered one large general merchandise store where clerks were few and purchasers many. Men bought tobacco, hardware, harness, guns, ammunition. Miners sorted out equipment; prospectors chose and rejected with a necessity for careful husbanding of money that Merryvale appreciated; hunters from the East were purchasing an outfit to use across the border in Mexico.

At last Merryvale got waited upon, and left with a gun belted under his coat, and shells, and a heavy parcel of clothing and boots, and other necessities Adam and he had so long lacked. He returned with them to Augustine's. Adam was nowhere to be found. Merryvale cut off his mustache, shaved his grizzled beard, and making a complete change of old for new attire, he surveyed himself with much satisfaction. He was willing to wager ten to one that Collishaw would not recognize him.

This accomplished, he went out again. If anything, there was an increase in bustle, in number of passers-by, brightness and variety of color, and most certainly of heat, dust and wind. He awaited his opportunity to cross the street.

This famous main thoroughfare of Yuma was ankle deep in dust. It rose in sheets and puffs and clouds from the hoofs of the horses and mules and oxen, to form a yellow haze that obscured even the buildings on the other side. Indians came riding by on ponies;

cowboys on spirited horses that pranced and reared, hating the dust; prospectors, leading laden burros; freighters with their six mule wagons; buckboards and buggies of the Mexicans from the ranchos down the valley; and then a stagecoach white with dust.

Merryvale risked his neck to get across. "By gum!" he ejaculated, spitting out the taste of dust. "That Hank Day was shore correct. Yuma is one hell of a hole!"

In another store Merryvale essayed to purchase the articles he considered necessary for Ruth. The veil and linen coat were easily chosen, but when it came to shoes, stockings, gloves and a dress of some kind, he had indeed assumed appalling responsibility. The shoes seemed the most difficult. Merryvale's recollection of Ruth's feet was that they were small and shapely. He finally made a choice, not without trepidation, and paying for his goods left the store.

Again he had to run the gauntlet across the dusthazed street. Upon entering Augustine's house, Merryvale was mightily concerned to find that Adam and the Mexican were still absent. Where had Adam gone? He was known in Yuma. Moreover the town was such a mecca for desert wanderers, prospectors and other travelers who might recognize Adam, that the risk was considerable. Adam certainly could not very well disguise himself. Still what did it matter, after all? For some wayfarer to meet Adam and remember him could hardly be calculated to hinder the work at hand. It would take an avalanche to stop Adam, once he started.

Merryvale waited for a while, then restless, and growing uncertain, he went out again. The hours had flown. Already it was mid-afternoon, and the street activity had markedly decreased. Still there were numerous individuals passing, and many loungers under the arcades and in the areaways. Merryvale sauntered along, keener than ever. There wedged into his mind a possibility of his rendering some service for Ruth. He had always been lucky. Why waste precious time when he might learn something himself?

To that end. he walked by the Del Toro, across the intersecting street, and down, to turn back again. Viewed by daylight Sanchez's place looked its reputation. It was a very old building, with painted and white-washed plaster covering the walls. There were many patches. At some points the plaster had fallen off to disclose bricks of adobe.

Merryvale proceeded down the side street, so as to get a view of the rear of the building. A wide alley separated this from a high vine-covered wall running along the back of the other half of the square. Down this side street there were but few pedestrians. Merryvale ventured to cross and enter the alley, where he discovered that Sanchez's house had two wings overlooking a courtyard. A stairway led up to a double-decked porch. What easy means of entrance and egress from the rear!

Merryvale continued along the alley to the end, and turning out was soon on the main street once more. When he again neared the main entrance of the Del Toro, to see the dark stairway leading to the upper floors he experienced a sensation that not only thrilled him but drew the prickling cold tightness to his skin. He halted to lean against the dirty whitewashed arched doorway. There were men going in and coming out of the saloon. No one entered the stairway. Why not risk going up? He could make some plausible excuse, if he were questioned. The idea took him by storm, in a most unaccountable manner.

With stealthy glance to and fro, Merryvale ascertained that no one appeared to be noticing him. Then he mounted the stairway. It was wide, high and old. The steps were cement or stone and worn into hollows. When he reached the first landing he faced a long corridor, blank painted wall on one side, with doors of rooms widely separated on the other. Behind Merryvale the corridor ended at a second stairway leading up. The hand of a giant might have been pulling Merryvale.

Walking naturally he ascended this flight of steps, which were of wood and very badly worn, and from the top looked down another corridor, identical with the one below, except that the ceiling was lower. It looked and smelled like many Mexican hallways Merryvale had seen.

What should he do now? He had gotten thus far without the slightest idea of any preconceived plan. He had followed an inexplicable impulse, which still beat at his blood vessels and tingled his nerves. Ruth might be, and probably was a prisoner behind one of these massive doors.

Merryvale did not stop to reason with himself, to consider risk of meeting Collishaw or Stone. He never thought of either. He had a cold tight knot within his breast, which, had he but been conscious of its meaning, boded ill to any man who might cross him now.

Stepping to the first door he knocked with bold, yet trembling hand. No answer. He went on to the next door, with like result. At the third rap he heard voices and steps inside, and waited with all his blood rushing back to a contracted heart.

The door opened, and a young Mexican, lean and yellow of face, with beady little eyes, encountered Merryvale's gaze.

"Excuse me, Senor," said Merryvale, bowing. "I seek one Senor Garcia."

The Mexican shook his head and closed the door.

This incident emboldened Merryvale. On down the corridor he proceeded, keen-eyed, alert, succumbing more to the spell of the thing that drew him, until he reached a point where arched doorways opened out upon the porch he had observed from the alley.

Merryvale heard voices of women, laughing. He located the room and knocked. The sounds within ceased and the door was not opened, nor was there any response from the other doors on that side.

Merryvale went out upon the porch. Then he perceived that there were two outside doors, far apart, on the section of the house between the two wings. Merryvale kept on round the porch, looking everywhere, until he came opposite to the first door. It was of solid heavy wood, with large brass knob and big keyhole.

He knocked. Again and nervously! A slight rustling step caught his keen ear. He knocked a third time.

"Who's there?" came the query in a voice that made Merryvale's tongue cleave to the roof of his mouth. Fearfully he gazed everywhere, forgetting to be natural.

With trembling hand he rapped: "Ruth! Ruth!" he called, as loud as he dared.

He caught a low cry, soft footsteps, a guarded knock from the inside.

"Who is it?" she whispered.

"It's Merryvale."

"Oh, thank God. . . . Is Adam with you?"

"He's heah in Yuma. We come to get you. Who fetched you heah?"

"Collishaw and Stone," Ruth replied, in tense whisper.

"What aboot Larey?"

"All his plot. But don't tell Adam."

"Are you—" Merryvale choked over the words, "safe an'—an'—"

"I'm all right—only badly bruised from fighting Collishaw. He was a beast. But for Stone he—"

"Never mind now. I must go after Adam. Keep up courage, lass. We'll come pronto."

"Bring something I can put around me. My clothes are torn to pieces."

Merryvale put all his strength into an effort to force open the door. It was beyond him.

"I can't break down this door. But Adam can. Keep up heart, Ruth."

"Hurry—oh! hurry!" she whispered back. "Any moment *he* may come."

Merryvale wheeled away, his heart pounding, and

under his breath he muttered: "I hope to Gawd *he* does come—jest as Adam gets heah!"

It was almost impossible for Merryvale to keep to a natural walk along the corridor, and down the first flight of stairs. Reaching the second and seeing them empty, he ran down, two steps at a time, and hurried into the street. Here he forced himself to walk without attracting undue attention. What endless distance these two blocks back to Augustine's!

Merryvale burst into the patio and raced on, to reach their quarters breathless and triumphant. Adam was not there. Augustine was not there.

"Gawd! This is tough," he muttered. "But I caint do anythin'. I've got to wait."

He paced the stone-floored room, crushing down his dismay, telling himself over and over again that the delay, while terrible for Ruth, was not necessarily serious. He saw the red sunset haze darken through the window. Interminable moments wore on. When Merryvale had almost become desperate he heard quick footfalls. Adam entered, followed by Augustine.

Merryvale approached them, aware that neither of the men recognized him. The room was not light. Adam bent down to see the better.

"Where'n hell *have* you been?" demanded Merryvale, hoarsely.

"If it isn't Merryvale!" ejaculated Adam. "Augustine can't find the man who'll know where Ruth is—if she's at Sanchez's."

"Never mind him. *I* know where she is," broke out Merryvale.

Adam's two great hands closed on Merryvale's shoulders.

"Pard! You know? How? Where?"

"Don't waste time makin' me explain now," returned Merryvale. "I've talked with Ruth. She's locked in. It's a strong heavy door. We'll need—"

"I could smash any door," interrupted Adam, hoarsely.

"Come, then," said Merryvale, snatching up the package that contained the linen coat and veil he had bought for Ruth. "Augustine, wait for us heah."

Adam asked no more questions, and stalked beside Merryvale, trying to keep down his stride.

"Adam, if we have the luck I had it'll be shore easy," Merryvale was whispering, as they hurried along. "We could go by the backstairs, but I reckon the front will be better, if we meet no one. Keep your eye peeled. We'll have to go out the backway. . . . It's the Del Toro, as shore you've guessed."

They stalked on up the street, and Merryvale was powerfully aware of the great arm, hard as iron, on to which he held. A few lights illuminated the shops. The volume of traffic in the street had not been resumed, but the sidewalk was crowded.

Adam's swinging stride, with which Merryvale kept pace with difficulty soon brought them to the Del Toro.

Sanchez's saloon was roaring. Merryvale edged out of the middle of the sidewalk, and reaching the stairway he drew Adam in. They went up to the corridor, turned to the second flight—ascended that. The upper hallway was almost dark, except at the far end, where the arched openings emitted light.

"Never met—a soul!" panted Merryvale. "Shore my luck held."

The porch, too, was deserted. Merryvale no longer looked fearfully in any direction. He saw only the door he wanted.

"Heah we—are—Adam," he said, drawing a deep breath.

He rapped. A moment of intense suspense followed. Adam's breathing was deep and labored.

"Ruth! Ruth!" called Merryvale, in low eager voice, knocking again. No answer! Then he hastily gazed along the porch to get his bearings a second time. "Shore this heah is the room."

Then Adam knocked and called in his deep voice: "Ruth, it's Adam!"

A dead silence greeted them.

"She had to wait too long," whispered Merryvale. "Reckon she's give out an' fainted. Her voice shore was weak."

"Get back," ordered Adam, and laying hold of the handle he pressed his shoulder against the door and shoved. It creaked and strained and shook. Adam drew back and lunged with tremendous force. The door cracked loud, broke from lock and hinges, and fell in with a crash.

Merryvale followed Adam into the room. It was empty. A small adjoining closet, dark and full of rubbish, showed no sign of Ruth.

"Aw!—she's gone!" ejaculated Merryvale, in blank disappointment.

Adam swooped down upon a little handkerchief. It was Ruth's. It was faintly sweet with the perfume Merryvale recognized.

"Wal, you see—she was heah!" he burst out, after examining the handkerchief. "She caint be gone long or far."

He saw Adam's swift glance take in the heavy Spanish bed, with its old yellow lace and faded curtains—the table, where sat a tray of food still untouched—the small high iron-barred window.

"Yes, she was here, pard," said Adam bitterly.

"She's been taken away from heah," returned Merryvale, getting back his wits, and rising under the crushing blow. "Last word Ruth said was for me to hurry—that—" Here Merryvale caught himself and bit his tongue. He had nearly betrayed Ruth's fear of Guerd Larey's coming. "She was awful afraid of Collishaw," went on Merryvale. "She was *all right* yet, she said, but bad bruised from fightin' Collishaw—"

Merryvale's hurried speech died in his throat. Adam had turned white to the lips. With giant strides he crossed the threshold, out upon the porch. Merryvale plunged after him, into the house again, and down the stairs. Two doors opened, and the startled faces of Mexicans peered out. A man was rushing up the lower flight of steps, but gave way before the impetus of Adam and Merryvale, making no attempt to stop them. Once on the street, Adam made directly for the swinging doors of the Del Toro Saloon.

10

In that day the Del Toro was the largest, if not the worst, drinking and gambling hall in the Southwest.

Merryvale entered close upon the heels of Wansfell.

An immense long wide room ran the length of the Del Toro. Many yellow lights, hanging high, shone on a smoke-hazed scene. Men stood four deep at the bar, and they had to shout to make themselves heard. Gilt-framed mirrors and crude paintings of nude women showed garishly above the endless shelves of glittering glasses and bottles. But few of the numerous tables were unoccupied by gamesters. Women were conspicuous for their absence. Music coming from somewhere, however, suggested that the feminine element was not altogether lacking at Sanchez's. The riotous drinkers and the quiet gamblers were in odd contrast. The stream of visitors appeared to begin and end in front of the long bar.

Adam stalked down the center of the hall and halted where he could see everyone to the greatest advantage.

It was indeed a mixed crowd. Merryvale, himself, searching with sharp eyes for the two men they wanted, scrutinized every one within range. Tall gamblers in black frock coats and high hats and flashy vests mingled in the throng, drinking little, watching with their intent hawk-eyes for victims to be plucked. Chinamen were not wanting from the changing mob at the bar. A lithe young man, stalwart in build, clad in beaded buckskin, with gun and knife in his belt, paraded by alone, his thin dark face, his glance like that of an Indian, arresting Merryvale's attention. Miners were many and the loudest of the drinking groups. And they, with the freighters and teamsters, in their rough garb and dusty boots were bent merely on a good-natured drink or two. When they imbibed these they passed noisily out to leave their places to others.

Mexicans predominated at the bar, while at the gaming tables most were white men. It appeared to be a Mexican rendezvous, patronized by all classes and types of desert Yuma. High above the bar stood out the stuffed head of an enormous bull, and across the horns lay a *matador's* sword, with his red flag draped upon it.

A prospector wandered in, perhaps more to see the sights, to have one evening of excitement, than to drink or gamble. Merryvale had met him somewhere, yet could not place him. Small of stature, with shrunken frame and face warped by exposure, and gray weathered-stained garments spotted by many patches, and boots held together by pieces of string, he was indeed an object to hold Merryvale's seeking gaze.

Arizona Charlie, a local character, whom Merryvale knew by sight, appeared with a group of friends, all bent upon conviviality. He stood head and shoulders above the crowd, a picturesque frontiersman in cowboy regalia, red of face, blinking of eye, with a mouth that was a thin hard line except when he laughed.

A group of riders, booted and spurred and belted, gun-packing, sombre-visaged men, entered to share Merryvale's scrutiny. How keenly Adam sized up these riders! And they had the same sharp attention for him. Merryvale placed them as bandits, and if not that, then surely hard-riding strangers who kept close together and avoided contacts. They took seats at an empty table.

"Horse thieves from the Gila Valley," explained

Adam to Merryvale. "They come here often after a raid. I knew—"

But Merryvale, who was gazing somewhere else, clutched Adam's arm.

"Heah comes Collishaw!" he said, with abated breath.

"Sanchez with him, but I don't know the other," returned Adam and his relaxed posture changed strangely.

"Shore it's not Stone, an' that's jest as well. You can make him talk, but you caint never Collishaw."

"I'll try," muttered Adam.

"Pard, he's a Texan," expostulated Merryvale. "Don't waste time on him. An' shore, Adam, I don't need to tell you, if he gets ugly, that you'll have to beat him to a gun."

Collishaw appeared to be listening impatiently to Sanchez, who talked fast and gesticulated vehemently, after the manner of Mexicans. He was a burly man short, with a head like a bull-dog, and a very dark skin. His attire showed the richness and color always affected by the prosperous of his nationality. Collishaw wore the long coat and wide black sombrero and flowing bow tie, which would have stamped him as a Texan. The man accompanying them was American, and certainly not prepossessing to Merryvale.

Adam advanced as they came on toward the center of the hall, but, at close range, they appeared to be too absorbed in themselves to notice outsiders.

". . . want in on Lost Lake deal," Sanchez's sharp low voice penetrated Merryvale's keen ears.

"That's not for me to say," replied the Texan.

These remarks certainly overheard by Adam no doubt accounted for the fact that he did not confront Collishaw. Instead he walked to the side and a little back of him. Merryvale followed. Sanchez opened a door leading into another room, and went in, with Collishaw at his heels. The third man reached for the door, to close it, when Adam, with a swing of his long arm, sent him staggering back. Adam entered the room, while Merryvale, quick witted and swift, followed, closing the door behind him.

It was a sumptuous private gambling parlor, with a game going on at the far table.

"The girl's gone. Stone stole her. I've just come down. Door busted in," Collishaw was saying, angrily, as he turned.

"Senor Collishaw has double-crossed me before," replied the Mexican.

The Texan suddenly espied Adam. He stared. His jaw dropped. His one eye, light and hard, expressed astonishment that, as Adam advanced, gathered a darkening suspicion.

"Wal, stranger," he began, blusteringly. "This heah room's private."

"Collishaw, I may not be so much of a stranger as you think," replied Adam, deliberately.

Sanchez promptly stepped aside, and Merryvale warily did the same. The door opened slightly, to show the curious face of the American who had been prevented from entering. He whistled low and disappeared, leaving the door ajar.

Collishaw's mien had shifted. From a man whose privacy had been intruded upon, he became the ex-sheriff Texan who had made innumerable enemies.

"I've met you somewhere—long ago," he remarked, coolly. "But I caint place you."

"You'll place me presently," returned Adam, somberly.

"Wal, I'm glad to heah it," drawled Collishaw in slow expectation that certainly belied the content of his words.

Sanchez, quick to sense the undercurrent there, put more distance between him and the Texan. In fact he backed against the table, disturbing the gamblers.

"Hey, Sanchez, you're mussin' my cairds," remonstrated one, whose back was turned.

"What's up?" quickly asked another, who faced the other way.

"Senor Collishaw meets an old friend," returned Sanchez, with significant sarcasm.

Adam took a long step, instantly bridging the distance between him and Collishaw. The amazing swiftness of it caused Collishaw to jerk up stiff. The ruddiness faded from his face. Merryvale leaned against the wall. He could see only Adam's profile, cold, gray, clear-cut, with the cast of the eagle striking at his prey.

"I want Ruth!" Adam shot the words too low for Sanchez and the gamesters to hear.

The cool nerve of the Texan betrayed another shock of surprise.

"Who are you?" he burst out, as if involuntarily.

"Where's the girl? *Quick!*" flashed Adam, lower and fiercer.

Collishaw laughed with grim humor at the idea of any man making him talk when he did not wish to; while at the same time his stern grasping mind was searching through the scenes of the past.

Suddenly he began to nod his bullet-like head, and his one eye gleamed sardonically.

"Wal, I've placed you, stranger," he said. "Reckon I've the doubtful honor of meetin' Wansfell, the Wanderer."

He had lowered his voice, evidently not caring to acquaint Sanchez with the identity of this man.

"Yes," replied Adam.

"Ought to have placed you quick—considerin' what I heah from Stone. Sorry, Mr. Wansfell, but I caint oblige you aboot the lady, an' help you to one of your desert tricks. But fact is—an' I'm admittin' it damn sore—the little hussy is aboot makin' up to Stone this very minute."

"You dirty Texan!" Adam's voice was cutting. "You who brag of being raised where women are respected! You low-down tool of Guerd Larey!"

Then Adam's big open hand flashed to hard contact with Collishaw's mouth. The blood flowed. He uttered a hoarse gasp, and jerked spasmodically, as if checking a violent move to draw his gun. Something withheld him; probably not the icy coolness of the man who had struck him; not that the indignity did not call for the retaliation of gunplay; but something in the name and presence of this man Wansfell.

"Collishaw, you were once a hanging sheriff," went on Adam, relentlessly. "I knew of one innocent man you hanged. You were a gambler and a thief. Now you are worse. You try to bully and rob an old man. You plot with that miserable partner of yours. You abduct an innocent woman for him. Then you betray him by wanting her yourself. . . . You manhandle her! You bruise her tender flesh! . . . *You dog!*"

"So it was you broke in her room!" rasped out Collishaw, and he lurched for his gun.

Swift as light Adam's hand pressed his gun into Collishaw's prominent paunch.

"Draw!" hissed Adam, pushing hard on his gun.

"You've got—the drop!" hoarsely stuttered Collishaw.

"Bah! You need two eyes to deal with a man," went on Adam, in studied contempt. "You hideous one-eyed brute! Why they'd laugh at you in Texas."

Collishaw's face turned a livid hue, his big head wagged so that it dislodged his hat, huge beads of sweat popped out on his brow.

"Who put out that eye for you?" continued Adam, leaning closer, in suppressed cold passion that was terrible.

"I've shot—men—for less'en—that," panted Collishaw, drawn inevitably beyond all reason.

"Yes, but what kind of men? Try it on *me!*" taunted Adam.

Then he waited, insupportably menacing to Collishaw.

Merryvale failed to draw breath. He felt all the eighteen years of agony and passion that Adam owed equally to his brother Guerd and this ex-sheriff, who had specialized in hanging men.

"Collishaw—remember Ehrenberg!" went on Adam.

The Texan's one eye lost its fixidity and dilated wildly.

"Picacho!"

Collishaw's frame seemed to expand with slow quivering pressure from within.

"Look at me! Look at Wansfell the Wanderer! Look close!"

That one eye, evil, with all of hell burning in its depths, glittered on the verge of appalling recognition.

"Look close at Wansfell! . . . At *me!*—I put out that eye for you! . . . *I am Adam Larey!*"

"*Hellsfire!*" screamed Collishaw.

His stiffness broke. With hate-driven speed he snatched out his weapon. As it gleamed blue in the light Adam's gun bellowed with muffled report at Collishaw's abdomen.

Merryvale heard the heavy bullet thud into the wall. It had passed through Collishaw. The terrific impact hurled him back. Yet it did not check his instinct to pull trigger. His gun spouted red and boomed —waved up wildly—to boom again. Shot through as he was—shocked, staggering and sinking there still lived the desperate desire to kill. And with superhuman will he was steadying the wavering gun when Adam shot out that burning eye.

Collishaw dropped the gun. His hand remained outstretched. For an instant he stood upright, dead on his feet, with visage of horror—then he swayed and fell, a sodden weight.

The gambling hall was stilled. All faces were turned to the door where Adam and Merryvale emerged. No man moved or spoke. Merryvale, helped by the hand dragging at him, kept the rapid pace across the hall, out the side entrance, into the darkness.

Then Adam, still holding to Merryvale, drew him into the throng in the main street, and soon passed beyond sight and sound of the Del Toro.

"Adam, shore you ain't forgettin' Stone?" queried Merryvale, moistening his dry tongue.

"No more than I forgot Collishaw," was the reply.

"Shore you ain't trustin' to chance?"

"No. Augustine has men on Stone's trail. But I believe if I walked blindly—something would lead me to him."

"Wal, reckon I understand that. It's a safe bet Stone made off with Ruth. Don't you agree?"

"We heard what Collishaw said to Sanchez."

Soon they gained Augustine's quarters, where Adam briefly explained to his Mexican friend the probability of Stone's having taken Ruth from the Del Toro. Whereupon Augustine, tense and excited, argued that Stone could not have ventured far in the daylight, that he must have left the Del Toro by the back stairways, and had hidden her somewhere in the adjoining block, which was wholly a Mexican quarter.

"Senor, come," urged Augustine, and rushed out, turning from the patio into a narrow passage that led into a side street. Here he strode quickly with Adam on one side and Merryvale on the other. All the time the effervescent Mexican kept up a running talk, into which now and then crept a word in his native tongue. His contention was that Stone had not dared to approach the main street with a captive girl, whom he very likely had to carry or drag. This seemed plausible to Merryvale. If a quick canvass of the quarter back of the Del Toro immediately did not produce the girl, Augustine assured them a thorough one, by daylight, most certainly would.

They reached the section the Mexican was bent upon searching. Most of the houses opened on the street, and natives were sitting in the doorways and out in front. Augustine questioned this one and that, proceeded swiftly from house to house, crossed the road and went down the other side. Adam and Merryvale kept pace with him, standing back when he questioned some one or knocked at a dark open door. It was another hot night. Soft laughter and low voices, a singer with a guitar, greeted the searchers at one house.

That block and the next were canvassed by the indefatigable Mexican without producing a clue. But he kept on into a narrower and less pretentious street, where only an occasional dim light shone. Augustine turned into an archway while Adam and Merryvale waited in the shadow.

Merryvale, giving way to gloom, leaned against a stone wall. He heard soft padding footfalls and imagined Augustine was returning. A dark form slipped into the dim flare of a light above the archway.

Adam leaped like a tiger. The man uttered a low sharp cry and tried to swerve aside. But Adam's long arm swept out and the heavy hand spun him round like a top. Next instant that hand clutched his shirt at the neck and swung him clear off his feet, hard against the wall.

Merryvale saw the light shine down upon Stone, bareheaded, without coat or vest. He was gasping. Merryvale, in a fury of amaze and glee, bounded closer. Stone's face was distorted, his tongue protruded. Then Adam released his grip, allowing Stone to drop down upon his feet. He choked and his hands beat wildly at his assailant.

"Keep still or I'll smash your head," ordered Adam.

"Don't hit me—Wansfell!" cried Stone, in terror, ceasing to struggle.

"Collishaw is dead," returned Adam.

"My God! . . . Don't kill me, Wansfell!—I have Ruth—back here—locked in. I stole her from Collishaw. . . . Let me go—an' I'll take you—to her."

Then Stone, in the iron grip of the stalking Wansfell, led them down the dark areaway. Augustine met them, to clamor to his saints, and run along beside them. In the dust a light with reddish tinge shone through an iron-shuttered window. Stone halted at a door, and fumbling in his pocket found a key which he tried to insert in the doorlock.

"Let go my arm—Wansfell," he panted. "You paralyze me. . . . My hands shake so."

The key dropped to ring musically upon the stone doorstep.

"Merryvale, pick it up. Open the door," ordered Adam.

A poignant exclamation from inside that door pierced Merryvale, as he bent to find the key.

11

Ruth seemed to feel herself waking from a dreadful nightmare. Her consciousness returned with heavily lifting eyelids and was attended by dull pain.

She saw faded curtains, bed posts, old plaster walls from which the pink tint had worn, a small barred window. All unfamiliar! This was not her room. Where was she? Still in a hideous dream?

But she was awake. The place had substance, reality, not the vague distorted outlines of a dream. Ruth raised herself, suddenly conscious of extreme weakness. She lay on the yellow lace coverlet of a high bed in a room she had never seen in her life.

Then successive waves of memory welled up, to overcome her with the flood of incidents that had rushed her to this sad pass.

Stone's confession that while under the influence of drink he had stolen money from Guerd Larey's office desk; his persistent and abject importunity to her to intercede with Larey in his behalf; her reluctant consent and foolish walk down the path; the sudden enveloping of her head and shoulders in a blanket, and the violence which stifled her scream and subdued her struggles; her sense of being thrown into a wagon and held there, of being carried by rapid rolling wheels off into the desert. Then the smothering blanket had been removed. She lay face up to the stars, with Collishaw on one side, Stone on the other. Like a tigress she fought to escape—fought until her strength was spent. Then she lay there panting, with rage giving way to fright. Collishaw could not or would not keep his hands off her. Her scathing scorn and then her impassioned appeal seemed only to incite him the more; but they affected Stone. He remonstrated with Collishaw and finally used physical intervention.

That dreadful night wore to gray dawn. The rolling of wheels ceased. She lay with hands bound by a scarf, in the wagon, which had been drawn under an ironwood tree. Hot and still the day came. She slept off and on through the heat, seemingly aware, even in her slumber, of these men, so fiercely at odds over her. Weary interminable hours of fear, of bewildered conjectures, of physical pangs! Then dusk and the lessening heat and the rolling wheels again. She remembered being lifted out of the wagon, carried on into the blackness—then oblivion. And here she had awakened in a strange room, weak and suffering, her white thin gown soiled, minus sleeves and otherwise torn, her arms showing dark bruises, her slippers gone.

Ruth took serious stock of these black and blue marks, and of sundry painful places, ascertaining with great relief that she had not been otherwise injured or harmed. With difficulty she arose. Then she noticed a table in the center of the room. Some one had entered with a platter of food and drink, which was not yet cold. She had to rise on tiptoe to see out of the small window. Yuma! The river, the church, and many tiled roofs and colored walls came within line of her vision. The sun was westering towards the purple ranges of Arizona.

Next she examined the room, the adjoining dark closet, and then tried the door. Locked! The door and walls were heavy and solid. From the barred window she could see only the roofs of buildings. She thought of screaming for help, and decided she would wait a while. Then she ate and drank, with difficulty, though the food was clean and appetizing.

No other conception than that Guerd Larey was the instigator of this plot occurred to Ruth, However Collishaw and Stone had been influenced by her actual presence, had nothing to do with the idea of the abduction. Suddenly Ruth's clearing mind flashed with the thought that as sure as the sun shone, Adam would come to her rescue. She had not the slightest doubt that he was already on the track of these men. What would he do to them? Wansfell! A shudder ran over her, despite the heat.

She must save herself until Adam found her. She must employ all a woman's craft and courage to that end before Guerd Larey appeared on the scene. If he got to her before Adam—too late! Then once again Adam must become a fugitive from such hanging sheriffs as Collishaw—go back to the desert, with the real and not imaginary blood of a brother red on his hands, once more to the lonely life of Wansfell, the Wanderer.

Ruth was terror-stricken at the very thought. In that moment she hated her beauty, her body, the poor frail vessel of flesh about which men became mad. No —not Adam! He loved her soul, her suffering, the thing she felt was her innermost self, the womanhood she had all but abased. Her kisses, her embraces that last night, her pleading to take her far away from the ghastly desert, had racked and torn him, but he had stood at the last like a rock. Not until she was free— and never could he free her! Even then the shame of her weakness and her failure burned within Ruth. What must he have thought of her? The same woman's wiles she had used upon Stone! Passionately she repudiated the consciousness.

Suddenly she sat bolt upright, all her thoughts suspended. Had she heard a step outside? Yes—another and another! A knock on the door brought her to consciousness of her captors. Hastily she covered her bare shoulders and arms with the bed coverlet. Then she heard her name called, low but surely. She ran to the door—knocked in reply—whispered. It was Merryvale. He spoke again, told her Adam was in town— they would come to get her. Ruth hardly knew what she was saying. Merryvale had tried the door and could not budge it.

"I caint break down this door. But Adam can," he whispered. "Keep up heart, Ruth."

"Hurry—Oh! Hurry!" she whispered back. "Any moment *he* may come."

Merryvale's light footsteps soon ceased. Ruth, with hands pressed over her pounding heart, leaned back against the door. Through the window she saw golden sunset—flushed clouds and blue sky. Adam was in Yuma. Would soon be there! What were doors or walls or chains to him? She prayed that there would be no hitch in Merryvale's plan—that they would rescue her before Larey got to Yuma. What vile intention had actuated Larey? To get her away from home—to break her spirit and drag her down—then back to Lost Lake, submissive and lost to all except the life of a squaw! What a madman he was not to realize that she would kill him and then herself!

Ruth began to pace the room in her stocking feet. Where had the fools lost her slippers? It enraged her to see the condition of her dress. Throwing aside the lace coverlet, which she had wrapped around her shoulders, she detached the faded curtain from the bed and tried that as a cloak. It would not attract undue attention. As for walking without shoes she would have been glad to tread upon hot sand and cactus. . . .

A key clicking in the lock interrupted her meditations. A rush of joyous excitement—and some emotion striking deeper—brought her erect, quivering. Merryvale and Adam had conceived to get the key. They were here.

The lock rasped, the handle turned, the door opened. Stone entered. He was pale, determined.

"Oh!" cried Ruth, with a shock of sickening disappointment.

"Say, you must have read my mind," he flashed, his glance running over the curtain which enveloped her. "Come. I'll get you out of here."

"No," replied Ruth, rallying.

"Don't be a fool. I can pack you an' I will. Come," he replied, angrily. He was nervous, cautious, and it was evident he did not have his ear near the crack of the door by accident.

"Where do you want to take me?" she demanded, suspiciously.

"Anywhere, but you must hurry. It'll cost me my life to be caught."

"Did you—have you seen anybody?"

"No. I'm in this deal alone. I'll save you from that one-eyed Texan."

"Save me from Collishaw! . . . Why?"

"Because I really love you, Ruth," he returned, with agitation.

"You'll save me for yourself?"

"Sure, if you must know. But I love you an' Collishaw doesn't. I saved you from him on the way here, didn't I?"

"Yes. And that goes a long way toward making up for your part in this. Don't spoil it now, Hal."

"Listen to sense," he replied, his throat contracting as he swallowed. His motive was powerful, but his fear seemed equally so. "I don't want to pack you out of here fightin' an' kickin' like you did last night. I'd excite curiosity. But I'll do it, if you won't come willingly."

"Hal, I'm afraid to trust you."

"But you'll be worse off if you raise hell an' spoil my game," he declared, impatiently. "Collishaw is dickerin' right now with Sanchez, and may be here any minute. He's goin' to double cross Larey an' *sell* you. . . . Oh, don't look that way! These men *do* these things. Besides if Collishaw an' Sanchez don't make away with you, Larey will be here tonight."

Ruth hesitated. If Adam did not come at once, before Collishaw, she would be in much greater danger than if she went with Stone, whom she felt sure she could manage for a while, at least, or else escape from him. Adam, not finding her at the Del Toro, would hunt for her, and the chances of tracking Stone were more favorable than of finding Collishaw. And, if Guerd Larey were the first to arrive—Ruth did not allow herself to finish the thought.

"I'll go with—you," she faltered.

Swiftly, then, Stone drew her out of the room and locked the door. It was almost dusk. The red afterglow of sunset lingered in the West. Stone took Ruth's arm with no light hand and almost lifting her along, he hurried down the porch stairways to the courtyard. From here he led her into the side street and away from Sanchez's place. They met several people, who apparently took no notice. Stone talked in forced casual tones. They went down a block and turned again, and proceeded to the poorer section of Yuma.

"You said Sanchez, didn't you?" asked Ruth. "Then that was the Del Toro?"

"You bet it was, an' no place for a white woman," he returned, suggestively.

"This path hurts my feet," complained Ruth. "I haven't any shoes. Don't go so fast."

Stone slowed down to oblige her, and slightly relaxed his grip on her arm. Ruth had suddenly been seized with an idea to break away from Stone and escape. She could certainly have done it the moment they emerged from the Del Toro. If she had fled into the main street she could have eluded him or surely have been protected by some passerby. Yuma was always full of miners, freighters, teamsters, cowboys, gamblers, any of whom would deal harshly with such as Stone. Why had she not thought of it? They were now in the less frequented part of the town, far from the main street. She would wait until they encountered someone. But they went on half a block farther without meeting a single person. Moreover twilight was settling down thick.

Ruth slipped out of Stone's grasp and ran. She was light of foot and fleet. Fear lent her wings. She ran so fast that the wind whipped the curtain from her shoulders. She kept on. Then she heard Stone gaining on her. His boots thudded faster and faster. She felt that her heart would burst, that her last breath was leaving her and she could not draw another. Her pace broke. She labored, and was staggering on when Stone caught her.

As he fiercely jerked her off her feet she tried to scream. But little breath was left to her. And Stone's hand stifled her feeble cry.

"You—wildcat!" he panted. "Try that—again—and see—what you get!"

Ruth could not resist. She was not even able to walk. Dizzy and weak she would have fallen but for his support. Then he carried her along the street, into a gloomy areaway, where coming to a door, he put her down. Unlocking the door he dragged her into a dark room, where she sank to the floor. There she partially lost consciousness, though she heard Stone moving around and saw the darkness lighten.

Then Stone lifted her into a chair. Ruth recovered presently to see that she had been brought into a large, high-ceilinged apartment, stone-walled and stone-floored. The furniture and the iron-shuttered window indicated that this was the abode of Mexicans. Stone wiped his wet face and breathed heavily while he glared at her. He betrayed no apparent consciousness of her pitiable state. His bold eyes gloated over her bare arms and shoulders, over her dishevelled hair that fell like a shower of gold about her.

"I heard Larey call you a wildcat an' swear he'd tame you yet," said Stone, almost with admiration. "I understand how he felt."

"Hal Stone, you have—no mind—no heart," returned Ruth, weakly. "You're just animal."

"Well, if you're a wildcat what would you expect me to be?"

"I was foolish to expect—you might have—had real pity. And I'm amazed at your lack of sense."

"I had sense enough to block Collishaw's deal, which you don't appreciate," he returned, sullenly.

"Your motive is selfish, not noble."

"I've yet to see *you* upliftin' anybody to noble deeds, Ruth Larey."

"What's the use of attempting the impossible," retorted Ruth. "But listen. You don't reason things out. You're not bright, Hal Stone. Suppose you have got me now? I'm certainly helpless and miserable enough to excite pity in even a dog. Now that you have me—what're you going to do with me?"

"You're a white elephant, all right," he acknowledged. "But I don't care."

"But answer me. I've got a right to know your intentions."

"I'm going to take you away from Yuma if we have to walk."

"Suppose you do elude Collishaw and Guerd, and —but that's silly of me. You cannot escape Adam Wansfell."

"Who? That wanderin' desert rat? Aw, damn him! I tell you I don't care," he retorted, with a sullen passion that showed he hated to be made to think.

"You love life as well as anybody."

"Ruth Larey, I don't love life or God—or anythin' but you. I'd throw them away—like that—just to possess you one minute."

"But Hal, think—*think* before it's too late!" she entreated. "You cannot possess me, as you call it. Of course, as I'm unable to lift a hand, you can sink lower than a desert savage and—'"

"Guerd Larey means to sink that low," Stone interrupted, with flaming jealousy. "I read his mind."

"Oh, there's no hope to reach you," cried Ruth despairingly.

"Not that way, Ruth. So you might as well make up your mind to let yourself go."

Ruth closed her eyes. How it beat into her weary brain—the littleness, bareness, intolerant mindless desire, the brutal instinct of man! How she prayed that God would pity her, and spare her the retribution her senseless, selfish woman's deceit and vanity deserved!

"Listen. One more word and it's the last, Hal Stone," she began again. "I misled you. I didn't realize the cost or didn't care. But I did mislead you. I beg your forgiveness. I beg you to remember your sister, your mother, and spare me. . . . If you do not—if you lay an evil hand on me—*I will find means sooner or later—to kill you myself!*"

"And I tell you—*I don't care,*" he replied, in his desperation. "I'd be willin' to go to hell an' burn for-ever!"

Ruth felt that she had spent her force in vain. What transformation a month had wrought in Stone! In her despair she wished she had remembered her decision to use all possible charm and blandishment and deceit to Stone's undoing. But anger had dominated her. Anger—and the bitter mocking memory of this seductive trait in her that had often been exercised wittingly! She could not stoop to it again even to save her life.

It dawned suddenly upon Ruth that Stone was no longer staring at her. His head was turned to one side, lowered a little, in the attitude of intense listening.

Ruth's tired heart quickened. She heard footsteps, then a knock upon a door, surely another door in this very house—then sharp quick Mexican voices.

Stone cursed under his breath, and leaping up he guardedly opened the door, which he had forgotten to lock. The voices came distinctly now, somehow different from natural conversation. They must have startled Stone for he glided out of the room, and turning whispered to Ruth: "If you yap it'll go bad with you!" Then he closed and locked the door noiselessly; and his swift soft footfalls died away.

Ruth huddled there, trying to struggle, against the rapture her intuition inspired. But she could not resist this thing that was stronger than her intelligence and reason. Deliverance was at hand. She divined it, she felt it. Adam and Merryvale were again on her trail. She could have cried out in her transport.

The voices ceased, other footsteps passed the door before which Ruth stood so wild with hope. Had she made some delirious mistake? Sudden cold despair beat her down. She tried to scream, but her tongue was dry, her lips stiff, her vocal cords paralyzed.

More footsteps—louder, coming back, the same Mexican voice, shrill, excited, answering deep tones that lifted Ruth's sunken heart! Men had halted outside the door. A key clinked upon the pavement.

"Merryvale, pick it up. Open the door."

The same dry tones! Ruth's voice released itself in a cry.

The lock shot back with a rasp. Violently the door swung in. Then the black doorway seemed filled by a gigantic form. Adam strode in, dragging Stone by one great hand clutched in his shirt. Other men followed, closed the door. Adam gave Stone a fling. He catapulted against the wall and slid down.

Adam knelt before Ruth, bent close to search her face. She could not speak just then, but she met the gray lightning flash of his eyes, and smiled with all the gladness that filled her breast to bursting. He did not speak, but the relaxing of an iron tension spoke more eloquently than words.

Ruth lifted a shaking hand, which he instantly enclosed in his. Merryvale came to her side. "Wal, now lass, brace up. We're heah."

The fourth man was a dark-browed Mexican who stood beaming down upon her, rubbing his hands. "Ah, Senorita, the Blessed Virgin be praised." My *grande senor* has found his lily! The house of Augustine is at your service."

Merryvale bethought him of a package he carried, and tearing it open he disclosed a long coat and veil.

"Ruth, I been packin' these heah all over Yuma," he said, trying to be gay. "Reckon you'd like the coat on anyhow. Sit up an' let me help you. . . . There."

"Thank you—oh, thank you," was all Ruth could say.

Adam's emotion seemed too deep for smile or word or movement. Yet his look was beautiful and soul-disturbing to Ruth. At last he released her hand and arose.

Then he gazed down upon her while he pointed to Stone.

"Why did he fetch you here?"

"He wanted to—to save me from Collishaw," faltered Ruth.

"Did you come here of your own accord or did he force you?" went on Adam.

"Both. He frightened me into coming. Then on the way I tried to escape from him. Oh, I ran! But I had no shoes and the rough stones bruised my feet. And he caught me."

"Stone," began Adam, in a deadly calm. As he turned away Ruth caught his sleeve, stopped him.

"Adam, let him be," she asked, not in any sense entreatingly. "At least he did save me from Collishaw's utter brutality last night, and no doubt today, also."

"I don't want your pity, Ruth Larey," declared Stone, flaring up.

Merryvale took a couple of steps in Stone's direction. "Did you heah what I told you aboot Collishaw?"

"Yes, I did, you old ferret-face. An' I don't give a whoop in hell. I played my game an' I lost."

Adam turned once more to Ruth. "It is evident to me that you want Stone let off."

"I do, Adam," she replied, quickly. "Partly because I feel to blame for his downfall, but mostly because I would not have *you* do him injury."

"Is he to blame for this plight of yours?" queried Adam, and his eloquent gesture not only intimated the disorder of her apparel, but her mental and physical state.

Ruth's rallying wits had been gathering fortitude for this very question. For herself she could no longer have lied to Adam. But she could stand being flayed alive before confessing truth that would wreck the storm of Wansfell's wrath upon his brother.

"Adam, I think I am to blame," she said, as unflinchingly she met his stern sad gaze.

"You mean merely because you happened to be at Lost Lake when Stone came. But that's too far-fetched. You are not to blame for being alive. You are not to find yourself guilty because you have wished men to find you fair. That is any woman's right . . . But was not Stone only an instrument in this deal—and Collishaw another?"

Ruth lied, encompassing all the innocence that she could muster.

"Aw, hell, Wansfell," burst out Stone, getting up. "You listen to me if you want the straight of this. Guerd Larey hatched this deal. He'd got a tip from Collishaw about how to fetch his wife to terms. Well, Larey didn't want to figure in it. He had deep schemes at Lost Lake, an' he was too smart to queer them. So he sends Collishaw off north as a blind. He got me to fit in with his game. That wasn't hard to do, for I had a game of my own. Dabb was in it, too. I was to steal money from Larey's desk. Then my part was to go to Ruth and beg her on my knees to come down and persuade Larey to let me off, because I was drunk or crazy. I did go, and Ruth fell into the trap. I daresay she didn't dislike the idea of trying out her charms an' tricks upon her husband. We went down the path. Collishaw was hidin' with a blanket. He threw it over her head, an' grabbed her up. We ran to the wagon waitin', an' got in. The Mex drove off.

"So far so good for Mr. Larey, but right there his deal ended. Ruth fought that one-eyed devil, like the little cat she is. He'd have torn her to pieces but for me. Then when she was beaten, lyin' there white in the moonlight, with her dress nearly torn off, that damned Texan couldn't keep his hands off her. If I'd had a gun I'd sure have bored him. But I hadn't an' I was afraid to snatch at his. I saw that he had doublecrossed Larey. The sight of that girl was too much for him, the old buzzard. I cussed him an' begged him an' fought him all night to let Ruth alone. An' so help me heaven, if I never did anythin' good for her before, I did *that*.

"But my plan was to doublecross Larey myself. I was to get the money I stole. Larey—who thought he was so slick—believed I could be bought. But I loved the girl an' I meant to fool him an' take her away. An' you can bet your life I'd have done it but for that bead-eyed Collishaw."

Stone's hurried, coarse and impassioned story had the ease and strength of veracity. If it impressed Wansfell he did not evince the slightest sign.

"Stone, you lack a good many things," he said, coldly. "And one is that you can't see ahead. I could crack your neck and think no more of it than to crack a stick by the camp fire. But this girl asks that I do you no injury. She misled you and that galls her. . . . Well, you go your way. But never cross my trail again."

In the silence that ensued Stone made for the door, opened it and passed out. The light flared upon him, dogged and sullen of mien, and then he vanished in the gloom.

Adam, at Stone's departure, seemed to be released from stern and implacable absorption. Perhaps while Stone was present he could not get away from the side of him that was Wansfell. Only Merryvale knew how Stone had been edging a precipice.

"We will go now," said Adam.

Ruth put her bruised feet gingerly to the floor and rose to rest her weight upon them. She flinched, but managed to limp a few steps, when Adam stopped her with an encircling arm.

"I'm afraid I can't walk very well," she replied.

"You need not walk."

Stone had left the door open. The Mexican, smiling and eager, backed out.

"I hope Stone doesn't go tell Collishaw. I—I've had about all—" said Ruth, breaking off falteringly.

Adam lifted Ruth in his arms. She wondered at the sphinx-like impassiveness of his face.

"Wal, lass, shore you needn't worry none aboot Collishaw," spoke up Merryvale, in a voice that held an unfamiliar cold note.

Ruth sagged against Adam. She felt only an exaggeration of her weakness, but she knew what Merryvale meant. What little strength she had left was scarcely enough to resist a stealing faintness. Then her mind seemed vague. She had a sensation of resting laxly in Adam's arms, of being moved out into the night, of gloomy walls and dim lights, of whispering voices.

Gradually that spell passed. Adam was striding swiftly, carrying her as if she were a child. Merryvale and the Mexican strode ahead a few paces, stopped a moment here and there, then went on. They crossed the street, with Adam following; they kept to the deep shadow of trees; passed on into an open park or square; entered a black passage between high walls. Ruth heard voices and laughter of persons near at hand, but she did not see any of them.

It required effort for her to hold her head erect. As she dropped it back, her hair, always unruly, massed against Adam's face. She smoothed it down and her hand touched his cheek. It was cold, like marble. She turned her palm against it.

Again Ruth heard the low hum of Yuma's night life. She was being taken back into the heart of the town. The passageway led into a *patio*. Then they were mounting steps. Adam carried her through dim-lit halls and rooms, at last to let her gently down. Their Mexican guide appeared to be issuing orders. Soft sandled footsteps sounded through the house; the darkness of this room gave place to light. Ruth found herself given into the kindly hands of Senora Augustine and her two daughters.

"We will be near you—in the next room," Adam said.

"Senorita, it is well for you here," added the Mexican, courteously. "Augustine has many friends. They are yours. Be happy again."

"Ruth, I'll fetch the things I bought for you. I did my best. Promise you won't laugh," said Merryvale.

"If I ever laugh again, it'll not be at you, my friend," replied Ruth. "You were good to think of my comfort."

Merryvale went out with the other men, and presently returned with several packages, which he deposited on the floor beside Ruth's chair.

"Heah you are, lass," he said, with a smile that wrinkled his lean face. "It shore was a mighty job, but I never enjoyed one more."

She gave him her hand, and drew him closer, whispering: "What did you mean—about Collishaw?"

The smile smoothed out and the keen kindly blue eyes clouded.

"Wal, now, Ruth dear, haven't you had enough shocks for one day?"

"I shall not be shocked," she went on, clinging to him. "At least anything is better than uncertainty—for me. You said I—I need not worry about Collishaw."

"Wal, you shore needn't."

"Just tonight—or—or—?"

"Never again in this heah world," he replied, solemnly and stalked out.

Ruth sank back, to close her eyes and surrender to the Mexican women. She scarcely felt their ministrations. All within her breast seemed stilled, frozen. It passed, leaving a numb sickness. Slowly the horror faded out of her mind, like a spectre retreating down an empty hall, where mournful winds of darkness blew.

Wansfell had killed another vulture of the desert. Many times during the last forty-eight hours Ruth had prayed for Adam to come and free her. Her fierce rage had been one of the factors in the havoc wrought in her. But when the mood had passed she was not the same. Must Adam again become a fugitive? His present actions would not presuppose such a thing. The death of a man in a fight was common on the desert, and an event of no moment in Yuma. Yet dread again came to haunt Ruth's thought; and it seemed to concern the future more than the present, a far-reaching ill omen, a harbinger of the fate she had brought upon herself.

An hour later Ruth entered the room where Adam

and Merryvale waited. She had been bathed, and her many bruises had been anointed with some soothing Mexican balm, and her tangled dust-laden hair combed and brushed, and she had dressed in the garments Merryvale had provided.

She halted in the lamplight with a curtsey. She had expected to create a sensation and was not disappointed. The Mexican girls were giggling in the doorway. Merryvale was stroking his chin in great perturbation while Adam's face slowly broke into his rare smile.

"Wal, shore I might have done wuss," remarked Merryvale, trying to bolster up his judgment.

"Little old lady!" exclaimed Adam.

Ruth laughed merrily: "You hit it right," she said. "Merryvale bought me a little old lady's dress! . . . And look, sir, you unflattering wretch—look at my new shoes. Spanish, with buckles! And my feet are lost in them."

She lifted the hem of the black dress and extended her foot for them to see. Merryvale's eyes popped out.

"Them big things? Why, Ruth, I swore they'd be too small," he said, in distress.

"Never you mind," replied Ruth. "Everything is splendid, especially the shoes. If they were tight I couldn't wear them at all, my feet are so sore."

"You should not have dressed," remonstrated Adam.

"I feel better, but I'm very tired."

"Can you eat something? Tomorrow will be a long hard day."

"Perhaps I can—a little. . . . Adam, are you taking me home to Lost Lake?"

"Of course. Where else could I take you?"

"The world is wide," she replied, gazing steadily at him.

"Ruth, there's your grandfather to look after."

"I know. It's my duty. But—if I have to go through all this again!"

"My hope is this will end your trouble," returned Adam.

"If my trouble isn't ended it'll end me . . . But, Adam, don't look so. I'll go willingly. I want to do my duty. I'll pray to learn to love the desert. I'll crush that rebellious savage in me. . . . Provided you are near me all the time."

"But Ruth!" he expostulated. "That is impossible—all the time."

"You think the situation will be different at Lost Lake—now?" she queried, with gravity.

"It can't help but be."

"That is my opinion. Different and worse!" returned Ruth, unable to repress what she felt to be the truth.

At this juncture they were called to supper. It was Merryvale who gallantly stepped to Ruth's assistance. Adam apparently had not heard the summons.

"Come Adam," said Ruth, from the door, reproaching herself for the bitterness that would crop up. Merryvale helped her to a seat at the table. But Adam did not join them. Ruth heard rapid footsteps coming down the hall. They recalled her nervous dread. Adam was not yet safely back in the confines of the desert.

Someone entered the other room to greet Adam, and Merryvale hurriedly went back.

"Senor Adam, it is well," said a man Ruth took for Augustine. His voice was low, sibilant, but she could hear: "Sanchez is my friend and therefore yours. He told the sheriff that Collishaw had at last met one old enemy too many. 'It was an even break'—And to his friends he said: 'Wansfell, the Wanderer, has made a call on Yuma. May he live to come again!' "

In the darkness of a cool stone-walled room Ruth lay, prey to conflicting thoughts and emotions that stubbornly resisted the encroaching sleep.

Many of them rushed on to oblivion, but some lingered. Genie Linwood and her story! The face of Tanquitch, the god, bright like the sun, which no Indian

maiden could look upon without love! The faith of
Mrs. Linwood, who said God abided in the desert, and
when she prayed—a saviour had come. The desert
Indians who could liken a man to an eagle! The thunderbolt that swooped down from the heights!

Ruth now had objective proof of the meaning
desert men gave to Wansfell. He was a wanderer, an
obscure name, a mystery, a force, they believed, more
mythical than real, a man in whom the natural elements of solitude and loneliness and wilderness were
mixed. He had become to Ruth what Tanquitch had
been to Genie.

Outside, the hum of the street grew fainter and
farther away. She heard the moan of the wind—desert
wind—seldom idle—from off the great open wastes.
She could smell the sand and the heat that was moving
away. The moon crossed the window, an orange-
colored, misshapen, strange orb, not pitiless like the
white stars, but melancholy, a lifeless desert planet of
the heavens.

In the room between Ruth's and the corridor slept
Adam and Merryvale. At least the latter slept, for
he had the snore of an old man. Faithful old Merryvale!
For years the sharer of Wansfell's wanderings! What
was his story? He had no home, no kin, no children, no
work, no one to love him—nothing except this giant
of the sands, this aloof and saintly avenger with
blood-stained hands. Yet, tragic as it was, that
seemed enough.

Ruth had been tortured into a changing awesome
outlook on life. She was being reborn. She was being
torn and riven and divided. That passionate, selfish,
intolerant egoist was no longer the sweet blind intimate creature she had been. Ruth saw her with hard
accusing eyes. She saw her as something to destroy.
And the old self, which had been all of Ruth, fighting
like a lioness, wild-eyed, mighty being of the habit
and mastery of years, was being driven and flayed and
beaten to the wall.

12

It was scarce daylight when Merryvale awakened Ruth, telling her to hurry. She tried to comply, but her cramped sore muscles hindered her to such an extent that she could hardly get up to dress. But she made valiant effort, and found it a painful process.

She had breakfast alone, with the dark-eyed little senorita attendant upon her. Merryvale came to the door and asked her to be ready in ten minutes to go with him.

"Where is Adam?" asked Ruth, anxiously.

"He's waitin' outside," replied Merryvale.

Ruth was ready a little ahead of time. The senorita, helping her with the veil, said shyly: "*Adios, l'luvia d'oro.*"

"Goodbye, dusky eyes," replied Ruth, returning the compliment; and then bidding the other kind Mexican women farewell she pulled down her veil and went out leaning on Merryvale's arm.

He did not at once take her clear out to the street, but halted in the areaway, explaining that it would be just as well for them to await the stagecoach. Before Ruth had time to grow more concerned the stage rolled up to the sidewalk, out of a cloud of dust.

"Heah we are," said Merryvale, cheerfully, and he almost lifted Ruth along.

"But Adam?" she whispered.

"Don't worry, lass. Adam ain't far away," he replied, and led her out.

The stage door was open, and as Merryvale helped her up someone approached her: "*Adios, Senorita.*

181

May the gracious Virgin watch over you!" Ruth recognized the voice as that of Adam's Mexican friend. She thanked him. In the stage were several passengers whom she could not distinguish clearly through her veil.

"I'll ride on top," decided Merryvale.

Just then a quick step checked Ruth from demanding of Merryvale why Adam did not come. She knew that step. It stirred her pulse. Adam's tall, dark form appeared. "Drive on," he called, and when he stepped up the stage was in motion. He closed the door, and sat down beside her, with a greeting. Ruth was relieved and overjoyed, too conscious of sudden tumult to reply.

What with her veil and the cloud of dust that rolled through the open windows Ruth could not see Adam very well; but she felt her shoulder against his arm, and she seemed all at once to be filled with a great palpitating sense of comfort.

The stage rolled rapidly out of town, and the dust lessened so that it was no longer stifling.

"You can put up your veil now," said Adam.

Ruth was not sure whether he meant that he wished to see her face, or that it was safe now for her to remove the veil, which was a nuisance at best. But when she lifted and fastened it back, and looked up at Adam, she decided he had meant both, and especially the former. It sent a sweet warm rush through her.

"How are you this morning?" he asked. "I saw that you limped."

"I slept well. But it was terribly hard to move this morning. I've aches and pains—when I think of them."

Besides Ruth and Adam there were only three other passengers inside the stage. A stolid Chinaman with a bundle on his lap and a Mexican laborer, sat across from them. The corner on the other side of Ruth was occupied by a rough looking miner who appeared to be sleeping off a debauch. How fortunate, Ruth thought, that there were so few passengers, and none who would be curious about her, or who would be apt to be familiar with last night's happenings!

She gave vent to a long sigh. Yuma lay behind, and the happenings there could be put out of mind. Lost Lake with its problem was a whole day and more distant. She could not comprehend why this early morning hour seemed wonderful, different from any she had ever lived, unless it was because of her escape. She was content to let the present moment suffice.

The sun came up white over the Arizona mountains, so stark and ragged, and soon the air was hot, though fresh still and redolent of the river lowlands. The road wound between dust-laden thickets of arrowweed, and sometimes afforded sight of the broad belt of lowland greens and the sullen swirling red river.

"I don't like the look of the sky," observed Adam.

"Why? It looks heavenly to me."

"Wind," he said, indicating the thin curled wisps of clouds now losing their sunrise tint. "That strip of desert from Pilot Knob to the dunes is bad in a dust storm. And to be caught in the sand is far worse."

"Let the wind blow," returned Ruth, smiling up at him. The desert had no terrors for her while she was with him; nor had its beasts of men. If it had not been for a crowding sense of past events and a vague impending shadow of the future, Ruth would have actually been happy.

The stage rolled on and around and upward, at last emerging from the river basin, and the rising dust. The air cleared. And the grand desolate variations of the desert wilderness stood out in the white morning light. Away wandered the red green-bordered ribbon that was the river, at last piercing the dark mountains, so crinkly and bald and rugged. Away spread and rose the gray gravel slopes, fringed with green-spotted gullies, swelling to the level rim of the escarpment.

Ruth suddenly realized that she was not for the moment gazing drearily, mournfully, hatefully at the ghastly desert, with its ever unattainable horizon. But the instant she thought of it the binding fetters shut upon her. Was this but the untruthful conception of her imagination?

"Adam, don't you hate the desert?" she queried, suddenly.

"Why, no child," he replied, surprised.

"I'm not a child," she said, impatiently. "You don't hate it? Surely you cannot *love* it!"

"Of course," he returned, simply. "It is the only home I know."

"Home! . . . Don't you hope ever to have any other home?"

"Yes, sometimes I dream of one—with you."

That disconcerted her momentarily, but her roused searching mind would not abide any sentiment blocking her curiosity.

"Do you think the desert beautiful?" she went on.

"Infinitely. Beyond words. I remember sunrises, storms, avalanches, sunsets, nights when the blackness has been blazoned white by streaking comets and shooting stars, moonlight from the peaks—a thousand scenes. My memory seems full of them."

"Isn't the desert hot, terribly hot, and again cold at times, lonely, hard as iron, bitter as acid, cruel, destructive? Doesn't it shut you in? Isn't that blue sky now a delusion, and won't it presently be a copper lid roasting down on you? Isn't the sun horrible, the wind frightful, the solitude unbearable? Aren't the Indians poor starved wretches? Aren't prospectors and water-hunters poor deluded blind fools? Isn't the dream of gold a passion that is never satisfied? Aren't most desert men—like—like all these things I've mentioned?"

"Ruth, I am bound to say yes," he replied, gravely. "But for me these things were something to conquer. In the fight I survived. In that survival I found my salvation."

"I can understand that," she replied, as earnestly as he. "But you are one man in a million. The desert's influence cannot be judged by you. Have you ever known any men who did as you?"

"Oh, yes. Many old desert rats, as you would call

them, and never look a second time. But these men have lived through all you mention—yet would never leave the desert. Some day I will tell you the story of Dismukes. He was almost superhuman."

"Do you mean that a man's struggle to find what he wants or thinks he wants out there—his fight against heat, cold, thirst, starvation, solitude, makes him superhuman?"

"I think that is what I mean," replied Adam, thoughtfully.

"How about the majority of men, in whom the spirit to fight is just as mighty, but who sink down to perdition?"

"They become superhuman, too. The evil in them magnifies with survival. Lust, hate, greed, blood, fanaticism—these all become superlatively abnormal. It is the mystery of the desert dominating their minds. It is the devil in man, and not the godlike, that gains the ascendancy."

"Very well, then. But how about a woman? I believe that she could sink to the uttermost depths, even lower than a man. But could she scale the heights—rise through this survival you speak of—so that *she* would be superhuman?"

"Yes, she could. I knew a one-eyed woman at Tecopah who was more bestial, more horribly deformed and distorted than any man I ever saw on the desert. Your own mother proved the opposite. By birth, breeding, character, by her defeat in life, and her frail physique. She was one whom the desert might have been expected to debase. But she rose above all."

"Through *you*."

"I only showed her the way, as Dismukes showed me. . . . But, though your mother died by accident, she could not have lived much longer in any case. The desert, not to say Death Valley, is fatal to white women. Even the Indian women cannot live long in some places. They are constituted differently from men. In white women, I don't believe it a matter of sex. It is the mind of a woman that kills her."

"Ah!—We have arrived at the thing I felt, but never have understood," declared Ruth. "I am justified in my shrinking, my discontent, my horror. Am I not?"

"Ruth, I never said you were not."

"Is it wholly my fault that I have been—oh, such a wild, raving, changeable, deceitful and hateful woman?"

"You have not been that. But even had you been—it could not all be blamed on your heritage and your beauty and weakness."

"There. You give me heart to go on," asserted Ruth, with agitation. "I can hate myself less and understand the desert more. . . . But, you admit this desert is fatal to white women—and to such as my mother and me it is death."

"Yes, in time, and as the years go—nothing like the normal life of woman."

"Then—are you going to take me away from the desert before it's too late?" she shot at him, with a glance of fire.

"Ruth! Of course I am. I did not apply the things I said to you."

"But I did. And I want to know when."

"As soon as you are free," he said, very low.

"Free!" she exclaimed, leaning to whisper. "You think *that* will come before the desert eats my heart out?"

"It will come soon. It will come by the very nature of life and events on the desert. That is what sustains me here—and stays—"

"Don't speak beyond me," she interrupted him, entreatingly. "I need every single little atom of help possible. . . . You mean—the way *he* is going—he'll not last long?"

"Not on this desert!" returned Adam, with dark and somber sadness.

Ruth laid her head back and closing her eyes let silence and thought subdue the emotion that had mounted in spite of her. A long silence ensued. The stage creaked and swayed up the slope; and the time came when the wheels began to roll on a level.

"Look!" said Adam, touching her.

Ruth's eyes opened to the vast colorful plane of desert, with its lacy fringe of green growths and its pale shimmering mirages, and at length rested upon a huge buttressed mountain, purple in hue, noble in outline, rising in a grand solitude.

"Picacho!" It was not so much the austerity of his look as the melancholy of his tone that affected Ruth almost to tears.

She slipped her trembling hand in his. She had just begun to get a glimmering of this man's spirit, a glimpse into the abyss of his soul. What could she say to comfort? How impossible to reach him in his aloofness! Yet in the poignancy of the moment she could not resist voicing a woman's childish vain sympathy.

"Never mind, Adam," she whispered. "Picacho brought us together, and if there is a God, we will be happy yet."

"Perhaps that is the strange feeling it gives me now," he replied dreamily. "Picacho called me for many long years. It is calling again."

The heat began to burn through the old coach and a fine alkali dust that irritated eyes and lips sifted in the cracks and poured through the windows. Ruth commenced to feel a drowsy fatigue that encroached upon her active mind. She let her hand remain in Adam's, and gradually, as the coach rolled and bumped along, her head slipped down against his arm and rested there. There seemed to be something sad and sweet, and very restful in this contact with him. It ended in her falling asleep.

She was awakened by Adam lifting her gently back from the shoulder she had appropriated. The stage was at a standstill.

"Ruth, I've got to take a look outside," he said, and opening the door he stepped out.

"Shore looks pretty bad," said Merryvale from on top.

"I've a good notion to turn back," added the driver. "If we was across the sand I wouldn't mind. But I ain't crazy about bein' hit along here."

Adam appeared to be gazing upward in thoughtful perplexity. "You can't go back to Yuma," he said to the driver.

"Why not? It'd be safer—if that storm turns out as bad as it looks."

"We are not turning back for any kind of a storm," replied Adam.

Ruth heard this conversation with a growing apprehension and she gazed out at the small part of desert and sky that was visible to her. Then she rose and stepped down to the ground.

A weird and marvelous change had transformed the white glaring desert. A frowning pall of angry cloud, yellow and purple and storm-hued, was rapidly reaching the zenith. It blanketed the sun, which shone a strange sinister magenta through this moving medium.

"Well, what do you make of it?" queried the driver impatiently of Adam.

"It'll be bad. And I believe you'd risk as much going back as if you go on or try to find a windbreak."

"Hell, mister! No man could go on in the face of that," growled the driver.

"I could," returned Adam, quietly. "But we'd probably do better to find a clump of thick ironwood trees to get behind. Have you an axe?"

"Yes. An' I see a tolerable big clump of ironwoods out ahead a couple of miles. Pile in, an' we'll rustle."

Once more the coach rolled on, rumbling and swaying from the faster gait of the horses. The driver whooped and cracked his whip as if they were pursued by Indians. The shadow began to spread deeper and farther over the desert.

"There is danger, of course," said Ruth, looking up at Adam. She had never been out in the dreaded sandstorm. It was dreadful enough to endure one safe in a close shut house.

"I have been through a thousand storms," replied Adam.

The coach bumped off the road, over rocks and brush, to halt in the lee of some large thick-foliaged ironwood trees.

Adam got out as the driver and Merryvale descended from their perch.

"Ruth, you won't be comfortable anywhere, but you'd best stay in the coach," advised Adam.

"But I want to see," replied Ruth, resolutely.

All the passengers but the miner left the stage, and while Ruth walked to a vantage point to view the oncoming storm, the men set about necessary tasks with the horses and the providing of as good a windbreak as possible.

It appeared to Ruth that the storm was yet a long way off. But it had cast its marvelous and formidable spell far over the desert. An amber twilight, thick and unreal, preceded the advancing sky-high pall of dust. The sun had become a dim dark red ball. Back toward the south sky and earth were still clear, though darkening in the fading light. Pilot Knob, far away now, showed coal black against the pale blue. Picacho loomed all the higher for the distance. Its purple bulk had a golden crown. To the east the Chocolate Range seemed receding, diminishing in size, fading in color. And away to the north and left of the storm, spread the vast sea of sand dunes, billows and waves and hollows, crested ridges and scalloped hills, thousands of slopes bronze and yellow and red, rising higher and higher to merge into the sky.

The storm was fast swallowing up the sand dunes. For the first time on the desert Ruth stood transfixed, her unwilling heart grudgingly forced to a tribute of awe, of wonder, of exceeding amaze. It was magnificent, this menacing mood of the desert storm-wind. The heat was oppressive, slumberous, hanging like a belt over the land.

Then the magenta sun faded and vanished. The far-flung top whorl of the dust pall swept over the travel-

ers at a lofty height, while the body of it, heavy and
dark, sweeping along like a flood, was still far from
them.

"Ruth, get into the stage, now," called Adam.

"Oh, one moment more," she cried.

And before that moment was up the roar had ac-
celerated to an all-engulfing shriek. A sombre transparent darkness preceded the wall of sand. The air all
about Ruth seemed trembling. She saw the running
streaks of dust that shot ahead of the wall, the balls of
weed rolling like mad things over the desert, the beating down of the greasewood, the shower of *palo verde*
blossoms like golden sparks flying aloft, and then the
dusky dense base of the storm, a rolling, coalescing,
mushrooming fury of sand-laden wind.

Adam broke her transport by seizing her arm
and commanding: "You must get in the coach." Ruth
went with him reluctantly. There was something in
this phenomenon that symbolized her gusts of passion
—the wild storms that swept her soul.

All save the driver were huddled inside the stagecoach, when Adam helped Ruth in. The Chinaman
had a blanket over him; the Mexican his colored scarf.
Merryvale lifted handkerchief and coat to show his
bright blue smiling eyes and to yell at her: "This
heah's one of Adam's *fiestas*."

There was a moaning out in the trees and a sweeping rush of sand under the coach. But the roar seemed
still at a distance.

Adam's swift capable hands hurried Ruth into her
linen coat, and tucked the flowing veil around her,
leaving roomy space within but no aperture. Through
the veil Ruth saw him cover his head with a silk scarf
and settle back in the corner.

Then, as a terrible bellowing came and a yellow
darkness, and a whistling of sand right through the
coach, Ruth seized Adam's arm with both hands,
and sinking against him, she shut her eyes in a kind of
strange exultance. She had no fear. What could blowing sand do to her? Let the fiendish sand come in palls

and mounds, and bury her and Adam, deep as under the ocean, forever and ever.

Her ears were assailed by terrific din, until they became deaf to sound. She did not lift her eyelids, but she could see the blackness as of night through them. The sand weighted her down, and the dust, sifting through her veil, choked her. The air grew vitiated and her breathing labored under oppression. Once that might have been a terrible ordeal. But now she made endurance a passionate defiance. This desert would make a weak and crawling beast of her. Drag her back to her forebears! Could any man be mightier of spirit than a woman?

Closer she clung to Adam. She felt the bands and cords of muscle in that arm. She would hold on there, with love of this man and scorn for the wretchedness of physical distress, until death came, if so it chose, without one single protest. It was the flesh that had ruined her—worship of her golden skin and graceful contour, and a madness to have these ever beloved by men. Let the storm howl like the demons of hell, and swell to the skies, and roll the sand dunes into one colossal avalanche, and give her a sepulchre like her mother's!

Her breast strained against the crushing need for oxygen. A million tiny sparks burst into the blackness before her eyes. Slowly beat her heart, and slower the pulse in her temples. And into her brain seemed to be beating the wind, the sand, the storm, like ruthless desert talons, cruel and agonizing.

She drooped lower and her head lodged on Adam's breast. She felt the heat and dampness through her veil. His mighty breast heaved and his heart pounded, regularly and evenly, without stress. Had he not weathered a thousand sand-storms? Ruth clung to the massiveness of him, and yearned for the soul that seemed beyond her.

She drifted then, losing at the last the consciousness of her revel in the storm, and wearying to the extremity of physical endurance, to the elemental instincts, and finally to oblivion.

Ruth opened her eyes to clear day. She was lying under a tree and Adam was bathing her face. Merryvale too was kneeling anxiously beside her.

"Aw, now," he said, with a great burst of relief, "she's come back!"

"Where did—I go?" asked Ruth, faintly, as she smiled up at them.

"I think you *would* have gone with the sand, if that storm had lasted longer," replied Adam.

She could see the brown hue of his face returning.

"Shore it was a rippin' snortin' blow, but short, thank the Lord," added Merryvale, wagging his head. "Once in a while this old desert acts pretty decent."

The driver hailed them from his seat.

"Hey, if you folks get aboard we can make Bitter Seeps by sundown, an' the post by midnight."

"Keep your shirt on," replied Merryvale, irascibly.

While being helped back to the coach Ruth saw the rear of the great storm, a horizon-blotting yellow cloud. Pilot Knob and Picacho, the landmarks to the south, were invisible. The sun shone again as hot as fire. It seemed that all the wind in the world had passed by. Horses and conveyance were sand burdened.

Adam folded blankets in a corner next to the window, making a comfortable seat for Ruth. It was on the shady side, a circumstance that made it possible for her to look out toward the glistening white sand dunes.

Once more they rolled on and Ruth was grateful for the motion. The air fanned her cheeks and blew her hair, rendering the heat less intolerable.

Her fellow passengers lounged asleep in their seats. Even Adam nodded with closed eyes and seeing him thus she fancied she could trace the havoc the last few days had wrought. Was not his hair a little whiter over his temples than on the day he had encountered her with Stone in the canyon? Ruth had to avert her gaze.

Must a woman always be a destroyer? Were there no women who made men stronger, nobler, happier?

The hard gravel road slid behind the rolling wheels, and the miles could be counted by the ever-changing nature of desert plants. This was the zone where ironwoods, *palo verdes, ocatilla,* mesquite, catclaw, and the hardy greasewoods attained their greatest size and perfection. Probably the soil in that fertile belt stored and held more water than zones to north and south. Observed from the distance, these desert growths resembled a forest of different shades of green, with the gold blossoms of the *palo verdes* and the red of the *ocatillas* shining out in beautiful contrast. But the rising heat veils and the shimmering mirages betrayed this illusion of the eye—that this wonderful stretch so seemingly verdant was not forest but the caustic bitter wasteland.

Ruth leaned at the window and watched till her eyes were tired, and then resting them, dozing the hot hours away, she awoke to watch again. Her mind was as wearied as her emotions and her body. But in spite of that she felt something new, dawning, unaccountable as it was prophetic, beginning to work upon her.

The sand dunes again! Clear, soft, blown clean by the wind, rippled as by shore waves, rising from the desert in long smooth rounded slopes, climbing and swelling and mounting, curved, scalloped, knife-edged, lacy, exquisitely silver, on and up alluring steps toward the infinite blue!

The stagecoach rolled on through the pass, down hill to the northward, and slowed only at places where fresh sand had piled across the road.

The sun was setting when the stage emerged from the pass, and turned somewhat westward, facing the bare, stark and naked basin in which Lost Lake shone a green spot in all that ghastliness.

But it was somehow a different place at the end of this strange day. Ruth had never before seen that vast hollow between the dunes and the black range to the north free of haze, drifting palls of sand, driving yel-

low dust-devils, and always the omnipresent and deceitful mirages. This hour it was silver and gold, an
endless desert scene, beginning to tinge with the slow
stealing red of sunset.

They presently turned a ridge corner, to roll down
a gentle slope into Bitter Seeps.

"All out. Thirty minutes for refreshments," shouted
the driver facetiously.

Ruth let Adam help her. It was relief to stretch her
cramped limbs. For food and drink Merryvale preferred to offer what he had fetched from Yuma rather
than what the Indians could supply. The water was
warm and the bread gritty with sand, yet Ruth forced
herself to appease hunger and thirst.

"I must leave you here," announced Adam, presently.

Ruth gave him a swift stare of surprise.

"I left my burros and packs here," he went on. "I'll
find them and come on to Lost Lake tonight."

"Oh!—You'll walk?" she returned.

"Surely. It will not take more than six hours. I'm
used to walking, Ruth, and like night best. Why do you
imagine they called me a wanderer?"

"There'll be another wanderer—if you abandon me
to the tender mercy of your brother!" retorted Ruth,
rebelliously. Then the instant the rude retort was out
she regretted it. But the thought of Adam not being
near her gave swift release to the dread that always
hovered under the surface.

"How like a child you talk!" he remonstrated, pa-
tiently.

"How like a cowardly woman," she added. "But I
can't help it. I thought I could. But have I changed?
Will I ever change?"

"Ruth, must I tell you again—what torture I endure
—at the thought of Guerd recognizing me?"

"No. No. Forgive me. I understand why you ought
not to take the risk. . . . I am as fearful as you. Not
to save me—even though what I've lived through
these last three days—would I have you meet him.

But I forget. And then I always slip back to that other Ruth. Alas, the real Ruth!"

"If my brother is at Lost Lake now, then we may doubt Stone's story. But if not——"

"Oh, Stone lied!" interrupted Ruth, hurriedly, guiltily conscious of her own falsehood. "He swore he would get even with me. Merryvale heard him. Well, Stone inveigled Collishaw somehow; and each had his own treacherous motive. Stone told me Collishaw tried to *sell* me to Sanchez."

"How terribly I want to believe that Stone lied about my brother!"

"Adam—that ought to make it easy," faltered Ruth.

"Yes. I will believe until I know surely."

"You will see me tomorrow night, without fail?" entreated Ruth.

He gazed down upon her with the strange look that always troubled her soul.

"Ruth, what will become of us if you make it so that I'll have to see you all the time?"

"It would be very wonderful for me," she returned, ashamed yet unabashed. "But I never can make it so."

"Take care," he warned, but with pathos. "Even the loneliest of desert eagles has a mate once in its life."

"Wouldn't you be happy, too,—if such a wonderful thing came true," she asked, softly.

"Happy if I killed my brother!" he ejaculated, sternly.

"My God—You—you—I didn't mean that!—Oh, I can't see why—" cried Ruth, breaking off in anguish.

"Ruth, you *can't* see. That's the trouble. But let me tell you. The noblest way you can be true to your mother's prayer—and save me, is to keep me from killing Guerd."

"Adam, I would sacrifice my life for that," she answered passionately.

"Then fight it out. I don't mean alone. I'll help all I can. For let me swear this to you. If Guerd ever finds

out I am Adam Larey—that I am your friend and protector—that I love you, he will be a fiend. Nothing
on earth or in heaven could hold him in his hate. . . .
Then I'd be driven to kill him!"

"Adam, I promise you I'll fight it out, and never
forget," replied Ruth. "But I'm only a woman—unstable as the winds—weak as water up to this very
hour. . . . I must know you are near me."

"I shall be," he replied, in earnest relief. "Listen, I
have a plan which I talked over with Merryvale. I
know a hiding place in the rocks near Lost Lake. I can
see your home. I can even see you with the field glass
I bought at Yuma. I can see your signal. But there is
no water at this place. I shall leave my packs there
tonight and take my burros to the canyon where Merryvale found me. Then I'll come back to this new
camp. I'll have to fetch water from Lost Lake.
But that'll be easy at night."

"You will be quite near?" asked Ruth, eagerly.

"It is scarce two miles."

"Oh! That big jumble of rocks to the east of Lost
Lake?"

"Yes."

"Grandpa has a field glass. I might even see you."

"Merryvale will show you where to look."

"Then I think I'll manage to exist," she concluded,
looking up with a coquetry as natural to her as breathing. "It is romantic, don't you think? . . . Ah, the
eternal woman!"

Merryvale approached them at this juncture.

"Wal, Adam, we ain't had a chance to finish the
talk we began in Yuma this mawnin'. An' if you're
leavin' us heah—"

Adam told him briefly and substantially the plan as
outlined to Ruth, and then he added:

"I think it advisable for you to live at Ruth's house
now. There will be no longer any reason for secrecy.
Everyone will know you and I brought Ruth back
again. You can make some pretense of work, if it's
only to run errands."

"I shore will be tickled to death," returned Merryvale. "An' I reckon I will see you some nights at Lost Lake?"

"You will see him every night," interposed Ruth.

"Ahuh! Wal, that'll shore be fine."

Here Adam put a brawny hand on Merryvale's shoulder.

"It's a hard place for me," he said, with emotion. "I am used to facing the desert, and men and events. But I am powerless here. . . . The trust I give you is this. Never let Ruth out of your sight. I mean when she is not in the house. She can't be cooped up all the time. Never let her out of your sight. And if any man lays a hand on her—shoot him!"

"Wal, pard, I savvy. An' I shore have a hankerin' for my job," drawled Merryvale.

Adam loomed over Ruth then, with smile and touch that thrilled her. *"Adios, lluvia d'oro!"*

"Ah, not gold. You should say 'shower of trouble' . . . and I should say, *'Adios, grande Senor!'* "

Ruth walked a little way down the road, watching Adam, as he strode among the mesquites. Presently he disappeared and she stifled a deep sigh.

The sun had just slipped below the wavering line of western hills. The low desert had succumbed to shadow. But the sand dunes, rising far out from Bitter Seeps, were bathed from their lowest steps up and up their million slopes to their magnificent heights, in a glory of sunset gold.

These were Ruth's stairs of sand—the golden stairway over the insurmountable barrier of the desert. The great sloping wall of sand—the million dunes that constituted a mountain—the shifting, changing, blowing atoms—these reflected the sunlight in one glorious blaze, transparent and magnifying, through which the successive steps with their shadows, like waves of the sea, rose so gradually and so symmetrically that only in the grand ensemble could any ascent be discernible.

Here were the physical details, the innumerable details that made up a colossal hill of sand.

But it was impossible for Ruth's sensitive and morbid mind not to symbolize this phenomenon of nature and see in it the stairway of her imprisonment, the barrier and gateway to her freedom, the deceit and allurement and pang and uncertainty and strife of love, the slipping, sliding footsteps of her fate.

While she gazed the glory dimmed, the gold paled, the high light shaded, the pale silver intervened, and then the dark cold shadow of the desert levelled all.

Darkness caught the stagecoach traveling down from Bitter Seeps. Toward the end of that long journey Ruth slept from sheer exhaustion, too wearied to give one more anxious thought to Lost Lake, or home, or self or anything. Merryvale watched over her as if she had been a child.

The hour was late when the coach, with weary horses at a walk, reached the outskirts of Lost Lake. Merryvale had the driver stop at the gate of Ruth's home. There were lights at the post, but elsewhere was darkness.

It was all Ruth could manage, encircled by Merryvale's arm, to climb the winding path to the house. Had she been gone only a few days? She smelled the dank weedy pond and heard the sweet low tinkle of running water. Insects were humming. The night wind moaned softly in the *palo verdes*. Over all hung a mystical blue sky fretted with white stars. The desert brooded, slumbered, waited. Lost Lake was the same lonely, isolated shut-in, silent abode for a few miserable souls of humans. But Ruth felt that she was not the same.

Resting on Merryvale's arm she called in her grandfather's window:

"Ruth—Ruth!" he answered, as a man in a dream.

"Yes, it is I, grandad," she replied, somehow glad. "Home, safe and sound, but very very tired."

"Who brought you, child?"

"Who could, but Adam and Merryvale. I did not

run away from you this time, grandad. But I'll tell you tomorrow. . . . Are you well? And—and is Larey at the post?"

"I'm well, I guess, though the heat and worry have dragged me low. Larey left the post three days ago and has not come back."

"Do not worry anymore, grandad. Goodnight."

Ruth found her door open and her room as she had left it.

"Lass, go to bed an' get the rest you need," commanded Merryvale. "I'll fetch my bed up an' sleep heah on the porch."

Ruth bade him goodnight, and closing the door, with slow and thoughtful action, she dropped the bar in place, and stood motionless in the little moonlit room. The night wind, cool, dry, with the fragrance of the open barrens, fluttered the curtain of her window.

13

Sometimes, though rarely in summer, there came a day which was hot, but not so hot that Ruth could never forget it for a moment, in sun or shade, asleep or awake. The light wind was north, from off the far-distant snow-capped peaks of San Jacinto and Gorgonio, visible from Lost Lake on such a dustless day.

Ruth suffered a physical reaction from the severe hardship and loss of sleep to which she had been subjected, but on no other morning of her desert experience had she felt so revivifying a joy, so inextinguishable a buoyant spirit. And never had she known the unintelligible, expanding fullness of heart that awoke her this day, and would not yield to thought, and utterly destroyed the old mocking self-depreciation, and the sword of dread.

Guerd Larey was gone; the post was in charge of freighters, as Dabb had mysteriously disappeared; Merryvale had taken up quarters under a dense low-branched mesquite that flourished across the pond below Ruth's door; and from the porch Ruth could see with naked eye the rugged unheaved rocks and cliffs that marked Adam's new hiding place.

How different this morning! The deceitful old desert was in gentle mood. The sun was not white, the sky not copper, the waste of ground not so ghastly. Birds and rabbits visited the pond. Ruth embraced something sweet and blinding, and hugged it to her. This day held much for her, and though she yearned for the starlight and Adam, she wished there were double the intervening hours, so that she could give them to a profound analysis of her perplexing self.

Merryvale, passing along the path with some of his belongings, encountered Ruth limping from her room, with apron on and broom in hand.

"Wal, you are shore surprisin' to me," he ejaculated, as he stared at her. "I expected you'd be half daid in bed. An' heah you are with jest a little limp."

"Merryvale, I could run over rocks and cactus today," she exulted.

"Shore you look it," he replied. "Ruth, I never seen the likes of you in all my born days."

"Likes! Is that a compliment or—" she returned, breaking off with an interrogating smile.

"Jest plain truth. . . . You gold, purple-eyed blossom of the desert! Ruth, if I were young I'd be mad, too. I'd have to wear you on my heart or die."

"Why, Merryvale!" exclaimed Ruth, amazed, and deeply pleased.

He laughed at his own sentimentality and passed on down the path, wagging his gray head as if cogitating a weighty problem.

Ruth halted in her work, and gazed with dreamy unseeing eyes out into space. Did Adam think she was like that? So many men raved about her beauty, but Adam could not see it. With him it did not seem to be how she looked, but what she was! The paradox of Ruth's life was that the desert had given her many of its attributes: its changeableness, its fiery depth, its mystery and moods and passion, and its beauty; and withheld its freedom, its strength, its indifference.

Ruth was surprised to have a visitor in the shape of Mrs. Dorn. She was a little woman, of middle age, dark like an Indian, with finely serrated skin and sharp eyes. She wished to borrow some household utensil, she gave as an excuse for her visit.

"So you come back?" she asked, curiously. "I should think once you got away from this hot hole that you'd stay."

"Well, Mrs. Dorn, I didn't have any choice about

leaving, and very little about coming back," replied Ruth.

"See here, Ruth Larey, you don't expect anyone to believe that, do you?" queried the woman.

"Come to think of it, I don't," said Ruth, with a laugh. "I'm sure I don't care what anyone believes."

"That's plain enough," snapped Mrs. Dorn. "It's a pity you don't care more. But some one ought to tell you a few things."

"You seem to be bursting to do so," returned Ruth, with sarcasm.

"Everybody here, even the Indians, feel sorry for that young Stone."

"Indeed. You're all very kind. I think I felt sorry for Stone myself."

"Yes, you acted like it. Guerd Larey told my husband you made a thief of Stone. And when he left, he swore he'd drag you back by the hair of your head."

"My husband's lies are the least of his villainy, Mrs. Dorn. Perhaps you will be enlightened some day."

The woman gave Ruth a suspicious uncomprehending look, and shrugging her thin shoulders she passed on down the path.

Ruth sat down, conscious that her rare beautiful day had sustained its first break. Then her grandfather emerged from his room, manifestly having heard Mrs. Dorn's remarks.

"You are being made the subject of vile gossip, Ruth," he said, severely.

"By whom?" she asked, lifting her head.

"By everybody who lives here and who passes through."

"What do they say, grandad?" she asked, with an interest that surprised her.

"Many things I could not repeat," he said. "But they say you are a beautiful hussy. That you have been an unfaithful wife. That you have made men mad about you and then flouted them. That you made young

Stone a thief. That your husband should whip you naked through the post."

"I deserve it all," flashed Ruth. "And no more than a day ago I could have grovelled in the dust with shame. . . . Now I am above and beyond slander, however just. Poor miserable desert creatures! Warped, dried up, poisoned, these withered souls—I pity them."

"It might be better to reserve some pity for yourself," he said.

"Grandad, you believe I ran off with Stone, *again?*"

"Didn't you?"

"No! . . . I was kidnapped. Stone came to me pleading that I use my influence with Larey. He had stolen money from Larey. It now seems such an absurd story. But I was sorry, excited. I let myself be led without considering. You know how impulse governs me. Well, before we got out the gate I was seized and smothered in a blanket and thrown into a wagon. Driven away in the night! . . . My captors were Collishaw and Stone. They fought over me. They took me to Yuma, to that dive, Del Toro, where Merryvale found me. Later Adam rescued me, and they fetched me home."

"Most extraordinary, if true!" returned Hunt.

That was indeed a rebuff for which Ruth was ill prepared. The hot blood burned her face, and a sharp retort trembled on her lips. But this was another day and Ruth Virey seemed far behind with the bitter yesterdays.

"Grandad, you will not believe, either, that Guerd Larey is behind all this. He and Collishaw got their heads together. They made Stone their tool. They hired him to let on he stole the money, just as a ruse to get me out of the house. Stone did it, but he had his own plan. Collishaw, too, betrayed the trust Larey put in him. It was Larey's plan to follow to Yuma, break my spirit there, and drag me back. But the plot

failed. They did not consider my friend Wansfell.—I
saved Stone's life. But Collishaw is dead."

"Ruth! Has the desert madness gotten into you?
Are you in your right mind?" ejaculated Hunt, incred-
ulously.

"You will hear of Collishaw's death from others,"
replied Ruth, coldly.

Hunt paced the porch in nervous agitation. "Ruth,
I didn't tell you Larey made me another proposition
—a most surprising and friendly one. Made it before
others! I—I have been considering it."

"Pray save youself the trouble of confiding in me.
I don't want to know. Anything Guerd Larey proposes
is fair on its face, but foul underneath."

Ruth left her grandfather then, with pity and horror
and amaze storming the door of self-control. But she
was victor. She saw as in an illumining flash the net
of circumstance and evil drawing closer around her
grandfather and herself. Yet she was unfalteringly sustained by new-found strength in herself and faith in
Wansfell. She had a divination that she had been on
the verge of destruction, but had been drawn back by
something she had not yet mastered.

Merryvale hailed her from his mesquite tree; and
Ruth, forgetting her introspection and also her physical disability, started to run to him. Quickly, however,
she discovered her soreness again, and limped as best
she could round and down to Merryvale's new camp.
He had a canvas stretched for a low open tent, under
which he had snugly arranged his bed and belongings.
On the moment he stood a little away from the tree
with his hands behind his back and a wonderful smile
on his face.

"Oh—I—I know," cried Ruth, out of breath.
"You've seen—Adam!"

"Wal, what'll you give, young woman, to lay your
eyes on him right this heah minnit?" drawled Merryvale, provokingly.

"Give? Why, my friend, I have nothing to give. But
oh! please—please—"

"Shore couldn't think aboot it for nothin'," he replied.

"You tease. You fraud. You don't mean it.—But you're holding my field glass behind your back. Let me have it—show me! . . . I—I will kiss you, if you do."

"Wal, in that case I'll reconsider," replied Merryvale, drawing her to where he stood. "Now look over the fence, out across the desert, at that wall of broken rock. Reckon it doesn't look like a big country from heah. But what you see is only the top an' that hides as rough a badland as I've seen. . . . Wal, now take the glass an' focus it to suit your eyes."

Ruth, with trembling hands levelled the glass, and endeavored to adjust it to her vision.

"My hands are so unsteady," she whispered. "I've got the glass clear, but it wobbles so."

"Lass, Adam is lookin' at you right this heah minnit," said Merryvale.

"No!" cried Ruth, radiantly. "Oh, I've got to control myself. . . . There. I see the rocks quite close. But the size of them! What broken cliffs!"

"Wal, move the glass along slow to the right—up a little—till you come to a dark shadow. That's shade. Adam is there, an' I'll bet he's wavin' to you right this heah minnit."

"Oh, I can't find him," whispered Ruth, almost frantically. . "How silly of me!—I *feel* so—so much over nothing. . . . I'll try again. . . . Yes. I see the shadow. . . . There's something red. It moves."

"That'll be Adam's scarf."

Then Ruth straining all nerve to achieve a tense body and keen sight, finally discerned a man standing on a cliff, waving. It was Adam. She recognized the stature, the pose, the action. How tiny that dot of red! Then a commotion in her breast upset all delicate mechanism of vision, and even the huge gray rocks blurred.

"I saw him, but this pesky glass or my sight has failed. Oh, I will wave to him."

"Wal, I reckon that'll be safe. I've been lookin' around, an' nobody sees us," replied Merryvale.

Ruth had only her apron, which she took off and waved again and again, wildly and eagerly.

"Fine. Adam sees you," said Merryvale, who had taken the glass. "There he goes down off the rock. Gone! . . . Wal, it shore worked fine. An' the idee is this. Adam hasn't much to do but walk out there often an' see if you're heah. If he sees you or me wavin' somethin' *red,* he's to come fast as he can get heah. But of course we ain't to wave anythin' red onless we need him awful bad. Savvy, senorita?"

"Yes, indeed. And it makes me feel so happy, so strong," replied Ruth; and quite weak from her exertion and excitement she stepped back under the mesquite to sit down upon Merryvale's blankets.

"Wal, I reckon I feel aboot the same," rejoined Merryvale.

"Have you been down to the post?"

"Shore. Early this mawnin'. It's been closed for three days, an' you bet the greasers an' injuns were mad. Dabb went away before Larey, an' somebody told me he got hold of Salton Springs ahaid of Larey. It was a freighter who told me. Said Larey was drinkin' hard an' poison sore."

"Ah! Things are not going to suit him," mused Ruth. "I hope he doesn't return here that way."

"It's daid sartin he will, an' be wuss'n ever."

"Was the post open? I must send Marta down to buy things."

"Yes, it's open. An' I reckon that's queer to me. Frank Dorn got word on last night's stage that he was to take charge. Now jest who sent that word? Who knew in Yuma the post was closed?"

"Who except Larey?" queried Ruth, gravely questioning Merryvale.

"No one else, by thunder. He's in Yuma."

"Then he knows—"

"You can bet he knows. Sanchez wouldn't be slow to

tell him what Wansfell did to Collishaw. . . . Larey is drunk or sick right this heah minnit!"

"Sanchez could only guess that Adam went to Yuma after me."

"Aw, it'd be easy for Larey to figger out, 'specially if he met Stone. An' it's a thousand to one Stone will tell our part in the deal, an' leave out his."

"Soon we may expect Guerd Larey back here?"

"Shore. An' at the end of his tether," replied Merryvale, forcibly. "It'll show whether he's yellow clear through. An' I expect him to show yellow."

"You think he'll be afraid of my mysterious friend Wansfell?"

"Precisely. He'll shore get a snook full of news aboot Wansfell. An' if he's not a rum-soaked desert-eaten fool he'll quit or at least go powerful slow."

"Merryvale, this is not my idea at all," said Ruth, compellingly. "I know Guerd Larey, both intuitively, and from personal observation. I believe he will react to this defeat in a deeper, blacker way. Larey is a moral coward, but he's not afraid of any man."

"But Ruth he's heard aboot Collishaw. Ten to one he's seen him daid. An' that'd be no pleasant sight—with Collishaw's other eye shot out. That may strike Larey most damn strange. It was a strange thing for Wansfell to do. Eighteen years ago he put out an eye for the Texan, an' now he shoots out the other."

"It was horrible. Beyond my understanding. . . . Did Collishaw guess who his assailant was?"

"Guess! I guess not. Wansfell *told* him. An' I hope to Gawd I never see another man as turrible lookin' as Collishaw."

"Oh, that was worse," said Ruth, with a shudder. "How could Adam do it? . . . I begin to understand a little more what Wansfell means."

"Ruth he's the desert Nemesis," returned Merryvale, in a kind of awe. "An' if Guerd Larey doesn't realize this he's doomed."

"Oh, Merryvale, don't say that—don't think it!" implored Ruth, wringing her hands.

"But, child, facts are facts," declared Merryvale, stubbornly, "an' we've got to face them. If you're right that Larey will be all the wickeder now, then I'm right in figgerin' what he's goin' to get."

"I will have to save Adam from killing Guerd."

"Shore. I approve. But how you goin' to do it—if Guerd keeps on after you? Shore you're not goin' to tie Adam's hands so he caint defend himself?"

"Never!" cried Ruth, firing up.

"Wal, then, when Guerd an' Adam meet—*if* they do—an' Guerd recognizes his brother—which the devil would see to—it'll be Cain an' Abel over again. Only this time Abel will kill Cain. It is written in blood on this desert."

"Suppose—I—went back to Guerd—to be his wife —truly?" whispered Ruth, hoarsely.

"Aw, woman! What're you hintin' at?" queried Merryvale, in dark passion. "It'd be better to let Guerd kill Adam outright. . . . Ruth, lass, you couldn't send Adam back to the desert with that awful wound? To crawl into some lonely canyon, like a deer shot through, an' die a slow an' lingerin' death! Not Adam with his wonderful love for you? Ruth, say you *couldn't* do that?"

"No! No! No!" she cried, fighting herself. "Anything but that! Death to us both before that! . . . I talk at random. But there must be some way to prevent this tragedy."

"Shore I hope so, with all my heart," replied Merryvale, fervently. "But I've lived long on the desert. An' when life heah begins tragic for a man or woman it shore ends tragic. There ain't no help for it. That is the desert."

"But it began—so—for me" whispered Ruth, fearfully.

"It never did," denied Merryvale, with strong feeling, as if he were cornered. "I know your story. An' me an' Adam are agreed. You were a weak, vain, hot-blooded girl. An' you fell into the last place in the world for a girl to find what she needed most—love an' happiness. Your parents' death was tragic. But if you only see clear you'd know up to now your experience on the desert hasn't been honest reason for agony. Now, Ruth, ain't that true?"

"Yes it is. But I believed in my misery."

"Shore. An' that misery was jest discomfort an' longin' an' wilfulness. Wal, so far so good. You ought to be finding yourself now."

"Perhaps I am," replied Ruth, dreamily, and left him.

Ruth had a great need to be alone. Merryvale had given her an inspiration. It took shuddering hold of her heart and mind.

Alone in her room, with door barred and window darkened, she had courage to voice the insidious thought. She could kill Guerd Larey. The recognizing of her consciousness of this inspiration threw her into tumultuous passion, that blinded her and held her in thrall one sickening appalling moment, before she fell prostrate before the temptation. It was irresistible. It was justice. It was fate. It would save Adam from staining his hands with the blood of a beloved and prodigal brother.

She lay on the bed, realizing the enormity of her decision, marveling at the tigerish leap of her instinct, bewildered at the revelation of her nature. Here it was stalking from ambush—the raw elemental force of the desert.

If Larey sought her again to bind her and break her, to make of her a fallen despicable creature, she would kill him. The decision had all the heat of the desert sun and the power of the wind and the ghastliness of the naked wasteland. It shook her as if a superhuman hand had gathered her up and shaken her. And then it left her in strange somber peace. If the worst came to the worst she knew how to meet it, to save Adam and herself.

But her peace was shortlived. With her mind settled ruthlessly, she had flung at her the mighty question, "Why?" Why would she stoop to a deed of blood, so foreign to her breeding, and the gentleness that had once been hers? The answer was love. It was desert love, and Ruth suddenly fell prey to a paroxysm more riotous than that in which she had received the inception of murder.

The room, the house could not hold her. She could not breathe there. She must flee to the desert, to the boundless open and the illimitable air and the infinite sun. But once outside, flying up the path, without limp or twinge now, the thought of Adam restrained her. She remembered that it would not be fair to him to take such risk. Instead, then, she threw herself on the sand under the drooping *palo verde,* and there, with her rapt gaze enveloping half the circle of horizon, she looked through the veils of heat, the white glare, the purple haze, through the silver sand dunes and the dim ranges, through all the vastness and terror and beauty of the desert into the mystery of her own heart.

Ruth had loved Adam at Santa Ysabel, with a strange dreamy girlish reverence; she had cherished that for long; when Adam had first met her in the canyon with Stone there had come again the perplexing attraction she had felt in other men, and then afterward what she took for love; and on the way home from Yuma, with her hold on his arm, with the consciousness of what it had dealt in defense of her honor and life, with the sand storm bellowing the menace of this desert hell she had come to the first real honest love of all her life. But that had been nothing to this white flame, this noonday bursting molten fire of the sun.

Physically she was part of all she looked at—these terrible elements of nature that had transformed and transfixed her. Spiritually, she had given to her all the tremendous incentives to a woman's love and passion.

She went back in retrospect to her vain wild weaknesses for this and that man. How slight, how shallow, how selfish those pale little gleams! She had stooped lower than flirtations. She had lent her beauty, her hands, her lips, her lying tongue to the winning of men. Unconscious? Only steps in her development? Just the mind—wanderings of a female, drawn by attractions she had no knowledge of? She had been vile. She should have perished in her self-contempt.

How lightly and with what gratification she had trodden the broad and easy path toward destruction. She saw herself from a great height and looked down with withering scorn, with infinite pity at the creature she had been. Not once nor twice, but many times had the desert tested her, always to find her ready for the sin of Eve. She had not known it then; she had held aloof at the end, as in the affair with Stone; but that had only been due to the maddening variations of her temperament. Only accident had saved her in those long-past, apparently trivial affairs. When womanhood stripped away her girlish illusions, and she had met Stone, to work a stronger and more perilous charm on him, only God, using Adam Wansfell as his instrument, could have saved her.

Ruth confessed it. She burned into her soul the brand of what she had been, of what she had escaped. Her mother's prayer to Wansfell now clarified. She had been born with beauty of form, of face, of eye; and with their deadlier parallel—the longing—the passionate need to love and be loved. She saw it all, and abased her spirit in humility and gratitude. She lay there on the sand, propped against the *palo verde,* gazing out at the transfiguration of the desert she had hated, marvelling at this evidence of her changed soul, and at the freedom which had come like a lightning flash out of the heavens.

Just yet she dared not surrender to the thought of her love, to the intimate and terrific sweetness of it, to the deluge that must sweep away all before it. She must make forever hers the truth of herself, of the fate that could no longer be miserable and could never have a tragic end. . . . She understood Adam's love. He was all love. He loved every creature on the desert, the beasts of men, even this illegitimate brother with all his malignance and corrupt maturity. That explained Wansfell, the Wanderer.

Ruth would never have the past changed now, were that possible. By the memory of the past she might climb to the eagle's crag.

Wansfell, the Wanderer, that was to say the desert. The same supreme force that had moulded her stairs of sand had fashioned the boy Adam Larey into the man Wansfell.

Out of the boundlessness of her woman's heart, that vessel of perennial and eternal fertility, she must give to the desert that had saved him, give good for evil, give in place of the hate that had been a cancer in her breast, love—love for its ghastliness, its mutability, its ruthless cruelty and its eternal beauty, its driving iron to the Godlike in man.

14

Days passed that were happy ones for Ruth Virey. There was a week of unprecedented fine weather, for June in that low country. The desert seemed to be silent, watchful, waiting.

Ruth saw Adam every night, and one day, when the heat was tempered by a rain storm in the north, Merryvale took her out to Adam's hidden camp in the rock fastnesses. It was the wildest and weirdest place Ruth ever visited. A cataclysm in bygone ages had riven and scattered the stone crust of the earth; and the subsequent weathering had worn short canyons deep between splintered cliffs.

Adam helped her climb high, to the point where he had stood to watch for her. Part of the way Adam carried her, as he had often carried her mother in Death Valley; and for Ruth the experience was both sweet and sad.

From this height the view transcended that from Lost Lake. Ruth might never have looked at the desert, she thought. The whole ninety miles of silver sand dunes lay beneath her; and she caught her breath at sight of the endless slope of her stairs of sand.

Here, in the shade of an overhanging rock, with the magnificence and immensity of the desert filling her eyes, Ruth told Adam all that she had been. She was merciless to herself. She confessed the littlest and meanest of her motives. She bared her soul. No enemy of hers could ever have sought less favor for her than she sought for herself.

Then quite simply, without sentiment, or surrender to emotion, she told Adam of the gradual change which had come over her, from his arrival at Lost Lake to the last night in Yuma.

Here she gave way to the agitation that would not be denied; nevertheless she went on with her confession. Then when it came to exposing the uttermost depths of her heart she faltered and whispered, and at last gasped out the confession of her love.

Blind and spent then, she was snatched to Adam's breast and crushed there, and kissed with a savage abandon that once she had dared to dream of. She had repudiated a fruition of that dream, because of her unworthy past.

At sunset she was again with Merryvale, out on the red desert, returning home, with her body seemingly as light as thistledown, her feet like wings, her mind full of Adam's words of love, and wisdom for her future conduct.

And the next day Guerd Larey came back to Lost Lake with a string of freighters, stagecoaches, covered wagons, the van of the railroad workers.

The desert seemed to have broodingly awaited this day of Larey's return. For it let loose the blasts of the sand-furnaces, the ghastly shades and shadows of the wastelands.

Ruth was kept closely confined by the whirling clouds of sand and the intolerable burning heat. In the evening Merryvale told her that Larey had returned sober, but showed the effects of debauch and mental strain. They waited under the trees a long time for Adam, and waited in vain. Perhaps the heat and the crowded post had kept him away. Merryvale was told that the advance guard of freighters, surveyors, bridge-builders and masons, with an army of white laborers, Chinese, Mexicans, Indians, were on their way to Lost Lake, and the loneliness and quiet of the post were gone forever.

A new era set in for Lost Lake, and it was one that Ruth both welcomes and deplored. Tents and shacks and houses went up as if by magic. The increase of population went on, and it was good, Ruth thought. But she hated the rough element, and the hilarity of the night revellers.

Ruth kept her poise and peace, though the torrid summer had fallen, and she had to content herself with seeing Adam less, and writing notes to him, which Merryvale delivered at night. The days passed swiftly for her, because she lived her dream, and denied the outside influences.

Larey kept to the post, a changed man, Merryvale said: hard-working, hard-thinking, wary yet friendly to all, with ponderous brow behind which there was surely a seething brain. He made no attempt to see Ruth.

The day that Hunt went back to the post, once more to work with Larey, was an ominous one for Ruth. He had spared her, perhaps gladly, any confidences regarding his renewed relation with Larey. The shrewd Merryvale, growing more brooding and watchful every day, shook his head distrustfully. Ruth concluded he had more on his mind than worry. When she asked him point-blank if he was confiding wholly in her, the answer was not to her liking, not that it intimated any immediate trouble for her, but that it roused her to wonder if there was any dark growing project in Merryvale's mind.

That night in the gloom of the *palo verdes,* waiting for Adam, she deliberated on the situation as it stood. She sensed something she could not analyze. It was an invisible intangible pressure from without. It had to do with the torrid day, the sultry night, the return of her grandfather to the post and his assertions of the friendly reception he had there, the sombreness of Merryvale, the Indians and hard-faced unfamiliar men who sometimes peeped at her through the fence. Nature and the desert were bringing the festering sore of Lost Lake to a head. And the thorn in its flesh was Guerd Larey.

The advent of Adam checked the current of her thought.

"Where is Merryvale?" asked Adam, after greeting her.

' "He's usually around at this hour. Perhaps you'll find him in his tent. But, Adam, he has become strange. He worries me."

"I've noticed it," returned Adam, thoughtfully. "However, it may not amount to anything. He is growing old. And these last days have been trying."

Adam added that he would slip down to the spring to fill his canteen, and then see if Merryvale was there. While Adam was gone Ruth pondered over the inference she had deduced from his concern about Merryvale. Was he afraid Merryvale might kill Guerd Larey? And then a cold sensation followed—giving rise to a grim thought that between Adam and Merryvale and herself it did not appear Guerd Larey would live long enough to further his nefarious schemes.

Like a noiseless shadow Adam stole back to Ruth's side, to deposit his canteens on the ground.

"He wasn't there."

"Then he'll come presently," she returned.

"Ruth, I've got to tell you something. On my way here, not far from the gate there, I almost stepped on a man lying flat on the ground. I think he heard my steps, but couldn't see me, so he lay down."

"What did you do?" she asked with a stirring of pulses.

"I nearly choked the life out of him, trying to make him talk. But I couldn't. He was a greaser. It's pretty dark but I'll know him again. I didn't want to kill him, for he might not have meant any ill to you or me. So I let him go."

"Mexicans and Indians are always sneaking around," replied Ruth. "They always were. But lately I'm suspicious. Perhaps it is silly."

"Yes. But just the same be more careful than ever," he advised. "So will I be. I ought not come often, yet when I have to come for water it would seem overcautious not to see you."

"See me whenever you come," she said. "I shall not

leave the porch again unless Merryvale is with me."

They had their stolen hour in the shadow of the *palo verdes,* and prolonged it until Merryvale arrived, stealthily creeping to them from the inside of the fence.

It seemed that Adam was loathe to leave her, though he did not say so in words. Perhaps Ruth's portent of some untoward thing had communicated itself to him. At length he accompanied her to the end of the porch, and kissed her goodbye, which was unusual with him, then went back to join Merryvale.

Ruth stood awhile at her door, fearful of the night, of the opaque gloom of the desert. She had arisen above material fears. But out there gloomed inscrutable mystery. Only an occasional gust of hot dust-encumbered wind, whipped over the oasis. When it swooped down to the dim lights of the post it had the substance of fine snow. Dark figures passed to and fro. The roar of the saloons rose faintly.

It was the void out there that fascinated Ruth, the dark space whence swept the variable wind. Night, and the moaning wind or the dead silence! It seemed impossible that human beings could be isolated here, savagely surrounded by an untamed hostile desert. Ruth realized the futility of their lives. How fear of them conquered their rapacious instincts, over-developed in that harsh environment, let alone the ceaseless compressing influence of this desolate land!

The windy day had brought one of the dark nights, when there was no sky, no stars, only the thick moving gloom overhead.

Ruth felt as loath to go indoors as Adam had been to leave her. There was something neither could fathom. Ruth could never again feel herself as a tiny grain of sand tossed and blown by the winds of circumstance; nevertheless there abided a stunning sense of helplessness in the things over which she had no control. Once inside her room with the heavy bar in place, in the blackness and close atmosphere, she felt removed from a nameless peril that had loomed like the canopy of night. But that sense of safety did not extend to those few individuals with whom her life was indissolubly bound.

She went to bed without the use of a lamp. The casement of her window let in the grayness of the night, the omnipresent fragrance of sand and cactus and rock, the occasional discordant sounds from the post, and the desert loneliness. No longer did she mind loneliness or heat or wind, or any of the other things that had once been nightmares. There was nothing hideous any more, except the natures of some men. And she was reminded of Adam's story of the one-eyed female creature of Tecopah, more hideous than any man, more terrible than any beast. Ruth could no longer hate the idea of such an unsexed and debased being. How easily she herself might have sunk to such depths! The round of circumstance, the lack or failure of love, the blasting desert—these could make of any woman something lower than the lowest man. As for herself she was on the stairway to the stars.

Ruth always awoke these days at a late hour, and at the low ebb of her vitality, caused by the enervating influence of the summer heat. And this particular morning there was the weight of the preceding night's morbid visitations. Ruth had to combat all these, and extreme lassitude, and sluggish blood, and a weary questioning wonder at the limpness of her hands. But effort and movement wore these sensations away.

Opening her door Ruth faced the white daylight, and her first sight, as always, rested upon the far-stepping silver sand dunes. Her second was suddenly attracted to a group of men at the gate.

She called her grandfather. He did not answer. Ruth knocked at his door, opened it and entered. He was not there, and he had not slept in the bed.

In an instant Ruth was stung palpitatingly alive. Catastrophe had fallen, like the lightning flash of the desert. She did not need to see Merryvale come sombrely and haltingly up the path.

"Ruth, somethin' turrible—has happened," he said, in a husky tone.

"Grandpa!" she cried.

"Yes. . . . An' shore I hate to tell you, Ruth. But you must bear up. . . . He's daid!"

Ruth's legs gave way under her, and she fell into a chair. For several moments she could not find her voice.

"Dead!" she whispered at last. "Poor grandad! . . . He had been ailing lately. And I did so little. . . . Oh, I—I can't realize. . . . Was he ill, Merryvale? Was it one of his old attacks of acute indigestion?"

"No, Ruth. I wish to Gawd it had been. But he was killed murdered!"

Ruth turned icy cold, frozen doubly by fact and imagination.

"Somebody hit him behind the ear with a heavy stone or club. He was knocked so his haid fell under water. We caint say whether the blow killed him or he drowned. But it shore doesn't alter the fact that he was murdered."

"How horrible!" burst out Ruth, flaming now where she had been frozen. "Who—who did it?"

"Who indeed? That's what stumps me. The post's full of greasers, redskins, chinks, an' riff-raff from Yuma. He'd been robbed of money, watch, all he had of value. That might mean nothin' an' then again it might mean a lot."

"Merryvale! . . . Your mind runs like mine?" she gasped, with a hand covering her mouth.

"I reckon. We're both liable to lay anythin' to one particular source. It might be wrong. But I caint help myself," replied Merryvale, almost with despair.

"Adam! Get Adam!" she exclaimed, wildly.

"Wal, first off I thought of gettin' Adam heah," he said, deliberating. "But that wouldn't do no good, 'cept to comfort you, an' it might lead to harm. I'm going to find out who killed Hunt. If I know these yellow dawgs that won't be no hard matter."

"What—what shall I do?"

"Bear it as best you can, lass, an' leave your grandfather for me to look after. You mustn't see him. I'll have him taken to the post, an' get the priest, an' give him decent burial down there in the little buryin' ground."

"Shouldn't he be taken to—to—Yuma?" faltered Ruth, tearfully.

"It could be done, with heaps of trouble an' expense. But what's the use? Lost Lake is as good a place to bury a man as Yuma. It'd suit me better, if I had a choice. Leave this to me, Ruth dear."

"It's—such an—awful surprise," replied Ruth, breaking down.

"Go ahaid an' cry, lass. It'll do you good. Then brace up an' see this heah trouble as it is. We're on the desert, where few men die in their beds. Your grandpa was old and failin' fast. It's a pity. . . . But it happened. We're in deeper now, Ruth than ever, an' you must not give in."

"Merryvale, I'm shocked to my heart. . . . But—but I'll stand it. Do the best you can for—for him. And let me know if there's anything I can do."

"Ruth, I'm goin' down to the post. It suits me to be the first to tell Guerd Larey aboot this," replied Merryvale, with a queer intent flash of eyes, and he turned away with bent wagging head.

Ruth did not see him again until nearly twilight.

"Wal, it's over, all us poor mortals can do," he sighed, wiping a lined and saddened face. "An' I'll say a daid man doesn't mean no more heah than in Yuma."

Ruth asked a few questions about the disposition of her grandfather's body. And Merryvale, more than usually the verbose talker, told in detail the events of a long harrowing day.

"An' now he lays deep under a *palo verde*," concluded Merryvale, with strong emotion. "Too deep for the desert winds to uncover him. But they'll moan and whisper over him in the night. He'll not lie alone, Ruth. No grave on the desert is lonely. There are hosts out on the sands in the daid of night, wanderin' down the naked shingle of the desert. May he rest in peace. Lord knows he had no peace heah. Lost Lake was no place for Caleb Hunt."

Presently he remembered that he bore a letter to her from Guerd Larey.

"I had half a mind not to give it to you," he said. "But I shore was keen to know what he's up to now."

"Merryvale, what did he say and look like, when you told him?" asked Ruth, in low voice, as she gazed as if fascinated by a snake at the letter in her hands.

"Ruth, I'm shore bound to admit that Larey is innocent of any complicity in your grandpa's death—or he's the deepest, slickest devil this side of hell," declared Merryvale in long drawn-out speech.

"He may indeed be innocent. I hope to heaven he is. But just the same he's that last you called him," returned Ruth.

"Wal, we are agreed on some things, lass. I reckon Adam will not see this heah as we do. Sometimes I believe he blinds himself on purpose. But read the letter, Ruth."

She broke the seal and the clear bold handwriting took her back three years, to the time when letters from Larey were frequent. This epistle was one of condolence, and on the face of it was kindly, courteous, sympathetic, without in the least encroaching upon her with personal intimations. Life was hard on the desert, but never really appreciated as such until it came home in loss of someone beloved. Larey inclined to the opinion that some Mexican whom Hunt had refused credit at the post, or some Indian or Indians long nursing a grudge over the water rights, had committed the crime. He would personally endeavor to apprehend and punish the murderer. And he reminded Ruth that she now had greater responsibilities than ever—that she must not grieve unduly over this loss.

Ruth perused this amazing epistle twice, and then read it to Merryvale.

"Wal, I'll be doggoned!" he ejaculated, scratching his head. "Larey is too slick for me to follow. That shore rings like a gentleman. Yet we know his soul is blacker than the ace of spades. Ruth, what do you make of that?"

"I can't be fair to Larey," she replied. "It's not what I know, but what I feel."

"Wal, I believe in justice for any man. But Larey stands committed before us. An' it sticks in my craw that he had somethin' to do with your grandpa's death. His takin' Hunt back at the post on a new deal, lettin' it be seen by all how friendly he'd got— that I shore never swallowed whole. An' this heah letter is just another blind. . . . There, Ruth, you have an old desert-hawk's idee of Larey."

Ruth did not commit herself into betrayal of deductions more definitely inimical to Larey than Merryvale's.

"Adam will have to hear about grandfather," she said, earnestly. "But don't hint of your suspicions to him."

"No fear. I reckon I don't want Wansfell spoilin' my game," declared Merryvale. "An' that is to find out who did this dirty job."

Later when Adam came he sat with Ruth for many moments, while Merryvale paced his beat close by, and neither of them found courage to tell him. But he soon sensed Ruth's stress, and bent low in the shadow to see the pallor of her face. Then the sad story had to come out. He sat silent for a long while, thinking —thinking. Then he threw off the spell, and talked so beautifully to Ruth about age and death and loss, and the desert, which was a mother to all who came to her at the end, that she wept away the tight clamping ice from around her heart. If Adam entertained suspicion of Guerd Larey he did not manifest it in the slightest.

Ruth marveled anew at this human phenomenon of the desert. His mercy, his forbearance, his nature too great for suspicion, were in direct proportion to the avalanche of his terrible wrath and vengeance, when once they were loosed.

"Ruth, this property is now yours," he said, seriously. "Of course at this sad hour you do not want to think of the responsibilities and riches left you. Yet you must. This water right is very valuable now. If you held on to it for some years it would bring a fortune."

"What do you advise?" she asked.

"I would sell it now."

"Then we could go far away?" she queried.

"Yes. As far as you liked."

"Would you go with me?"

"My dear, do you remember the vow of your Biblical namesake? That is mine to you."

"Oh, I would give the place away," she cried.

Merryvale heard and took strong exception to Ruth's rash statement. Her grandfather had suffered and died for this desert water hole. She must never sacrifice it. She must never let Guerd Larey buy it for a song. Therefore she had still a duty, aside from the normal need of money to live upon in some happier environment.

"Merryvale is right, Ruth," added Adam. "You shall not throw this property away. Nor be robbed of it!"

Between them they won Ruth's mind from grief and indifference; and revived in her a spirit of defiance toward the man who would undoubtedly seek to coerce her.

Adam at length felt satisfied that they had roused Ruth to an unconquerable state; and taking up his canteens he strode off into the dark lonely melancholy desert night.

15

Ruth, in going over her grandfather's books and papers, was astounded at the written proof of the large sums of money he had from time to time advanced Larey.

Caleb Hunt had always been very methodical and painstaking and sincere in all matters of business, never trusting to his memory or the other man's, and always having deals, loans, debts and purchases put down in black and white. Ruth knew that if there were any debts, which she doubted, they would be as faithfully recorded as other details. Careful search and reading failed to discover anything owing to Guerd Larey.

She made a mental reservation that she would have something to say to Larey when he presented the claims, which he would do sooner or later. Ruth likewise mastered the complicated bookkeeping of her grandfather in regard to the sale of water. Here another surprise awaited her. Hunt owned the only supply of water at Lost Lake, that was to say, the only spring, the fine flow of water called Indian Wells. The post had paid nothing for months. The stagecoach company had paid up to the first of the month. The freighters were also in arrears. Both the post and the freighting, so far as Lost Lake was concerned, were under the supervision of Larey and Hunt—according to the papers available. There was a new contract, made with the railroad construction contractors, upon which Larey's name did not ap-.

pear. Hunt had already received a considerable sum of money, which Ruth found intact. The water brought more money than she had any idea of. For the rest the few whites living at Lost Lake, and the Indians and Mexicans, were never charged anything for the water they used.

Ruth did not see fit to make any changes in Hunt's way of conducting business, except to demand prompt payment from the post and freight company. She sent Merryvale with the bill, rather puzzled at the expression on his face as he left her. Upon his return he looked as black as a thundercloud.

"Ruth, I busted right into the post where Larey was drinkin' with some men," declared Merryvale. "You should have seen his look when I handed him the envelope. Why, his hands jest trembled. Ruth, that villain shore loves you. . . . Wal, he read the bill, turned red as a beet, an' cussed somethin' awful. Then he haw-hawed like a gleeful devil."

"But what did he say?" queried Ruth, curiously, as Merryvale ended.

"Wal, that's what riled me," rejoined Merryvale. "He tore up the bill, an' right before those men, strangers to me an' a hard-lookin' crew, he said: 'Tell my wife she'll soon be usin' her precious water to bathe my feet!' "

Ruth felt blank for an instant, and then, as her blood boiled, she restrained the outburst that flashed so swiftly to her lips.

"Merryvale, is there any way to make him pay?" she asked.

"Heah on this desert? Lord no! There's no law except might."

"Very well. You turn off the water that's piped to the post."

"Shore. I can do that. But Larey will only have it turned on again. An' then, if I turn it off a second time—wal, I'll need to look round pretty pert to keep from gettin' knocked in the haid."

"Try it anyway. If necessary I'll go down there my-self, and stand by that pipe."

"Lass, you could, an' I reckon it'd have effect, but you caint hang around the pipes an' water-trough all the time."

"I could until Larey's outfit got good and thirsty," retorted Ruth.

"Wal, shore Larey himself ain't drinkin' much wa-ter these heah days. Ruth, his thinkin' is done. His mind is made up. . . . An' heah's another idee aboot the water you never figgered on. Suppose the freight-ers an' the hosses come in off that desert, 'most daid of thirst. Could you keep from lettin' them have wa-ter to drink?"

"No! Of course I couldn't," cried Ruth, fierce with the hopelessness of her situation. "But no matter. I'll fight for my rights."

"See heah, Ruth, ain't it all narrowin' down to Adam?" shot Merryvale, with squinted gleaming eyes on her.

Ruth felt the blood rushing back to her heart, leav-ing her chilled; and she looked her mute distress.

"What's the use? We caint do anythin' with this Larey. We caint keep his deviltry from Adam much longer. 'Pears to me we are jest playin' tag with some-thin' stronger'n us."

"Merryvale, when I think facts, I get the same reac-tion as you," asserted Ruth, stern with herself. "But I live on hopes, prayers—on feeling that can't be put in words."

"Shore, but you caint stave this off much longer," returned Merryvale, stubbornly.

"This what?"

"Wal—this all, which ain't nothin' else but Guerd Larey."

"Dear friend, I must sacrifice everything, even my-self, if necessary, to keep Adam from killing this brother he loves."

"Ruth Virey, you shore won't get far with me on such talk as that. I mean this heah sacrificin' yourself talk. Don't let me heah that no more, or I'll fail you, one way or another."

"Merryvale! . . . Forgive me. But you know how wrought up I become, when that dreadful possibility threatens. It—it forces me to a logical, inevitable conclusion. But I *will not* be logical. I'll never let Adam face Guerd."

"Ruth, I'll tell you somethin," replied Merryvale. "I ketched Adam the other night peepin' into the post. He wanted a glimpse of Guerd. An' he got it, for I seen Guerd, too. I walked most a mile with Adam after that, an' he never knowed I was near."

"Oh, how strange!" exclaimed Ruth, with trembling lips. "Why did Adam do that?"

"Wal, I can figger only one reason. Adam was jest crazy to *see* Guerd's face once more."

"Let us—talk of other things," replied Ruth, haltingly. "We've work to do. . . . What was it?—Merryvale, you must have a room in the house. I will take Grandad's, and you may have mine. Get some tools and a man to help you. There's an Indian who's a good carpenter. I want a door cut through the wall. Then I'll use grandad's room as a sitting-room, and have my bedroom open into it."

That evening made up for the trying day. Ruth always found strength in Adam. It was like looking up at a mountain. Many of her perplexities she had meant to confide in him, but when the opportunity afforded she forgot them. They began at first to discuss her problem there at Lost Lake, but soon left it for inconsequential talk that was yet the relief and happiness she needed. And they ended, with Ruth's arm locked in his, gazing silently out over the black spellbinding desert, and up at the magnificent blue dome with its myriads of white stars.

Two days of work and bustle around the house, with a woman's pleasure and satisfaction in fixing up new quarters for her comfort, passed swiftly, while Ruth gave but scant time to worry. Merryvale took up quarters in the little room that had been Ruth's.

"Reckon I'm gettin' old enough to sleep under a roof," he remarked. "My days on the desert are about spent."

On the morning of the third day Merryvale did not as usual putter round the house, working on repairs badly needed. He absented himself until nearly noon and when he returned, one look at him made Ruth's heart sink.

"Ruth, I hate to be a black buzzard soarin' around," he complained, almost coldly. "But I caint keep all the bad news to myself."

"Let me share it," she replied, bravely.

"Wal, I've been nosin' around an' carryin' a bottle to more'n one greaser an' Injun. An' I've got results. I've loosened the tongue of a greaser, an' found out enough to verify my suspicions. Larey was no doubt responsible for the murder of your grandfather. It caint never be laid at his door, because the half-breeds who committed the crime came from Yuma an' went back there. Neither fire nor whip could make this greaser tell their names. But I know enough. When I have more time I'll explain in detail how I've worked all this out."

"It doesn't shock me. It doesn't surprise me," replied Ruth, through tight cold lips.

"Wal, heah's some news that will," he went on, as if driven. "There's a bunch of hombres, riders from across the Arizona line scourin' the desert for Wansfell."

"*Merryvale!*" cried Ruth, leaping up.

"Yes, an' it come straight from Indian Jim, who heard Larey say it."

"Go at once! Warn Adam!"

"Shore, I'm goin' pronto. But Adam's a fox, an' leaves few tracks. You remember the soft sand an' the hard rock we crossed to go to his camp? Wal, he caint be tracked. An' that canyon is the best hidin' place I ever seen. So I'm not worryin' aboot them findin' him yet."

"Why would Larey want to put men on Adam's trail?" queried Ruth, fearfully.

"Reckon Larey figgers he caint carry out his plans with this heah Wansfell alive. An' so help him Gawd, he shore caint!"

"Wansfell—*alive?*" she whispered.

"Shore. Larey reckons your new spunk comes from this Wansfell who killed Collishaw an' snatched you from Stone. That's why he's left you alone. He's afraid of Wansfell. An' he wants him daid!"

"You must hurry to warn Adam."

"I'll be there in less'n an hour. . . . An' Ruth, neither you nor I—nor anythin' can keep Adam away from heah any longer."

"But those Arizona riders!"

"Wal, Ruth, there's a heap of difference between them hombres huntin' to surprise Wansfell, an' Wansfell huntin' them."

"Find him—tell him I said—come!" burst out Ruth, wildly.

Merryvale wheeled down the path. And the moment he was out of sight Ruth bit her lips to keep from screaming for him to come back. What was it that had happened? The lull before the storm had ended. The vague misgivings—the strange dreams, the random intuitions, the intelligent reasonings, all had their answer.

Ruth faced the desert with the gathering might of a passion that for weeks had been fostered and kindled and damned in the unplumbed depths of her. The wasteland out there seemed to leap at her with all its ferocity. In the far distance the red ranges burned with dark and sinister fire; the mirages gleamed and paled and shimmered, and burned white, to fade and gleam again; the yellow dust-devils rose and whirled like furies across the barrens; the silver stairs of sand shone dim through the heat veils, unreal, illusive, deceitful, calling, treacherous.

Ruth had reached the end of trust in chance, hope, faith, in the mystery of retribution working out. It was imperative to match the spirit and brutality of the desert against the wretches who had thrived thereon, upon the men into whom had entered the flint and fire, the cactus and the poison sap.

That day or the next, or as soon as it pleased his snake-like patience, Guerd Larey would come to her and reveal himself, his lust, his belief in the success of his evil machinations. When that hour struck Ruth would be steeled to meet it. The longer Larey delayed the stronger, colder, fiercer she would be.

Meanwhile she could only wait.

The hours lengthened. Sunset, and Merryvale did not come! Night, and Adam failed her! She waited until a late hour, pacing the porch, and lastly her room, darkened and barred. She slept but little, and the voice of the desert haunted her.

The gray casement, dawn, and the sunrise! Wide-eyed she waited, and drove herself to those ministrations her physical being demanded. She saw her cheeks grow wan and thin, her eyes darken to bottomless gulfs. But night fell again and wore on endlessly, without her friends coming.

When another day dawned Ruth stood at the parting between her fear and her faith. Between the intelligence that spelled catastrophe and the sixth sense that sublimely held Wansfell as invulnerable!

She waited. It was one of the unbearable days—torrid with heat, ghastly with its white wraiths, destroying to flesh, maddening to mind. She drunk water copiously, yet could not allay her thirst. She waited. Yet there were moments which broke the strain.

What the day foreshadowed came at last. Quick ringing footsteps of a man who brooked no opposition to his will!

Ruth's door was open. She had halted by the table. She had hidden something in a drawer. With a hand that had no tremor she opened it part way.

"Pedro, set my bags here," Guerd Larey's resonant voice. Ruth heard the thud of heavy articles being deposited upon the porch. An amazed query tried to wedge into her mind. It was dispelled by a shadow at the door.

Larey rapped. Ruth did not move so much as a flicker of an eyelash. She was close to the table. One movement of hand! The heat of the room swirled around her, entered her veins.

"Howdy, Ruth," he said, coolly. "I've fetched up my things to stay."

His effrontery seemed more than Ruth could bear. It whirled her to face him, her eyes blazing.

"What do you mean?" she demanded.

He did not reply. His brilliant green eyes were taking her in from face to feet, lingering over her. He was clean shaven, and he wore immaculate white, and knee-high Mexican boots, embroidered in flowery design. His silver-buckled belt did not hold a weapon. His shirt was open at the neck, exposing his magnificent breast, matted with hair. The flush on the olive tan of his face was not from drink. Shades and lines of dissipation were there, but almost obliterated by a glow, a radiance, a wonderful outward shining of an inward flame. Handsome still, like an evil god, he stood there, possessing Ruth with his snaky eyes.

"What do you mean?" repeated Ruth, cold level gaze on his.

"It's too noisy and uncomfortable at the post for me any more," he replied, leaving against the door. "So I've come up here to stay."

"You can't stay here."

"Why not?"

"Because this is my house and I will not have you in it."

"Wrong, Ruth. The property is mine, land, water, and house. Your grandfather owed me money. So I take possession right now."

"You lie, Guerd Larey. Can you show me any proof of my grandfather's owing you?"

"My word is proof enough."

"Your word? Good God, the vanity, the brazenness of you!"

Ruth's quick wit grasped the subtle and remarkable assurance of the man. He had played his cards and from his standpoint the game was won. He was but a cat toying with a mouse. No sentiment, no tenderness, no genuine longing, such as she had often before divined, emanated from his presence this day.

"Still the same sweet old wildcat," he returned mockingly. "Well, it suits me. Spit, scratch, bite, fight! I'll like it. . . . But you're pale, Ruth, a trifle thin. If it wasn't for your eyes!"

"Will you get out of here?" she demanded.

"No. I won't."

"I have not strength to throw you out. Will you rob me of my home? Force me out?"

"The place is mine, I told you."

"You thief! You greaser bandit! . . . You murderer!"

"Ruth, you always had a wicked tongue. It used to bother me. But you can't faze me now."

"I know what you've done, Guerd Larey," she said, hotly. "You had my grandfather made away with—to further your greed. Your loathesome lust! . . . Oh, you unspeakable monster!"

He laughed at her, though the olive tan of his face began to whiten.

"Now you're like your old self. You lovely piece of flesh! Your purple blazing eyes! Your swelling breasts! . . . I almost remember I loved you once."

Ruth felt the futility of words. Yet she could no more have silenced her voice than she could have stopped the raging of her heart.

"Loved!—You?—Why, you never loved even mother—or brother, did you?" she flung at him.

That strangely pierced his degenerate armor. He stared at her, wondering, for a second, aghast.

"By God, I never did," he retorted, with bitter brevity.

"Let me out of here," cried Ruth, fearing to trust herself longer. The word brother had unnerved her. This man was Adam's brother. Could she not escape—

surrender everything—flee from him and the madness of vengeance, as if from a pestilence?

"If you run I'll drag you back," he rasped out, with first show of passion. "Once I begged for your love. On my knees I begged. You could have made me a better man. But now I don't want your love, your surrender. I want you to fight like the cat you are. I want to beat you, violate you. . . . I'll make you cringe and crawl—you white piece of ice. You damned staring-eyed statue!"

He had come out with his ultimatum. The fire of him matched its terrible portent. A great outward stillness seemed to possess Ruth, while internally all was chaos, a multitude of galvanic currents charging toward the fatal act, through which only there could be freedom.

"Ice? Statue? . . . You should have asked Stone," she taunted him.

"Damn you!" he glared at her. "Fling that in my face, will you? . . . You hussy! You cheat! . . . I should have killed that fool. But I thought you were only playing with him."

"I was, Guerd," she returned, with mockery. She had found the vulnerable place in his hard hide. Jealousy had always been his weakness. Who could stand before such jealousy? She would shake him as the storm shook the oak. "I played with Stone, as with all the others—until Wansfell came."

Larey's flesh quivered spasmodically. His green eyes took a lurid sheen. He slid into the room, back against the wall.

"Wansfell? That desert rat! . . . You—You—"

"He is the most wonderful man in all the world," she cried, and her voice rang with the sincerity of her feeling.

"You're crazy. This desert has acted queer on you," he declared, thickly, uncomprehendingly. "Not satisfied with young men like Stone! Or men like *me!* . . . You seek the abnormal—the hideous. Ruth Virey, you're a depraved woman!"

"I am what the desert has made me."

"But Wansfell—that wandering tramp! That desert hermit madman! They tell me he is old, gray, like a bald eagle."

"He is younger than you. And oh, indeed he is an eagle!"

"Sanchez called him a saviour of virgins. . . . Wansfell, the Wanderer. For years that name has haunted me. . . . Damn his soul! I wish I had . . . But, Ruth, I ask you again. You can't be *serious* about this giant beggar who thinks he's a knight of the desert. Who goes about redressing human wrongs! Who has the instinct to kill!"

"Serious?" queried Ruth, with slow sweet smile, and tone that did not require her passion to deceive. "I rather think I am serious. Once—the only time in my life. The first—the last! . . . I have awakened. I love Wansfell. I worship him. I am his slave. . . . I would bathe his feet with the water out there—that you swore I'd use on you . . . Bah, you toad! You slimy thing! . . . And I would wipe his feet dry with my hair."

Larey's face was distorted and purple, and his breath whistled.

"Woman!" he burst out, hoarsely. "Listen. You *were* his slave, then. For I have had him shot!"

The man was terrific in his sincerity, in an agony that was half fiendish joy. He blazed the truth. Before it Ruth staggered back, stricken to the soul, almost swooning. But her own hate would not relinquish clutch on the moment. She rallied.

"Yes, by heaven!" he continued, in husky exultation. "I had your Wansfell shot. My men have been on his trail three days. And this morning a messenger came. They'd got him. I had paid them beforehand. So they were off to cross the border . . . And he was your lover? Wansfell, the Wanderer! I sought only to free myself of a dangerous man. A protector of fair virtue! And all the time he was your lover. You white-throated harlot! You shiny-haired reptile! You destroyer of men! Your lover!"

Ruth swept close to him, to look into the writhing soul of him, to pierce him at the last, mortally, beyond recall.

"My lover. Yes. And he was more. . . . *Your brother!*"

Larey certainly thought she had gone mad. But the icy hiss of her voice and its rending content directly changed the current of his passion.

"You're out of your head," he growled, with evil speculation.

"Wansfell is Adam Larey," she shrilled.

"Liar! Shut up, or I'll—"

"Do you remember Margarita Arallanes? Do you remember the wheel on the sandy bank, where you stole that Mexican girl from Adam? Do you remember *why* Adam fought you in that gambling-hall at Picacho? Do you remember who put out Collishaw's eye?"

"Hell! I never forgot!" gasped out Larey.

"Did not Sanchez tell you Wansfell shot out Collishaw's other eye—that night at Yuma?"

Larey rallied from that swift volley, but white to the lips, he eyed her in awe, and something of horror.

"A trick to add to his name," he replied, doggedly. "Wansfell had heard that story, no doubt. And he has filled your mind with it. But you can't make me swallow it."

"Oh, can't I though?"

"No, you white fiend. No! . . . Make that wandering lover of yours my brother—who starved on the desert eighteen years ago? . . . No, Adam Larey is dead. And I'd give ten years of my life to kick his bleached skull out of the sand."

"Wansfell was Adam Larey!" she cried, with such triumphant exultance that he flamed anew.

"Proof! or I'll choke you quiet," he thundered.

Back from him and to the table Ruth glided, every move like bending steel.

"Guerd Larey, you bore Adam an inhuman hate. You hated your mother. From childhood you nursed your implacable jealousy. You tortured Adam with his mother's shame."

Larey's rolling eyes fixed upon this skeleton ghost of the past. His jaw dropped. His face changed convulsively, turned livid, and set in appalling expectancy.

"You bastard! *Bastard!* BASTARD!"

"Hell!" he screamed, as one whose flesh had sheathed a naked blade.

Ruth pulled open the table drawer and snatched out the gun. As she swept it round Larey bounded like a cat, struck up her hand just at the flash and report. Then he seized her arm and wrung it, sending the weapon flying. Violently he swung her away from him against the couch, where she sank. With baleful eyes riveted on her, with his hair like the mane of a beast, he moved to kick the door shut.

16

Merryvale filled his canteen, and hiding it under his coat he took an opposite direction from the post, down through the *palo verdes* and mesquite. Making a wide detour out of sight of any watchful eye, he headed at last for the wildly broken rock country to the west.

The day was hot, but the air free of blowing dust. Merryvale sensed that he had begun to fail during this last trying week. It was like something cold creeping up from his feet. And similarly his mood had altered. He had turned to Adam as the last resource. What days of racking pain might have been spared Ruth! Always Merryvale had seen clearly. For eighteen years it had been written that Adam must kill his brother. The hour had struck. And Merryvale's old slow heart thumped at the thought and his blood warmed and grew hot, and burned out the coldness of his veins. Old though he was the passion to see Adam beat and tear and crush the life out of Guerd made Merryvale young again.

He reached the end of the escarpment, and started down the slope into lower country. The sand had given place to stone. It appeared that the mountain range to the west had reached down a long arm into the lowland, a broken mass of rock like yellow lava, cut by the elements into every conceivable kind of break.

Entering the mouth of a canyon Merryvale trudged on, absorbed in his sombre brooding, yet aware of the changing growing ruggedness of the region. It was infernally hot down there, and the shade of stone walls was most welcome. Twice he had recourse to his canteen, and as he tipped it up he saw the splintered rock slide far above, where Adam had taken Ruth one day. Merryvale had forgotten to signal Adam, and now, if he were up there on the heights it was impossible to locate him. Merryvale would press on to his camp.

Suddenly a man stepped out from behind a rock to level a cocked gun at Merryvale.

"Howdy, old geezer. Hands up!" he called, with gruff grim humor.

Merryvale obeyed. And his breast seemed to cave in and his heart to turn to lead.

"Who are you? An' what you want?" queried Merryvale, quaveringly.

"Me? Aw, I'm a bold bad bandit from Arizonie. An' I'm invitin' you up the canyon to a picnic."

Merryvale's keen scrutiny took in a sturdy man of middle age, with a face that was a record of blasting desert years. Merryvale noted particularly the ruffian's eyes, gray, bloodshot, hard as steel, indicative of extraordinary character.

"Move on," he ordered, and as Merryvale complied he stepped in behind, and jerked Merryvale's gun from his belt. "Now you can drop your hands, pardner."

Merryvale strode up the canyon, head bent, eyes on the hot yellow stone and gravel. He had been too late. Larey's hirelings had found Adam's hiding place, and had killed or captured him. Merryvale's tortured mind reverted to Ruth. What would become of her? It was heart-breaking. Merryvale all but sank in the sand, spent, finished, ready and glad to have the bandit end his misery. Yet his spirit could not wholly surrender. He had seen so many miracles on the desert. What did this outlaw and his accomplices know of Wansfell? If they had not killed him from ambush or in a fight they were still in peril. Merryvale thought of the terrible battle in which Wansfell had rescued Dismukes from the claim-jumpers in Death Valley.

From time to time Merryvale felt a prod from behind.

"Say, Mister Arizonie, I'm doin' the best walkin' I can. You're a younger man than me."

"Air you tired livin'?" queried the man, roughly facetious.

"Wal, to be honest, I reckon I am," replied Merryvale, with a sigh.

"Air you the big fellar's pard?"

"What big fellar?"

"The one we got tied up hyar."

"Yes, I am," said Merryvale, immensely relieved and glad at this information.

"You're out of luck, old man. Fer the boss has orders to shoot your pard. An' you'll come in fer a pluggin' too."

"Whose orders?"

"Say now, ain't you the wise old fool? But I don't know that it matters. Fact is I ain't acquainted with whose orders they was an' what they was fer. Damn queer deal to me. An' I've had all I want of this hellhole in the rocks."

"Shore is pretty hot," agreed Merryvale. "Caint we rest a bit. I've drink, both water an' whiskey."

"I should smile we can rest a bit. You set there . . . An' I'll have the water first, thank you."

Merryvale watched this loquacious bandit wipe his wet face with a dirty scarf, and then drink lustily from the canteen, all the while holding the cocked gun on his knee, in dangerous alignment with Merryvale.

"I reckon you needn't cover me with that gun. Leastways you can let the hammer down," complained Merryvale.

"Sure. It is onconsiderate of me. You're a harmless old fellar, an' I ain't stuck on this job."

Merryvale clutched at straws. He knew men. And this bandit radiated something the best and worst of western characters had in common. Again Merryvale's mind began to cast off fatality and to work.

Presently he was ordered to move on again. Another long arduous toiling over rocks and washes, winding through recesses of the dividing canyons, brought them to a spreading of the gloomy walls. Merryvale smelled smoke. There were bits of green and yellow brush, cactus and stunted *palo verde*.

They came to a camp in the shade of a bulging wall. It indeed was a meagre outfit, as dry camps on the desert were likely to be. Four men sat playing cards. Two of these had their shirts off.

"Hey, can't you heah anythin'?" called Merryvale's captor, as they approached.

A big man, hairy of breast, with sallow cadaverous face and eyes of a ghoul, got up to greet the speaker.

"If it ain't Stark! Howdy do? An' who's the stranger?"

"He's the old geezer you said you was told to look out fer," replied Stark.

"Good. Tie him up an' let him be company for the big fellar. Then go back on watch again."

"Not me, Brooks," rejoined Stark. "You can send somebody else."

"Seein' we got the two of 'em we don't need any watch, except over them," replied Brooks, and squatted back to the game.

"Say, boss, what's the idee stayin' longer?" queried Stark, gruffly.

"That's my bizness. You rope the old gent an' come sit in the game," was the answer.

Stark bound Merryvale's hands behind his back, using first a scarf and then over that a stout cord.

"Come over hyar to your pard, an' don't make any queer moves. Savvy?" commanded Stark, and led Merryvale a few paces back toward the wall where Adam lay bound and propped on his side. Merryvale sat down, gladly, with his back to a slab of stone; and he bent anxious eyes upon his friend. Adam looked the same as usual. Certainly he had not been injured. When Stark want back to his comrades Merryvale spoke.

"How are you, Adam?"

"Ruth!" replied Adam, hurriedly.

"Wal, she was all right this mawnin'. Shore full of grit. An' I believe she'll hold her own for a little anyhow. But we haven't any time to lose gettin' back to her."

"Listen," rejoined Adam, whispering. "This is the Arizona gang I saw in Yuma at Sanchez's. Brooks is an outlaw. He knew me years ago. I can't place the others. But it's plain Stark is the man most to be reckoned with. I could break loose any time. But there's been no chance yet."

"Don't make a rash move. Let's wait. Somethin' may develop. This heah Stark seems square, an' he's sore. Let me work on him," returned Merryvale, in like whisper.

"Pard, if you ever thought hard do it now," groaned Adam.

"What's their game?"

"They left their horses at the post, and tracked me here. They've water but little food. Guerd, of course, put them on my trail. They surprised me, held me up, took my gun. Brooks recognized me, but kept it to himself. He's a deep one. He would doublecross Guerd as quick as carry out his orders to shoot me. But Brooks knew me as a prospector. He thinks I've found gold in this canyon, and that Guerd is after it. But for this, I'd probably have been shot at once."

"Ahuh! An' you've been helpin' Brooks think you have a gold claim up heah?"

"Yes. And all the time waiting for a chance to jump them."

"Keep on waitin'," huskily whispered Merryvale. "Don't risk your life unless you see a good chance. Remember Ruth! She may have hell with Larey, but that's not as bad as you bein' daid. Shore he'll not kill her."

Merryvale composed himself to wait and to listen and to think, while pretending to sleep. The hours dragged for him and Adam, though manifestly not for the gamblers.

At sundown Stark fetched them some biscuits and meat.

"You can slip me a nip of whiskey," said Stark. "I ain't mean enough to rob you of it all."

"Shore. Take a good big nip. My pard an' me keep it only for snake-bite," replied Merryvale, indicating where the flash rested in his pocket. Stark took his drink, but a sparing one.

"Thanks, old boy," he said.

"Say, excuse me, Stark, but I'm shore curious to know why a fine fellar like you is mixed up with this outfit."

"Haw! Haw! Thet's good!—See hyar, friend. Brooks an' his pardners are pretty easy-goin' fellars compared to me."

"Wal, shore that's what I meant," returned Merryvale, enigmatically.

Night fell. The bandits, having but little firewood to burn for a light, abandoned their game. One of them sat guard over the prisoners. He was surly and he knew his job. The moon crossed the belt of sky, flooding the canyon. Merryvale slept by fits and starts. Several times he heard Adam roll over, once to touch him. Some time during the night the guard was relieved by a bandit, wakeful as the other, and even harder of aspect.

Day came at last. And Adam, who no doubt had remained awake all night, fell asleep, until roused by Stark, who came with coffee and biscuits.

That morning ushered in another gambling session, in which Stark took part. Adam and Merryvale were permitted to walk along the cliff, between the camp and the wall. The thing that sustained Merryvale was a feeling he assimilated from his patient imperturbable comrade. Adam radiated inevitableness. Strange facts, opportunities gravitated toward him.

During the tedious hot hours the gamblers quarrelled a good deal. Merryvale suffered from cramp in his bound arms. Towards the close of that day Brooks came to Adam.

"Ain't you gettin' tired?" he queried, not without wonder.

"Not very," replied Adam.

"Humph!—Air you goin' to take me where your gold strike is?"

"I guess not."

"Why ain't you?"

"You'll kill me whether I take you or don't. So why should I make you rich?"

"No reason atall," returned Brooks, with a grim laugh. "I'd figger the same. But, Wansfell, supposin' I let you go?"

"That's different. But you'd have to make it so I'd trust you."

"Larey told me you'd struck it rich out hyar," went on the bandit leader, evidently hazarding a lie. "He's sure got all the old Mohave claim-jumpers beat. I'm tellin' you I've got all that's comin' from him. An' if you can show me some of the yellow dirt I'll let you an' your pard go, providin' of course you stay hyar until I get away from the post with my hosses."

"Brooks, I tell you I'm afraid to trust you," replied Adam, with apparent irritation.

"Natural. But I've nothin agin you. Fact is I always had a sneakin' pleasure in what I heerd about you. Now why should I want to kill you? Word given to as low-down a hombre as this Larey wouldn't count. Not with me. Think it over some more. My grub an' water are low, an' my men are stewin' hyar."

At this juncture Stark approached with a meagre bit of bread and meat, which he set down between the prisoners and then untied their hands. That, for Merryvale, at least, was immeasurable relief.

"Say, Brooks, what's the need of keepin' these men tied up day an' night? It's cruelty to animals," said Stark.

"Huh! You wouldn't ask why if you knowed thet man as I do," replied Brooks, pointing to Adam.

"Oh, wouldn't I?" returned Stark, doubtfully. "Excuse me."

Another night passed, quicker and less wearying to Merryvale for the reason that he could not keep awake.

The third day dawned hot, with wind at sunrise. Soon the sand began to fly.

"They won't last out this day," whispered Adam. "It'll be good or bad for us."

By mid-morning the canyon was a veiled vestibule of hell. Merryvale rested quietly, moving when he had to, and awaited developments. Adam lay propped against the wall, his eagle gaze on the restless, irritable bandits. They tried to keep at their game but it broke up. Brooks had manifestly won back most of the ill-gotten gains he had shared with his companions.

The reflection of heat from the canyon wall became blistering. By lulls and gusts the dusty, sand-laden wind worked upon the brains of these elemental men.

Merryvale heard parts of their conversation, and the tenor of it augured more ill than good to Adam and himself.

"We gotta git out of hyar tonight, at the furdest," said one.

"I'd vote for goin' right now," added another.

"Nix. Not till the sun sets an' the sand stops," advised a third.

"What's keepin' us anyhow?" demanded Stark, whose voice had not been evident before.

"Gold," rejoined Brooks, laconically.

"Gold, hell! Ain't you enough of a prospector to know float or quartz never shows in this kind of rock?"

"No, I ain't. Are you?"

"I sure am. I prospected all over the Mohave an' Death Valley. This fellar is workin' you."

"Thet idee has been eatin' into me, like the sand in my biscuit. . . . Stark, you go knock him on the head, an' the old geezer, too. Then we'll pack out of hyar."

"Me? Say, Brooks, I'm not doin' your dirty work," replied Stark, scornfully.

"You're gettin' most damn testy," growled the leader. "I thought mebbe you'd like the idee of layin' out Wansfell—"

"Who?" flashed Stark.

"Didn't I tell you?—Wal, this hyar big fellow is Wansfell, the Wanderer."

"Why'n hell didn't you tell me before?" yelled Stark, leaping up.

"Why'n hell should I?" shouted Brooks, in amaze and anger. "Is he anythin' to you?"

"Never seen him in my life," retorted Stark, and wheeling he rapidly approached the spot where Adam lay.

Merryvale sensed events. Stark looked as forceful and forbidding as before, yet with an extraordinary difference that was baffling. He sank on one knee and fixed a most penetrating gaze upon Adam.

"Say, big fellar, I want to know somethin'," he said, in low voice. "Are you the man Wansfell, the Wanderer?"

"Yes. The desert gave me that name. But it's not my real one," replied Adam, sitting up, suddenly intense.

"Honest to Gawd?" added the bandit, huskily. His ruddy skin had paled.

"Shore he's Wansfell," interposed Merryvale. "I've knowed him for eighteen years."

"My name is Stark. Bill Stark. Ever hear of me?" went on the bandit leaning closer.

"Stark? The name's familiar. But I can't place you," answered Adam.

"You once killed a man named Baldy McKue. A gambler, claim-jumper. Flashy man keen on women?"

His words were significant enough to thrill Merryvale, but nothing to his knife-edged tone and the quivering steel light of his eyes.

Adam labored to raise himself higher, and the bandit with a powerful arm, helped him. Then they locked eyes.

"Yes, I did," replied Adam, slowly, sombrely.

"You cracked the bones of his arms, an' busted his ribs—an' broke his neck—all with your bare hands?" whispered the bandit, his intensity growing terrible.

Wansfell nodded with a gloom that overshadowed his interest in this man.

"What'd you kill McKue for?"

"Well, I'd just wandered into that mining camp," replied Adam, grasping from the man's growing agitation the tenseness of this situation. "And I happened on a little woman, starving and ill in a shack. She had been pretty once. Baldy McKue had beaten her, abandoned her. I never learned who she was or her story. She kept her secret. I nursed her, tried to save her life. But I couldn't. She was not strong enough for childbirth. And they both died. She did tell me, though, before she died, that the baby was not McKue's."

"Oh, my Gawd! Oh, my Gawd! Oh, my Gawd!" moaned Stark, his face convulsed and wet, his body shaken, his big hands wringing each other. Then he bent to the wall and his broad shoulders heaved.

Merryvale gazed in wonder. Adam made as if to put a kindly hand on Stark's shoulder, but his arms were bound.

"She was—my wife," said Stark, raising his head, disclosing a havoc-lined face. "An' the baby was mine."

"Well! I always wondered," returned Adam, gently. "She had been a good girl. I could see that. McKue had got around her."

"He was no worse than me," responded Stark, growing stern and dark. "I drove her to her ruin . . . Wansfell, I always wanted to meet you."

"Queer we should meet here. Life plays us tricks. But I'm glad, too, if meeting me has helped you."

"Roll over on your face," returned Stark, opening a clasp-knife.

Adam laboriously moved, and turned, face down.
The knife blade flashed. Adam's great hands spread.
He sat up, rubbing them. Stark motioned for Merryvale to turn. Then in another second Merryvale felt
his numb arms drop free.

"Brooks, come hyar," yelled Stark, bounding up.
He was agile for so heavy a man. His aspect, as he
strode out, was sinister and formidable. He stalked
more than half way to meet the bandit leader.

"Brooks, there won't be any knockin' Wansfell an'
his old pard on the head," he announced, in a voice
that lashed the air.

"The hell you say!" retorted Brooks, furiously.

"You heard me."

"Who's runnin' this hyar outfit?" demanded Brooks.

"If you must shoot do it with more'n your chin," replied Stark, bitingly sarcastic.

"Ha! That's strong talk, Stark."

"Look. I cut them fellars hands loose."

But Brooks did not spare a glance in the direction
of the liberated prisoners.

"Stark, I never liked you no how," he snarled.

"There wasn't no love lost."

Both men lurched for their guns, and Stark was the
swiftest to shoot. Brooks emitted an awful groan, and
falling face down in the sand, he twitched a little,
then lay still.

Stark, smoking gun in hand, leaped over his body
to confront the other men.

"If it's anythin' to you—out with it," he hissed.
"But I ain't talkin'."

The followers of Brooks were intimidated. Perhaps
it meant no great loss to them.

"All right. Divide Brooks' roll between you, an'
then we'll pack to get out of hyar."

Adam moved then towards the camp and Merryvale followed.

"We're square, Wansfell," said the bandit, gruffly.
"Take your canteen an' go. Keep your mouth shut at
the post, till we're gone with our hosses."

As an afterthought he added to Merryvale: "Say, old geezer, do you need thet whiskey more'n me?"

"Shore I don't," replied Merryvale, hastily producing the flask.

Adam was striding out along the grim wall. Merryvale had to hurry to catch up with him. They turned a corner, to face the long blue-and-yellow-hazed canyon. The wind whistled through the rock crevices.

17

Merryvale's endeavor to keep pace with Adam back to Lost Lake, coupled with the stress of his emotions, well-nigh exhausted him. His heart warned him that it was being taxed far beyond its limit. But he would not retard Adam and he would have dropped dead in his tracks rather than miss seeing Guerd Larey and Wansfell come face to face.

The day was at its bitter worst. The desert yawned, like a ghastly furnace mouth, horizon wide, from which issued a roar, and a smoke of whirling sand, and fire-hot breath, consuming, devastating. Lost Lake was swathed in white dust, blinding, suffocating, burning like invisible embers.

Adam led Merryvale round to the back of the post, to the entrance of Ruth's yard above the house. What welcome protection behind the thick hedge! Adam wiped the dusty grime from his face. Merryvale, panting and spent, wet with sweat, cleaned his black face and hands.

They did not pause longer than a moment, nor did either speak. A monstrous urge kept Merryvale from sinking down. He was consumed with despair, yet upheld by hope. Ruth! If only—

They reached the porch. Adam paused at some sound within the house. Then he knocked on Ruth's door—knocked until Merryvale remembered this was no longer Ruth's room.

They strode on, and Adam's footsteps rang from the porch.

Suddenly the next door swiftly opened inward and

Guerd Larey filled the aperture. Bloody marks marred the pallor of spent passion on his face. His jaw hung down, quivering. His rolling dilating eyes set black upon Adam. His thin white attire was dishevelled and stained.

In one lunge Adam shoved him back into the room, so powerfully that he staggered clear to the back wall, crashing against it.

Adam leaped across the threshold, with Merryvale at his heels. But Merryvale halted at the door, as if held by an unseen power.

The room was in disorder. Table and contents had been overturned. Merryvale's panic-stricken gaze swept over the dazed Larey, on to motionless Adam, and down to the couch, where Ruth lay white as death.

"Ruth!" cried Adam, in a voice that would have called her back from the verge.

Merryvale's poor heart froze. Was she dead? Had they come too late? Her glorious hair fell around her shoulders, half hiding her naked breast, where crimson stains burned against its whiteness.

Then her eyelids fluttered and opened, to disclose purple filmed gulfs that stared blank, changed from dead to quick, and suddenly blazed.

"Adam?" she whispered, faintly, and tried to rise.

Even in that terrible moment Wansfell did not forget the rousing Larey, for he made no move toward Ruth.

"Yes. I am here," he said, with what seemed an unnatural, unholy calm.

His compelling voice lifted her. Straining she half raised herself on her arms. Her hair fell like a golden mass. How lovely, how terribly tragic her face! The great eyes, expanding, shining like purple leaping flames, set with awful accusation upon Larey.

"Kill him! Kill him!" she breathed almost too low for Merryvale's strained ears. It was a command, supreme in agony, from an insupportable hate. Then, fainting, she fell back on the couch.

Merryvale, out of the corner of his eye, had seen Larey stoop quickly, to pick up something behind him. He rose, he leaned, head out like a bird of prey, he stepped, all the time with his glittering green eyes riveted on Adam. But he kept his right hand behind his back.

"Look out, Adam. He's got a gun!" called Merryvale, shrilly.

Larey's dry lips framed words that did not sound clearly.

"Wansfell, the Wanderer!"

He was quivering from head to foot.

"No, Guerd. I am your brother, Adam Larey," returned Adam, in tones that had no life.

Larey leaned closer as he stepped. All that was stress and strain about him magnified. He peered with intense scrutiny into Adam's eyes—close—closer, until with a wondering, terrifying cry he straightened.

"So help me God! . . . *Adam!* . . . Mama's little goody boy! . . . Damn your soul—I know you!"

"Eighteen years, Guerd. It was written, out there," replied Adam, making a gesture toward the desert.

Then it seemed to Merryvale that this prodigal brother became an archangel of the devil in his godlike beauty. Whiter than a corpse, yet burning, with eyes like green jade!

"Ah! Eighteen years!" his voice rang out like a clarion. "A lifetime, in which I have gone to hell, as once you prophesied, and you have become Wansfell, the Wanderer. How things work out! . . . My ruin is great, but I'd live it again ten thousand times for this moment."

He halted, towering, beautiful, beginning to sway and choke over passion too terrible for human strength.

"You love—this woman, Ruth Virey," he panted. "Oh, I know. . . . You couldn't help yourself.—And she loves you—loves you—*loves* you, curse her. . . . I took her for a hussy—a strumpet—a twining white-throated harlot. . . . But she was pure. My jealous black heart could not see it. . . . Look at her now!"

Larey pointed with left hand that seemed rigid yet had an exquisitely slight and rapid tremor.

Merryvale's look followed Larey's gesture. Ruth in her pitiful frailty and tragic loveliness would have melted a heart of stone. But Larey's heart had burned out love, tenderness, mercy. Adam never shifted his piercing gaze from his brother.

"Look at her now!" went on Larey. "I have killed her soul! This woman who loves you! . . . Your wandering, knightly, Christ-like code has failed you here!"

Merryvale's tortured acumen read the intent behind Larey's denunciation. He shrilled a warning. Larey's right arm swept out with a glinting gun. Adam leaped like a panther. His hand caught the rising arm. The gun exploded. Then Adam's mighty frame wrestled into terrific motion. He swung Larey off his feet. There was a rending sound, a cracking of bones.

The gun flew at Merryvale's feet. He snatched it up.

Adam catapulted Larey against the wall with sodden thud. But Larey did not fall. His arm hung limp, dripping blood, but he appeared not to be conscious of it.

Adam extended those clutching hands, those talons of the desert, and they seemed to speak the death his gray mute lips could not utter.

Merryvale had existed for this, prolonged his life for it. But it was more than human nature could bear. Even at that awful moment he felt Wansfell's anguish. Raising the gun he held, he shot Larey—once—twice —through the heart.

They laid Ruth on the little bed in the room that had been hers.

Adam knelt, still mute, no longer rigid. Merryvale flew to fetch water. It was he who bathed Ruth's still white face, and called to her, hoarsely, hopelessly, until his voice failed.

But she was not dead. The sad pale eyelids moved, languidly opened. Staring black her eyes, through which she came back to consciousness.

"Ruth. It—is—over," whispered Adam.

She tried to lift her hand. She gazed at Adam, at Merryvale, around the room.

"Lass, it's all right—all—right," said Merryvale quaveringly, taking up her hand.

"Guerd!" she whispered.

"He's daid!"

"Oh, God! . . . Adam, I made you kill him. . . . Your brother. . . . After all my love—my vow—Oh my stairs of sand! I climbed only to fall—only to fall!"

"Ruth, Guerd's blood is not upon my hands," said Adam solemnly. "I meant to kill him. I would have done so. . . . But I did not."

"Ruth, I couldn't stand it," interposed Merryvale, huskily. "I wanted more than hope of Heaven—to see Adam break his bones—an' crack his neck. . . . But when the time came I couldn't let him do it. . . . So I shot Larey myself."

Then these two shaken men knelt at her bedside. Merryvale thought he saw a change that was not physical, though a shade seemed strangely to pass away from her face.

"Ruth, it is hard enough," said Adam, his voice gathering strength. "But Merryvale spared me this deed—fear of which has made your life and mine a hell of contending fires. It is over. . . . Now let me think of you."

"I—but Adam—I can only die," she wailed.

"Hush! Have I been blessed by God with your love —only to lose you? No! No!"

"Guerd Larey could not die before—telling you— what—"

"He'd killed your soul, he said. But Ruth, that was only a madman's jealousy. That was my brother's curse. Your soul is God's and love's."

"But do you love me—*now?*"

"More, my darling. More a thousand times."

"But could I make you happy?"

"Ruth, all that has made life significant for me is embodied in you. Your heritage of discontent, your weakness for men, your love—your fight—your climb —you toiled up your stairs of sand on steps of your dead self—and you reached the heights. I would love you the same if you had not. But think of my faith in you and the splendor of my happiness to know it was justified. I love you with all the passion and strength that the desert has given me. But the joy of that is little compared with my joy in your victory over yourself. I think your mother must know."

Ruth did not—could not answer, but her eyes spoke her unutterable love. Adam lifted her in his arms and carried her outdoors.

The mood of the desert was changing. A mellow light tempered the ghastliness. The white wracks of dust had settled. Nature had ended her harsh audit for that day. The sun had lost its torrid heat. Mystical, beautiful, illusive, beckoning, the dunes of sand stepped up to the infinitude of blue. And a brooding haunting silence settled over the wasteland.